FAITH IN THE MOUNTAIN VALLEY

CALL OF THE ROCKIES ~ BOOK 5

MISTY M. BELLER

Unless otherwise indicated, all Scripture quotations are taken from the Holy Bible, Kings James Version.

ISBN: 978-1-942265-44-3

And I will bring the blind by a way that they knew not;
I will lead them in paths that they have not known:
I will make darkness light before them, and crooked things straight.
These things will I do unto them, and not forsake them.

Isaiah 42:16 (KJV)

CHAPTER 1

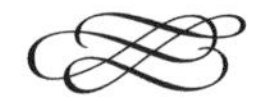

Spring, 1831
Clearwater River Valley, Future Idaho Territory

A person approached through the trees ahead.

French tensed as his spotted mare perked her ears toward the figures. He rode near the back of their group, a position that let him slip into anonymity but allowed him to keep an eye on the others. Step in and help where needed. Then ease back just as quickly, without his presence making much of a stir.

Beaver Tail, riding in the front, would meet whoever approached through the trees, assess any danger, and deal with it accordingly. Behind Beaver Tail, his wife, Susanna, never strayed far—his better-looking shadow, one might say. Meksem, another warrior, would be nearby as well, with her future husband, Adam, at her side.

The others—including French—settled in between and around, with Joel and his wife, Elan, bringing up the rear, ever watchful.

French never had an exact job. He was the one who adapted.

Stepped in to gather wood or help where needed. More often than not, he provided a story for entertainment when the rest of them needed a distraction.

He'd never planned for his life to be so haphazard, without focus or any kind of real plan. But here he was, a man of all work, yet with nothing to call his own.

Maybe if he'd been able to find Colette, all this would be different. His entire world would be different. Happy. His purpose had always been to please her. Because a smile on her sweet face filled him up like an overflowing canteen.

The day he'd lost her, he'd lost his purpose.

He'd never been able to find either of them again, so here he sat. Riding with his friends along the edge of a cliff, watching a cluster of pines and cedars for who knew what to step through.

Movement caught his eye beyond the trees, and his senses spiked. An Indian appeared through the branches. Not really a surprise out here in the mountain wilderness, yet... These braves wore the markings of the Blackfoot tribe.

And the Blackfoot had a reputation as a bully among the mountain tribes.

Not Beaver Tail though. He was Blackfoot, at least half so, though to look at him you'd never know his father had been English. But the man never took up arms without just cause. Which only showed you could never judge a person according to his nationality. Better to judge by each fellow's own actions. And be cautious.

In front of him, Caleb's big frame blocked the sight of the oncoming riders for a moment. But when the trail shifted again, French saw the strangers had multiplied to six now. The five in front were definitely Indian, probably Blackfoot. But the man in the back appeared white, although the slouch hat he wore pulled low over his face made it hard to see more than pale skin. The fellow's lean form seemed almost wiry, but French could tell little more than that with the bulky buckskins.

French's pulse picked up pace. A Frenchman maybe? The few trappers they'd met west of the Missouri had been part of the Hudson Bay Company, the sorry lot. And only half had spoken his native tongue, the rest being of British descent—a likely possibility since that country had won ownership of the Canadian colonies.

But still, what he wouldn't give for a conversation in his mother language.

Beaver paused their group a few strides before the strangers. The high-low cadence of the Blackfoot tongue drifted on the breeze, and French tried to focus on picking out words. He'd learned enough Blackfoot through the years to know they were asking where each was headed and what their business was. Friendly conversation, it sounded like. Good.

The word *Peigan* came clear. These five must be part of the more peaceful sect of the Blackfoot tribe. Maybe that would help ease any lingering concerns from the Nez Perce women in their group. Not a lot of trust existed between the two tribes.

His gaze drifted to the white stranger in the rear, but the man's horse was positioned so the brave in front covered much of him. Only the pretty palomino the white man rode could be seen plainly. The animal still wore its pale yellow winter coat, which would likely shed out in another month or two to produce a darker golden or coppery color. But the lighter tone brought out the pale blonde of the man's hair, which barely showed at his neck beneath the hat.

Not many grown men could boast hair that light. A painful memory swept over him. Colette's father was the only other man French could recollect. Colette's hair had been even a shade lighter than her father's.

Movement where Beaver Tail was speaking pulled his thoughts from Colette, thankfully. Even after all these years, she stayed too heartbreakingly close to the forefront of his mind.

Beaver Tail motioned farewell to the strangers, then nudged

his horse forward. The path spanned wide enough for two to ride abreast, with a steep slope rising on one side and a sheer cliff dropping off on the other. Both parties would need to ride single file to pass—a strong test of the strangers' friendliness.

As their group straggled out to pass in a single line, French readied the Blackfoot greeting on his tongue to offer as the men rode by. The lead brave appeared seasoned, at least fifty years old with plenty of salt worked through his long pepper braids.

French nodded and spoke the usual greeting in their tongue. "*Oki*."

The brave gave an answering dip of his chin as he passed. One by one, each of the four other Blackfoot rode by him in quick succession, some offering a friendly nod, the rest barely a notice.

As the last brave passed, French sent a hungry glance ahead to the white man bringing up the rear. Should he say *bonjour* or greet him in English?

The fellow gave no sign of his heritage. No word of greeting or even a smile. He wore his hat so low, the brim covered most of his face. The fur collar of his coat pulled up to hide the point of his chin, which left only his mouth and the tip of his nose revealed. Those features were small, almost dainty for a man.

The fellow must be young. Maybe even a white captive they'd raised as a Blackfoot? But why then would he wear a white man's hat? So maybe not raised as a Blackfoot, but possibly still a captive?

"Hello." French spoke the word quietly, almost intimately. To show the lad he would find a friend in them if he needed one.

The fellow didn't lift his head to reveal his eyes. Didn't acknowledge French in any way until he'd almost passed by completely. Then he lifted a gloved hand in greeting.

There was something in the motion. In those long, slender fingers that caught French's attention.

Those weren't the gloves a man wore. They were too well

fitting. Nor was that a broad male hand. But it was more than that. The elegance of the movement stole his breath.

The rider had already passed, but French pulled his mare to a halt and spun in the saddle to watch the stranger. The outline was lean, definitely not a full-grown man. But a boy? The figure sat too tall. A lad of that height would be awkward and gangly without the poised elegance this person possessed.

It must be…a woman. Should he do something? She hadn't seemed afraid. Maybe she was married to one of the men. He'd seen trappers marry Indian women. And Joel had married Elan, from the Nez Perce tribe. Adam would soon be married to her friend, Meksem. For that matter, it looked like Caleb would soon be wed to Otskai.

And the opposite happened also, though white women in this wilderness were scarce. But Beaver Tail had married Susanna, a white woman.

Since this female didn't appear in danger or desirous of help, maybe it would be best to leave well enough alone.

Maybe.

~

"You're awfully quiet tonight, French."

Caleb's words pulled French's gaze from the leaping flames of their campfire. The man had a way of seeing things a fellow tried to keep hidden. And a knack for making you want to confide in him.

During their years together, French had told him many stories from his eleven years of trapping, had even told Caleb that both his parents were dead. But that was the most he'd ever shared.

Not even Caleb's gentle steadiness could pull Colette from his lips. She was too important. And the rest…well, it was history. Another lifetime, and better left there.

So, he worked for a smile for his friend. "Just thinking about that group we met on the trail earlier." That was close enough to the truth. Seeing that white woman with the Blackfoot braves, trying to appear as a man, yet with hair almost as flaxen as Colette's, had resurrected too many childhood memories. The woman couldn't actually be Colette, not this far away from the Canadian fort her family had moved to. Yet the memories wouldn't stop.

He couldn't tell them to Caleb. Better to find another story.

"Reminded me of the time I spent with Jim Bridger and we passed by a group of Bloods and Gros Ventre. I'd never seen the two tribes travel together like that, nor have I since. But these fellows had spent the winter together and looked to be half starved." The rest of the group had shifted their focus to him and leaned in for the tale.

Maybe this really was his purpose in life, to entertain these friends. Maybe his eleven years on the trail had all been in preparation for this. First the nine years searching for Colette. Then the winter he'd spent desperately trying to forget her, and then this last year and a half with the men around him.

The women had joined on by ones or twos, mostly marrying up with his friends. Not that he begrudged Beaver Tail, Joel, Adam, and now Caleb happiness with their lady loves.

But once again, he was the odd man out.

He always would be, because he'd never settle for anyone but Colette. He'd promised her he wouldn't.

After he finished his story, Adam joined in with a tale of his own, one from when he traveled with the Mandan warriors on his way to find the Palouse horses. Adam had tried to get the rest of them to accompany him, but when Joel—his younger brother—had put his foot down and said they'd finish their trek up the Missouri as planned, Adam had sneaked off in the middle of the night, leaving a note to share his plans.

Though Joel had been angry at the time, if they hadn't spent the next summer and autumn looking for Adam, neither Adam nor Joel would have found these women they now loved so deeply. Beaver Tail either, most likely.

So did that mean Adam had been wrong for leaving? The others would probably say God worked it all for His plan. Once upon a time, French might've thought that too.

But if God had ever worked in his own life, the Almighty had left him the same day Colette had. The only difference was that Colette hadn't left of her own accord. She'd been taken away by her parents. If only he'd been old enough to travel along with them. But he'd been afraid to leave his mother alone. Not with the way his father sometimes turned violent when the drink took over. Colette had promised to write, but he'd never once heard from her. There must not have been a way to send mail from Fort York, or wherever her family had gone after leaving there.

Now, as he settled into his fur bedding, with a buffalo robe pulled over him against the cold spring night, he couldn't clear the figure of that woman on horseback from his mind. As a girl, Colette hadn't possessed that poise, not when they'd been running through the countryside, playing knights, or soldiers, or school teacher.

By the time she turned thirteen, her bearing had begun to change. That was about the time he'd kissed her, though he'd fallen in love with her long before then. Yet even the fourteen-year-old Colette who'd waved a tearful good-bye to him wasn't as poised and graceful—and tall—as the woman who'd ridden away from him today.

But that hair—the pale blonde. How likely was it another woman would have that same shade? It was a tad darker than her childhood color, but the same exact shade as her father's.

What were the chances she would be riding through these wild mountains...in a United States territory, no less? So far from where her parents had moved her. Weeks, maybe months away, depending on the season of travel.

But then, what were the chances any woman would be out here riding with five Piegan Blackfoot braves?

So many questions that they made his chest ache, and not an answer among them. Especially if he kept lying here on this bed pallet, then rose in the morning and continued riding westward with his friends. He'd never get the answers.

If there was a chance, even a minuscule chance smaller than the mosquitoes that harassed them through the summer months, that the woman was Colette… That the girl he'd spent a third of his life looking for and had traveled the whole of Rupert's Land more than once to find… If she was lying somewhere in her own bedroll only a couple hours' ride away, how could he not go make certain? What if she were a prisoner?

The thought burned within him.

He could do what Adam had done, leave a note letting the others know where he was going. He'd find Colette—he could call her an old friend in his note, since the others wouldn't know her name. He'd tell them he'd be gone a week or two visiting with the friend and would catch up with them at Otskai's village. If they'd already left that place, he'd meet them at the town where Elan and Meksem hailed from.

Even if there was some kind of trouble that had driven Colette to this place, something he needed to take care of for her, that should give him enough time to do whatever necessary. He'd promised Colette he'd always love her. Always be there for her. They'd both promised. Though he'd only been thirteen at the time, he'd meant every word.

Maybe he could even bring Colette to meet these friends who'd become like brothers, and even sisters, to him. After that, whatever Colette wanted, he would do. If she wished to return to the Canadas, he would gladly take her there. Though he didn't enjoy the thought of living around so many people again.

He'd much rather settle with her in these beautiful mountains. But wherever she was happiest, he would be happiest.

Easing down his fur covering, he scanned the sleeping forms around him. He could just make out Beaver Tail's steady breathing, only because the man and his wife lay nearest French. Sneaking away without waking him would be a feat, as the man seemed to sleep with one eye open and both ears cocked.

If Beaver woke, French would just have to explain what he was doing. That would save him a note anyway. Beaver would likely let him leave without a stir. The man had uncanny insight. French could make him understand the importance of this without having to share details.

Sure enough, though French hadn't made any distinguishable noise that he knew of, as he finished rolling his furs in a bundle, Beaver Tail slipped out from the blanket he shared with Susanna.

The man watched as French looped his possibles bag over his neck and picked up his other packs. Beaver didn't awaken any of the others, only padded quietly behind French toward the horses.

When he reached Giselle, the spotted mare he'd traded with the Nimiipuu for, French turned to Beaver Tail and kept his voice low. "I think I recognized the white person who was with the Piegan Braves earlier today. It might be an old friend. I'm going to ride back and find out for sure. If it's who I think it is, I'll probably stay with them a few weeks, then catch up with you guys at one of the Nimiipuu towns. I'll look for you at Otskai's first, then go on to Elan's if need be."

At least he'd gotten the whole plan out before Beaver Tail responded. The man usually took his time thinking through a situation before responding.

And it was six whole heartbeats before Beaver Tail finally parted his lips to speak. "A friend from before, when you were a lad?"

A knot of emotion clogged French's throat. How had the man guessed? That intuition at work.

He nodded. "Yes."

Beaver Tail didn't argue or beg him to stay, thank goodness. He lifted a hand to French's upper arm. It was the clasp of a brother, though Beaver Tail didn't usually show such emotion. "Go with God. And come back to us when you can."

The words seemed to say more than their simple meaning, but French didn't stop to read everything. He offered a returning grip to Beaver Tail's arm. "*Au revoir.*" The French farewell slid so easily from his tongue.

Then he released his friend, saddled his horse, and rode into the night.

CHAPTER 2

If her mother could see her now, Mama's color might well blanch as pale as the powdered white wig she told stories of wearing in her younger days.

Colette sat on her sleeping fur in the early morning light, head braced in her hands. The braves were stirring, but she needed a minute for her belly to settle before she rose. She'd forgotten to refill her pouch of roasted meat the night before, so she had nothing close by to eat before getting up.

Left Standing grunted as he padded past her on his way to the river. She lifted her head to smile a morning greeting, though with the sun barely lightening the eastern horizon, he might not see her expression. He was already striding into the trees anyway.

She could handle an early morning as well as the next person—Blackfoot brave though he be—but it was the roiling in her belly that made the early part of the day a challenge. Still, she'd better find a tree before the waking sun stole the shadows.

She pressed her mouth shut to hold in a grunt as she pushed up to standing. An icy wind slipped around her when she stepped from the shelter of the cliff they camped beside. She pulled her coat tighter, the buffalo fur protecting her from the gust. Raphael had traded for the hide more than two years ago, and she'd had the good sense back then to stitch a coat that leaned more toward function than form. The blockiness of the garment, along with the way she wrapped her chest to flatten herself, made it easy enough to conceal her shape and become believable as a man.

A young man, anyway.

After taking care of morning ministrations, she approached camp again. Young Bear was stirring something in the pot over the fire, likely leftovers from the stew she'd made the night before. As much as she would like to offer a little better fare than what some of the braves served up, she didn't cook any more than was her turn among the group. If she showed any tendency at all toward women's ways, they might give her a second glance.

She didn't dare do anything to endanger her position with these men. The situation was exactly what she needed for now. At least, until she could find a better plan.

She knelt by the fire with her cup and scooped a portion of stew, then offered a nod to Young Bear. The others liked to check their traps before breaking their fast in the morning, but Young Bear seemed to need sustenance before coming fully awake. Usually, she could go either way. But these last weeks, she needed her belly full first thing.

They sat in silence, both sipping hot broth. One of the many nice things about these new friends was that they didn't feel the need to pile on extra words.

Something must have caught Young Bear's attention, for he jerked upright, his hand going to the knife hanging from his neck. She spun in the direction the brave was staring, trying to make out anything in the murky shadows of the trees around them.

There. A branch snapped in the distance. She reached for her gun, the Hall rifle her husband had been so proud of. She'd recharged it after cleaning the night before, and she now raised it to her shoulder, bracing herself in case she had to fire the weapon.

She half suspected this rifle was the reason these men had allowed her to travel with them. Hawk Wing was the only other among them who owned a gun—an older fusee that the man had to constantly repair. She'd had the forethought to bring along Raphael's gun kit along with his traps, so she'd managed to put the fusee in better working order over time.

A rustle in the trees sent a tingle down her spine, and she tightened her grip on the rifle, positioning her finger alongside the trigger.

So early in the morning, this intruder would likely be game, not strangers. And she'd have a single shot to drop the animal. She'd learned quickly to aim that shot in an opportune location so she didn't ruin the hide. But if this was a small creature, she'd do best to let Young Bear slay the animal with his knife, lest her bullet cause too much damage to the meat.

"I come in peace."

The unexpected voice sent a jolt through Colette, and her finger touched the trigger out of reflex. She caught her breath and yanked the digit away from the metal so she didn't accidentally squeeze the trigger.

Who was this man entering their camp so early? His voice held an eerie familiarity. And a French accent, though he spoke English.

She summoned images of Raphael's brothers and tried to place the voice with one of their faces. No, Louis was too young, barely eighteen. And Hugh's rumbled much deeper. So this voice...

Young Bear jumped to his feet, and she did the same, though not half so smoothly. Though the only sign of her condition was a thickening at the waist, her balance had already shifted—or maybe fled altogether.

She braced her feet and repositioned the rifle at her shoulder, doing her best to look like a man accustomed to shooting. Not a woman cringing in preparation for a blast that would knock her backward three steps. She tried not to fire this weapon any more than she had to.

No matter who stepped through those trees, she would *not* spill his blood. Too much of that had been done already.

If this was Hugh or Louis… Well, she still hadn't worked out what she would do if faced with one of her husband's avengers. Flee again, probably. *Lord, don't let me have to make that choice today. Please.*

"I mean no harm. *Ikkinaa'pii.*"

That was the Blackfoot word for peace. She sent a glance toward Young Bear. He knew enough English that he'd probably understood the other things the stranger said, but he didn't seem eager to believe them. He still stood with his knife raised. She knew for a fact that his aim was true.

She tucked her neck to use her deepest voice, then called out loudly enough for the stranger to hear. "Show yourself."

Maybe she shouldn't be the first to speak, but she'd learned early that men thought it odd for another man to cower in the background. If she was going to play this role correctly, she had to be willing to step forward and act. Besides, the sooner they saw this fellow's face, the sooner they could move on with their day.

More rustling sounded in the leaves, and a figure formed from the shadows. He didn't wear a hat, and he moved with the easy grace of a man familiar with this wilderness. The trees partially concealed him, so she could only see his outline. Especially those broad shoulders, probably showing wider than they actually were because of his winter coat.

He stepped through a small patch of sunlight, revealing a

tousle of dark brown hair that almost blended with the fur of his coat. He carried a gun, but the shadows overtook him before she could decipher more.

Then he stepped to the edge of the trees and paused in full view.

Her gaze ran the length of him before seeking his face. She sucked in a breath as her heart stalled.

It couldn't be. Could it? No. How could...?

But the slight widening of his eyes gave her answer.

Jean-Jacques had come.

~

French could barely breathe, much less think. He'd found Colette. Here in this mountain wilderness. What was she doing here? And pointing a gun at him?

Before he could open his mouth to speak, she dipped her head so her hat covered the top part of her face, then took a step back and turned a little. Hiding from him?

Why? She had to know he'd seen her. Recognized her. So why did she still hide? And why from *him*?

The Indian grunted and stepped forward, forcing French to wrench his focus away from Colette. *Part* of his attention anyway, for he could never manage to ignore her completely. He'd spent so long searching for her, there was no way he would lose sight of her now. The Colette he knew would be happy to see him, but this woman...

He needed to talk with her. Catch up on over eleven years of life.

For now, though, he made the sign for peace and spoke the Blackfoot greeting. "Oki."

The man nodded, then glanced at Colette in question.

She spoke to him quietly, though her voice didn't quite sound natural. "He is a friend." Her tone was deeper than he would have expected. Sure, she'd been fourteen the last time he'd seen her, so her voice would have changed some. But she seemed to be altering the sound now on purpose.

Then she looked back to him, though she didn't meet his gaze and still kept her hat pulled low. She motioned him forward. "Come and sit. Are you hungry?"

She turned and bent over a pot, then stood with a cup in hand. When she held it out to him, she finally looked up. Her eyes fixed him, stilling his breath as he sank into their blue. But they seemed to be speaking to him. Pleading maybe.

He did his best to understand, but he kept losing himself in their familiar depths. *Colette*. She was here. And so much more beautiful than he'd ever imagined she'd be as a woman. Even with short hair and wearing that awful hat.

But what was she saying to him? He nodded in answer to their unspoken request. He would do whatever she wanted of him. He always had. But did she need protection? From these braves?

As he took the cup and she turned back toward the fire, he shifted his gaze to the Indian. The man had replaced his knife in the sheaf hanging from his neck but stood watching French as if waiting to see if he would turn out to be a threat after all. Colette didn't seem bothered by the man. When they'd spoken, the tone between them seemed almost...companionable. Yesterday, before he'd known this was Colette, he wondered if she was a captive. Could he have been right? She didn't act afraid of the Indian.

As if she'd heard his thoughts, Colette straightened and glanced between him and the man. "Jean-Jacques, this is Young Bear."

The power of his name on her lips, even in that deep, altered tone, sent a jolt through him. No one had called him by his given name in years. Not since McCann had labeled him *French* when he was barely sixteen years old. That nickname had eventually become a badge he wore, a reminder of his heritage. The name everyone called him.

But Colette knew the *real* Jean-Jacques.

Before he could linger on that thought, she spoke again. "The others are checking their traps. They'll be along soon." She sent a glance in the direction of the river, then turned her gaze back to him with a tight smile. "We've been trapping the outer edge of these stony mountains. Young Bear and his group let me join in with them about five weeks ago."

As that news sank through him, she motioned toward the ground at his feet. "Sit. Eat. Tell me what you've been doing." Her voice held little emotion. Only a tiny bit of interest. In her face, that tight smile that didn't touch her eyes.

What did it all mean? He had to know what had happened with her, but he couldn't ask in front of this brave. She was clearly hiding something, although he couldn't be sure if it was from him or from her new friends.

For now, he obeyed her bidding, dropping to sit cross-legged in front of the fire. She did the same, and he couldn't help admiring the grace in her movement.

Young Bear still stood, watching him. But Colette motioned toward the place the man had been sitting before, and he eased down, his gaze wary.

Colette turned to French and nodded toward the cup he'd forgotten he still held. "Eat up. And tell me what you've been doing since I last saw you."

French sipped the broth. Something floated in the liquid that looked like meat. The stuff didn't have a lot of taste but would help fill his belly. Yet the first swallow started a sour roiling in his middle.

Colette was watching him, waiting for him to answer her question. A question one might ask a casual acquaintance, not a lifelong love who she'd been wrenched away from almost a dozen years ago.

Should he answer honestly? He fought to keep from sending another look toward Young Bear. Maybe he needed to say something to shake Colette from whatever game she was playing. "Well, I've mostly been looking for you. Spent the last eleven years trapping, first in Rupert's Land. This last year and a half, I've been traveling with friends back and forth across these mountains."

She tipped her head, a hint of real interest slipping through her demeanor. "Were you with that group we passed yesterday?" No response to his comment about searching for her? He would let her ignore it for now, but he'd circle back later. Maybe when they didn't have an audience.

He dipped his chin in answer to her question. "I was." If she hadn't been hiding behind her hat, she'd have seen him.

He took another sip of broth to keep from saying the wrong thing. It would be rude to give the cup back full, and he'd not broken his fast yet that morning, so he needed to fill his belly with something. This swallow went down a little better than the first.

When he looked back at Colette, his gaze snagged on her empty hands. Had she already eaten? Realization slipped through him. She must only have the one cup, the one he was drinking from.

He handed it back to her. "Didn't mean to take your breakfast."

She shook her head, her hands staying in her lap. "Finish that, there's plenty."

He moved the cup closer to her. He wasn't about to eat when a woman sat hungry—when Colette sat hungry.

"Eat up." She nearly barked the words in that false deep voice.

He studied her expression. She seemed to be sending him a message again with her eyes, maybe begging him to go along with her ruse?

As much as he hated to, he pulled the cup back and took another sip. Then a gulp. The sooner he finished, the sooner Colette could eat.

As he swallowed the last bite, she spoke again. "Are your companions waiting for you? You must've camped soon after we saw you yesterday, but that was still a couple hours ride to here. I'm surprised you came so far to reach me."

He nearly choked on the last bit of broth slipping down his throat. Surprised he came so far? Nothing could've kept him away once he had an inkling she might be here. He stared at her, trying to decipher why she was talking this way. Could she really have forgotten him and all that had happened between them? All they meant to each other?

Maybe he'd simply been a childish pastime for her, not a lifeline to survive the turmoil of a hard childhood. And then...that kiss. It was the only time he'd ever kissed a woman—well, a girl, but he'd been a lad himself.

He'd meant the words he said to her back then. There would never be another for him. She'd said the same. He couldn't imagine, but maybe they'd not meant anything to her. Maybe he'd only been a passing fancy.

Her face gave nothing away. No sign of her thoughts. There was...something there he couldn't read. Maybe, a sadness?

Emotion clogged his throat even as he searched her eyes for more. He needed to get her away from this stranger to a place where they could speak freely. Colette had always been refreshingly honest with him. Never holding back her thoughts. He could find that place with her again.

He handed the cup to her. "Thank you."

As she scooped another helping of stew, he shifted his focus to the Indian. His Blackfoot was rusty, so he had to search for the words in that tongue. "Have you found many furs this winter?"

"Most of these men speak a little English and French,"

Colette murmured in a voice low enough not to disturb the conversation.

He gave her a nod and a small smile of thanks but kept his focus mainly on the man. He needed to establish good relations with these companions of Colette. That might help him later, once he figured out exactly what was going on.

Young Bear nodded, then pointed toward a stack of furs at the outer edge of their camp. "We will stay here to dry these and lay more traps."

Three other piles of pelts stood in different places around the outer edge of the campsite. There had been five braves, so likely there were more hides. And what was Colette doing with these men? Aside from the many larger questions, what specific role did she play in their camp? Did she cook for them?

Even at thirteen, her fare had been much better than the watered meat she'd just fed him. But then, there was only so much a body could do with the scant provisions available after a lean winter. Maybe they'd run out of corn and other staples. Too bad they didn't have camas root like the Nimiipuu women served. As much as he'd hated the stuff the first times he'd been served, it filled his belly well, and the taste had grown on him.

He kept a bit of his attention on Colette, enough to see that she'd already inhaled a cup of the soup. She sent a glance to the pot as though wondering whether it was safe to drink more. Did they not have enough food? He shouldn't have eaten what he did. Even when she insisted, he should've let her drink first. Finding his way with this new version of Colette was no easy thing.

He managed a little small talk with Young Bear, then Colette rose. "I need to check my traps. Do you want to walk with me?"

He was on his feet in half a heartbeat. Never mind how strange it sounded that she might have traps. Of course, Otskai, Caleb's wife, had trapped to help provide food for her and her son. Probably other Indian women did as well.

But Colette? She'd made him put the crickets and worms on her fishing line when they were children. And he'd barely gotten her to hold the slimy fish while he disentangled the wire from its mouth. Maybe she didn't mean the kind of trap that came to mind with the word.

She turned to Young Bear. "You'll tell the others he's a friend?" He couldn't get used to this strange deep tone she used. But hopefully her words would keep these new friends from planting an arrow in his back as he followed her to check her traps.

Young Bear nodded, then pushed to standing also. He moved into the trees, and Colette turned to the right, where a path wound a different direction. She motioned for him to follow, though he didn't need the invitation.

Now that he'd found Collete, only the Almighty Himself could keep him from following her.

CHAPTER 3

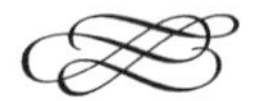

Colette had to work to steady her breathing as her heart hammered. Jean-Jacques had found her. After all this time.

All these years of missing him and more tears than she could count. Had he really been looking for her as long as he said? What of his wife? He'd married only three years after her parents moved her away from him. Had the woman died?

So much of her wanted to tell him everything—all the awful details of this predicament she was in and how afraid she was. She'd never been able to keep a secret from him.

But then, she'd never had a secret this important. As they stepped from the trees to the creek's edge, she inhaled a steady breath. She couldn't lose her cover yet. She'd have to make Jean-Jacques understand how important it was for the braves to think her a man.

And she'd have to be careful not to tell what she'd done. The Jean-Jacques she knew would keep her secret as best he could. But she knew too well how a man changed when under the influence of strong drink. She couldn't chance word of what she'd done slipping out when he wasn't sober. No man could be trusted when intoxicated—she'd learned that the hard way.

She started across the river, using the rocks she'd positioned to keep her moccasins dry. Each person in their group had chosen a separate territory to lay their traps. She'd picked a stretch farther away than the others so they could have the nearer locations. She'd happily settle for crossing the creek a few times a day if it kept the others from fretting over her presence with them.

And just now, having her trapping area at a distance to the others' would give her time to speak with Jean-Jacques in private. She had to make him promise not to give up her disguise.

As she leapt from the last rock to the bank, a mutter sounded behind her, then a splash. She glanced back to see Jean-Jacques with his moccasin planted firmly in the ankle-deep water.

He wrinkled his nose as he stepped the last distance to the bank, then shook out his wet foot. The expression was so much like his ten-year-old self, a smile slipped out before she could stop it.

He looked at her with one brow raised the way only he could manage, still shaking the water off his foot. "That should wake me up." Then his mouth tipped at the corners, and he sent her that look he'd always reserved only for her.

Warmth slipped through her. A sensation she hadn't felt in so...very...long.

Emotions surged up to burn her eyes, and her legs threatened to buckle right there. If she didn't have so much counting on her strength, she would have given in to her weakness and sat there in the grass to cry. How could that one smile loose so much she'd locked away for years?

She forced herself to turn away. Forced stiffness into her back. Forced her feet to march forward. She was no longer a child able to give in to any whim.

She'd murdered a man. And his babe grew inside her. She had too much at stake to let down her guard.

The muted tramp of Jean-Jacques's footsteps followed her as she made her way to the first trap. Last night's dusky shadows had been deep when she'd set these, so she might need to move a few of them. Assuming she could find the snares at all.

The first was easy enough to locate, a long spring set built to catch beaver. The arms had been sprung, but no animal lay inside.

She shifted its position and sprinkled fresh bait, then covered the metal with grass.

Jean-Jacques stood nearby while she worked, but she didn't spare him a glance. The weight of his gaze was enough to bear. The tension of all his questions hanging thick in the air.

The only thing she could tell him was that she had to keep her gender a secret. If she said anything more—about the reason she was out here, why she traveled with these braves, or anything else she'd done since she'd last seen him at fourteen, she might give away too much. As much as she trusted the boy she'd known back then, she knew better than to trust any man now.

When she finished with the first trap, she climbed back up the bank and pointed to an inlet not far ahead. "The next one is right there." Better to get most of this work done before she let their true conversation begin. That would give him less time to ask questions before they rejoined the others. Then, she could send him on his way.

The thought pressed hard, like a falling tree crushing her beneath its weight. Send her dearest friend away? The man she'd loved her entire life?

But she had to. How could she not? She had too much at stake to trust anyone. She had to start over on her own.

At least, far from anyone who knew her before. If she could manage to stay with these braves until they finished trapping and returned to their village, maybe she could find a home there. That fresh start she craved.

By the time she finished resetting the third trap and had a single beaver to show for her work, she could feel Jean-Jacques's frustration boiling around them. Like she was stuck in a cauldron of steam.

One more trap. She'd only set four last night and planned to lay out the last two this morning. But that would have to wait until she sent Jean-Jacques on his way. She couldn't possibly stand any more time with this tension than what was necessary to check these four.

The fourth was empty and not yet sprung. Maybe she should rethink the positions of these. But that would have to be done later—when she could think past the man filling her head with his presence behind her.

At last, she turned to him. He straightened, meeting her gaze. He looked like he might start in with his questions now, but she had to be the first to speak. She had to control this conversation.

She lifted her chin. "They think I'm a man." Perhaps she should have paused to think through that starting comment.

Especially since Jean-Jacques's mouth dropped open, his brows rising to widen his eyes. His jaw worked as though he were trying to close it, trying to speak. Apparently, he'd not realized she was trying to conceal her gender. Was her disguise really so bad? She'd cut her precious long hair to accomplish it. Had worked so hard to keep her voice deep and to mimic the careless gestures and habits that seemed to come naturally to the male species.

At last, he managed to close his mouth and recover a bit of control. "Who thinks you're a man?" His gaze flicked in the direction of camp, maybe trying to answer his own question.

"Young Bear and the others. It's important they not realize otherwise. Else it would be much harder to travel with them."

The truth in that statement should be obvious—all the layers of it.

These men had been good to her. But that was because they thought her an overgrown lad who wanted to tag along with their group. If they realized she was a woman...well, she didn't intend to travel that path.

"You can't think they really believe it. And why? What's happened? Talk to me, Colette."

She ignored the earnestness in his tone. The tenderness. And the questions. The only thing she could address was that first statement.

She sent him a scowl to rebuild her defenses. "Of course they believe it. I talk like a man. I work like a man. I even spit like a man." That last bit was only one of the tragic things she'd been required to do.

And he would know exactly what it cost her. She'd hated when he took up spitting for a few short weeks one summer. He'd stopped soon enough, just to make her quit nagging him.

He raised his brows at her again, then slid his gaze down the length of her and back up. The look was clearly intended to speak for itself, and it said enough to rile her.

She raised her brows right back at him. "I dress like a man. They haven't even looked twice at me."

He let out a huff and spun away, raking a hand through his unruly hair. He chuckled, the sound lacking any form of mirth. "Ah, Colette."

Then he turned back to her, his gaze piercing. "Why? Why are you doing this? And why are you all the way out here? Is it just to see the world?" His expression turned pleading. "Come with me then. I've met some good friends. There are even a few women in the group. I think you'll like them."

That face...the features she'd loved since he first found her pulling weeds in the garden and pitched in to help without her even asking. He'd been her hero even back then.

But now...so much had changed. Everything had changed. He wasn't just asking her to slip away from her book and go fishing. This was real life—a tiny life growing inside her, completely dependent on her to make the right choices.

Jean-Jacques's friends...there was no telling who they might know. How quickly news of her would get back to Hugh and Louis. She couldn't risk it.

"Talk to me, Colette."

She hardened her resolve against the tender pleading in his voice. "I can't tell you why. Trust me, it's important they not know I'm a woman. Leave it at that. Please?"

Once upon a time, adding that please would make him give in to whatever she asked. Her girlhood charm had fled long ago. But she let him see a tiny bit of her desperation.

He didn't speak for a long moment. His brows lowered, his eyes cloudy with thought. She used to read those eyes so easily, but she couldn't decipher their emotion now.

His throat worked. Then at last, he nodded. "I won't let on you're female, if they haven't already figured it out." He gave her a wry look. "It won't be easy thinking of you as a man."

Relief washed through her, along with the sudden impulse to wrap her arms around him and hug him just the way she used to.

But then reality pressed in. He was no longer the boy she loved. Not even the half-grown lad she'd kissed. He was fully grown now, a man she barely knew. A man who belonged to another—at least he once had. She had no idea if that was still the case.

That thought sobered her like no other, and she hoisted her satchel and catch, then started toward the creek crossing.

The sooner she took Jean-Jacques back to camp, the sooner she could send him on his way. Then, at least she wouldn't have this complication to contend with.

~

French followed Colette in silence as his mind played through what little she'd said. She'd ignored so many of his questions that he still knew nothing about what was happening with her. He'd have to renew their friendship before she would trust him again, apparently.

Would Young Bear and the others mind him joining their group for a while? He'd counted on Colette asking him to stay. But the way she'd placed a blockade around herself, he had a feeling she wouldn't be offering an invitation.

So, he'd have to work out that detail himself, just as he'd done more than once as he moved from one group to another to cover new ground in his search for Colette.

When they stepped from the trees into the camp, three men worked in different areas. One sat before the fire, a wooden bowl of stew in his hands. Another knelt by a stack of furs. The third was slicing meat on a flat rock.

All three looked up, honing their gazes on him. The faces were familiar from when their groups had passed the day before. Young Bear and the fifth man must be nearby.

Colette motioned to him and slipped back into that odd deep voice. "My friend, Jean-Jacques Baptiste." Then she pointed to each of the men in turn. "Left Standing, Hawk Wing, and Elk Runs."

The man with the stew bowl, Left Standing, raised a hand in greeting. "We welcome you, Jean-Jacques Batiste." Though he spoke with a heavy accent, his English was better than French would have expected.

French offered him an easy-going smile and a friendly greeting in the sign language most of the tribes used. "Most people call me French these days."

He nodded toward the furs piled near the trees. "Looks like you've been successful this winter." He cast his glance around the three to include them all in the praise. "My furs haven't been nearly so plentiful as yours." He would have had more if he'd focused his efforts on trapping instead of traipsing back and forth across the mountain ranges on missions of mercy with his friends, but no need to add that detail now.

The man by the furs, Hawk Wing, nodded with a grunt as he pointed to the lower half of his stack. "Many beaver. Good trade."

French sent an appreciative glance toward the healthy pile. "Those will bring a good price. It's been two winters since I met at the rendezvous. How much is a beaver pelt trading for now?"

"Two beaver bring bag corn." The man gave a nod and pushed up to his feet. "Good trade."

French sent a glance in the direction of the creek. "I need a place to lay traps. Might I bide here a few sleeps and set my traps down the river? I'll stay far from your own."

A sound that seemed half-grunt, half-gurgle came from Colette.

He used the moment to turn a smile on her and stepped close enough to slap her shoulder as he would a man. "That will give me time to visit with this fellow. My old friend." The fact he'd treated her like a man might help keep her from objecting. Besides, telling him to leave in front of these braves would not be a sign of friendship. Would be quite rude actually. And Colette's innate kindness had always been too strong to allow for rudeness.

He tried to send her a look that told her all would be well. He wouldn't give away her secret, but he *would* be a help to her.

He didn't let himself look at her long but returned his focus to the Indians.

Hawk Wing rose to his feet. "Young Bear is our elder. You met him, yes? He say whether you leave or stay." He started forward and motioned for French to follow. "I take you to him."

French sent Colette a final gentle smile as he followed the man back through the trees.

Young Bear's territory for trapping must be the area nearest camp, either in deference to his age or his leadership, for they found him before they even reached the creek.

Hawk Wing spoke a string of Blackfoot to the man, and Young Bear turned his gaze to scan French. Down, then back up.

After Hawk Wing finished speaking, the older man was still studying French, maybe waiting for him to say something.

French offered a friendly smile. "I have traps to set out, but I'll keep them far from yours and these others. I would like time to visit with my friend." He almost said *with Colette,* but if she was pretending to be a man, she might've given them a different name.

Young Bear nodded. "Place yours past the traps of Mignon." He motioned across the creek and down the stretch where Colette had placed her snares.

French nodded. "I will. Thank you. I have a horse too."

The man pointed to the right of the trees separating them from camp. "There."

Again, French nodded. "I'll see to her then."

As he turned toward where he'd tied Giselle, relief sank through him. But it tangled with too much apprehension.

Now he had to learn why Colette was hiding like this. Was she in danger? He would find out, even if he had to tickle it out of her, like she'd once done to him when they were young.

That thought added an extra spring in his step. He'd finally found Colette. Though it seemed, the search to learn the truth had only just begun.

CHAPTER 4

How had she let this happen?

Tension knotted in Colette's belly, starting a fresh roiling that kept trying to send bile up her throat. She dropped her trapping supplies and the catch and went for her food satchel. After pulling out a piece of smoked meat, she bit into the tough, flavorful bite, chewing only enough to swallow before biting off a new chunk. After a few bites, the nausea in her belly finally eased, and she refilled her pack to use for snacks.

She would have to do her best to ignore Jean-Jacques's presence.

Not that she'd be able to. He'd never been ignorable, even when he didn't look at her with so many questions in his eyes as he did now. He was too savvy to ask personal details in the presence of these men, especially if she didn't offer up any. Perhaps that was her best approach—keep from being alone with him.

After refastening the food pack, she pushed to standing. She'd heard his voice from the direction they hobbled the horses, so maybe he'd be occupied with getting settled for a while. This might be her best opportunity to set the last two traps and skin this beaver in the creek. Then she could flesh the hide where the others worked.

She trudged to the end of her trap line to place her last two traps first, so they would have time to work before the evening checking. After setting the first one, she bent over the final trap to reset the coil.

"Hello."

At Jean-Jacques's voice, she jumped sideways and barely kept in her yelp. She pressed a hand to still her racing heart as she straightened and sent him a glare. The melody of the brook had completely covered the sounds of his approach.

His face wore a look of concern, but then his expression softened. His eyes took on a twinkle, and one corner of his mouth tipped. The look washed through her with the shock of memory. How many times had he turned that mischievous grin on her to dampen her ire?

And it had worked, every time. Just like now.

She fought to keep a scowl and managed to at least stop herself from matching his grin. "What do you want?"

He blinked, maybe at her tone. She'd not meant to sound quite so sharp. But his grin stayed intact. "Young Bear said I can set my traps past your area. Where would you prefer I start?"

She raised her brows at him. Now, there was a question begging for a snap of truth.

He seemed to realize it, for he added, "Rather, is this your last trap? I'll move out of sight before I begin placing mine."

She'd always appreciated his quick mind. They were a matched pair most times, whether that be for good or bad.

With a nod, she turned back to her set. "This is my last one."

"I'll get started then." He nodded toward the beaver carcass lying beside her pack. "Leave that and I'll skin it for you."

She tightened her jaw and shook her head. "I'll do it." As much as she would love to hand over that awful task, she had to do her own work. All of it. If she was going to play a convincing role for her campmates, she couldn't slough off the unsavory portions like a squeamish female.

No matter that she'd lost her breakfast more times than she could count while performing that particular task.

His brows lowered in a frown as he studied her, and she met the look with another glare. If he was going to force his will on her, she would tell him to leave.

Maybe he realized that, for he finally turned away with a sigh. "If you insist."

He started downstream with a whistle. A jaunty tune she couldn't place. Before, she'd known all his songs. He whistled them often and had tried to teach her how. She'd never been able to manage more than a breathy squeak, even when he used his hands to position her jaw and wrenched his mouth in all manner of contortions to show her how to hold her tongue.

She'd finally learned how to whistle with a blade of grass, and that seemed to suffice for him. She couldn't carry a tune with the grass though.

He was almost out of sight behind a cluster of box elder trees before she let herself watch him go. How had he become so broad through the shoulders? And that lean waist begged for her to wrap her arms around him.

His hugs had been a balm, even when they were little. When her puppy had been kicked by a passing mule and the doctor couldn't do anything for it, Jean-Jacques had wrapped his nine-year-old arms around her and held her through her tears.

He'd done the same when she'd lost other pets through the years. And that final farewell...she could still feel both of their shoulders shaking with their tears. That good-bye had been awful. So much worse than losing a pet, and after the final ripping away, she no longer had his arms to wrap around her.

She'd tried to run away once—the second night on the trail from Montreal to Fort York. Mama must have had an inkling of what she planned, for when Colette had slipped out from under the wagon where they bedded down, she'd nearly screamed at the form standing over her. Not that she was afraid, once she realized it was mama. But the tears had started anew. They'd not stopped for weeks. Maybe even months, but that time was all a blur.

Then three years later when Mama told her Jean-Jacques had married…had taken another woman to wife…she'd been a little more careful to hide her tears. But they'd come.

She forced the memories back as she sprinkled grass over the steel trap. Hopefully, this one would catch a beaver too. Hawk Wing had shown her the best way to conceal a trap for a beaver. And how to find their trails. He knew the business well, as the stack of furs he'd showed Jean-Jacques attested to.

Grabbing up her supplies and her catch, she started back toward the creek crossing. As much as she hated this part, it had to be done. She just had to make sure she didn't cast up her accounts in the doing.

~

The sun had risen halfway to the high noon position by the time French finished setting out his traps and exploring the countryside a bit. Beaver Tail would've said the sun was three fingers high, the Indian's way of marking time.

He came back toward the creek, crossing by way of Colette's traps so he could see if any had sprung. She'd snared a beaver that he removed, and one of the other traps had been sprung, but had no animal inside. If he remembered correctly, this was the same set that had been like that this morning. Had a predator discovered the snare for an easy meal? There wasn't an obvious sign of blood or fur at the trap like something had been wrenched free, but he inspected the area a little farther out, doing his best not to leave a print or tramp down the bushes.

There. In the midst of a section of tall straw grass lay a flat bloody spot, littered with bones and scraps of fur. Something had ripped the furbearer from the trap and feasted on it. The predator was definitely an animal, the way it left the scraps littered about.

Colette would do best to move this trap, but he'd let her know and leave the decision to her. It was the right of the trapper to choose the best location, based on game trails and features of the land. Did Colette really know what she was doing out here? Her traps were set in decent locations. He might've shifted one or two a step to the right or left. But that was individual preference. She seemed to know at least the basics, more than many men who started out in this business.

Leaving that trap sprung so she could come and move it, he picked up the beaver and his supplies and headed back to the creek crossing.

When he reached the stone path across the water, Colette and two Indians were working on the far bank. All of them fleshing hides, from the look of things.

He paused long enough to watch her with her tongue clamped sideways between her teeth, her face in a grimace, eyes intent as she used a carving knife to scrape bits of flesh from the underside of the hide.

The two men, Elk Runs and Left Standing, had their own fleshing stations set up, but they were going about the job in a much more subdued manner. No fierce expressions, just steady scraping, their arms flexing with their efforts.

He knew well how much effort fleshing a hide required. Firm scraping for a solid hour, sometimes longer, depending on the size of the hide. His arm muscles would protest by the end, even if he was in regular practice of scraping several hides a day. For a woman, the effort must be exhausting.

But Colette went at the task with a vengeance. Surely the others saw how much harder she had to work at the job. They couldn't really be so blind as to think her a man, could they? If he squinted really hard—enough to make her only a fuzzy outline—*maybe* he would believe her an over-eager lad. A tall one, with an awful lot of grace for his gangly limbs.

But a man? So why didn't they tell her they knew her secret? Maybe the men possessed protective instincts. Maybe they realized she must be in danger and the best way to help her was to let her keep up the ruse.

He needed to know how much she'd told them about herself. That would give him clues about the men's behavior and also might be a way to get her to open up a little about the years since they'd last seen each other.

He started across the river toward them, taking care from one rock to the next to keep from slipping as he'd done that first time. Hopefully, he'd be able to speak with Colette alone later in the afternoon to ask what she'd told the Indians about herself. But for now, he'd better make himself useful.

Approaching Colette, he held up the beaver. "On my way back through, I noticed your trap by the rocky point had caught this fellow. I pulled him out and reset the teeth for you. I can skin him if you'd like me to."

She didn't meet his gaze and only flicked a quick glance at the beaver. "Thanks. Just lay it there, and I'll take care of it." She wiped her brow on her shoulder and went back to scraping.

"I don't mind. I've sure skinned a lot of animals these past years. I'll take care to keep the hide whole." She'd been too squeamish to pierce a worm with a hook back when they were kids. Was it *his* help she didn't want now, or any help in general? Maybe she thought it would make her look like less of a man.

He sent a glance around the group, then spoke loud enough for all to hear. "Since I don't have as many traps as you all, nor furs in need of scraping and stretching, I'm happy to help where I can. I can be the camp keeper and help skin and scrape when I'm done with my own furs."

Elk Runs acknowledged his words with a nod, and Left Standing added a smile. "Is good."

French turned back to Colette and did his best to keep his grin from turning smug. He'd found a way to help her without her losing face.

She met his gaze long enough to arch her brows at him. Then she nodded toward the beaver in his hand. "Suit yourself."

He'd never thought he'd be happy about the bloody job he'd just won. But this was a different kind of pleasure. He was taking the load from her overburdened shoulders.

As Colette turned back to her work, memory of his other bit of news slipped in. "One other thing." He waited until she looked up. "That first trap across the river had been sprung with no catch again. I didn't see anything there at the trap, but in the tall grass about ten strides past it, I found a kill site. Looks like we've got a predator stealing from the trap. I didn't move it. Thought you might want to."

She finally met his gaze and even offered a weak smile, though there was weariness around her eyes. "*Merci.*" The word of thanks slipping from her mouth in their native tongue eased through him like a warm drink on a cool morning. The word and tone together reminded him of the Colette he'd once known.

CHAPTER 5

After skinning and fleshing the hide, French built up the campfire and started roasting the meat from all their catches.

These men were bringing in a great deal of meat each day, more than they could eat. They likely traded the food along with the pelts and saved some for days when hunting wasn't as good. He applied salt liberally as he roasted to make the meat last longer. Some of this he would smoke instead of roasting, as that was the best method to preserve meat for the long term, if done correctly.

No one said anything about the midday meal, so by the time the sun had fallen two fingers past the noon mark, he ate his fill from what he'd cooked. Maybe the others carried food with them to eat during the day, as many a trapper did.

He checked the horses hobbled in the meadow and led each to drink in the creek. He'd not seen Colette in at least an hour, so perhaps she was by herself and they could have a few minutes to talk.

Aside from everything he needed to know about her situation, he had questions about the evening meal. He wasn't certain they would take him up on his offer to be camp keeper. They likely had an established routine they may not want to change. The last thing he wanted was to step in where he wouldn't be welcome.

Young Bear was the only one at the campsite when French stepped through the trees. The older man sat by the fire with a piece of meat in one hand and a pipe in the other.

French approached him. "I'm looking for...Mignon." He caught himself just before he used Colette's given name again. Where had she come up with Mignon? He'd have to make sure he asked that when he finally found her. "Have you seen...him?"

The man shook his head, then nodded across the fire. "Sit. Smoke."

No. French fought to keep his groan from leaking out. This was one of the Indian customs he liked the least. But Beaver Tail had made it clear that refusing to smoke the peace pipe was a strong offense against a brave. Especially an elder. He couldn't offend this man, the leader of the group.

After settling cross-legged on the ground where Young Bear motioned, he accepted the pipe. The tobacco filled his lungs, nearly choking him with its pungency. Some pipes he'd been forced to smoke had a sweeter taste, but not this.

He handed the tool back to Young Bear, and the man inhaled with a peaceful expression.

Maybe this was a good opportunity to clarify the cooking duties. "I told the others I'm happy to be keeper of the camp while I'm here. I can cook, if you'd like. See to the horses." He didn't mention the skinning. He'd volunteer for what work he could fit in among all these other jobs he was acquiring, in addition to his own traps.

Most trappers considered six sets to be a healthy line, since they were checked twice a day, and a man could reasonably skin and flesh twelve small hides each day. Since he only had two traps, he would, in theory, have some extra time.

After a slow, smoky exhale, the man nodded. "We all have turns. You have turn for all now."

All right then. He'd have to see if he could find herbs to throw in the stew pot. The fare he ate this morning filled the empty places but did little to satisfy his pallet. And salt could only go so far.

He acknowledged his new role with a nod. "You have food supplies?"

The man pointed his pipe at a leather pack against the rock wall lining one side of camp. "Hang in tree when sleep."

Again, French nodded. "I'll make sure I hang it high away from animals. Have you seen many bears yet this season? I've only seen one so far." And he'd been a hungry one. Caleb still healed from the wounds gained in that scuffle. But he'd saved the lives of Otskai and her son, so the claw marks and broken ankle had been worth the outcome.

"Only bear sign." The man bit into the roasted meat.

French rose to standing. "I'll take a look in the food pack, then do a bit of scouting in the area before I start the evening meal."

And hopefully he could still find Colette and get a few answers.

~

The warmth of sunlight soothed Colette's face as she opened her eyes. How long had she slept? She'd been forced to take these afternoon naps more often of late. Scraping hides hadn't exhausted her as much in the first weeks. Her arms had been fatigued of course, but this overwhelming weariness hadn't assaulted so strongly until the past couple weeks. Maybe the babe was responsible for this change too.

The little one growing inside had altered her body so much.

What she wouldn't give for a midwife or doctor to tell her what was normal. What she could expect, and what should worry her.

But she had no one. Eventually, her condition would be impossible to hide. Hopefully by then, she'd have followed these braves back to their camp and met women who would take her under their wing. Of course, Young Bear and the others wouldn't appreciate that she'd lied to them about being a man. Maybe they'd feel taken in and send her away. Surely they wouldn't do worse.

If she did find herself stranded again, she'd simply have to make another plan. This was the best idea she could come up with for the present.

A rustle in the grass jerked her attention sideways. A man's form stepped around the nearby trees, and she scrambled to sit up, reaching for her hat. She planted it on her head even as recognition slid through her.

Jean-Jacques.

Relief nearly stole her strength. At least he wasn't one of the braves, finding her napping in the daytime. But still, she struggled to her feet.

He sent her a grin. "Seems you have the right idea." He motioned to the flattened grass where she'd been lying. "The sun's warm this afternoon. Can I sit with you?"

The last thing she wanted was to talk alone with Jean-Jacques, but he was already settling himself on the ground. Her body seemed to still be gathering strength from her midday nap, her legs barely strong enough to hold her up.

So, she took the easiest route and sank back to the ground beside him.

Jean-Jacques rested his wrists on propped knees, but she struggled to find a good position. There really wasn't a ladylike way to sit in trousers, nor should she be looking for one, if she was going to keep up her ruse. But it seemed completely indecent to sit cross-legged without a skirt to cover herself. Especially since he knew she was no man.

She stretched her legs in front of her. With the position of the baby, she had to brace her hands behind her and lean back a little. Hopefully, that didn't show the bump she was gaining at her middle. Her jacket was loose enough to cover the small swell—mostly.

Jean-Jacques glanced sideways at her. "Do you ever take off the hat?" He eyed the leather brim with his brows dipped in a frown.

She shook her head. "Keeps the sun out of my eyes." And she could tug the brim down to cover part of her face if she met strangers. The entire thing made her look more like the man her companions expected.

Jean-Jacques reached toward the hat. She fought the impulse to jerk. She didn't move, even when he gripped the brim and eased it off her head. She shouldn't have allowed him —both the intimacy in the action and the removing of part of her disguise.

But this was Jean-Jacques. By her side again, feeling so familiar—and so very foreign. His nearness stole her breath, the familiar action almost intimate. She couldn't bring herself to move away.

After laying the hat in the grass behind them, his eyes still lingered on her hair. Her short locks must be a soiled mess. She'd only found a few opportunities in these past weeks to scrub her hair in the river when the others weren't around.

But the frown had left his expression, replaced by a tenderness in his eyes and a curve of his mouth. He reached toward her head and tucked a lock of hair behind her ear. When his fingertips brushed her skin, a tingle slid all the way through her. She had to fight to keep the shiver from showing.

Her body ached to lean into his touch. But he pulled his hand away and draped his wrist over his knee again. His eyes found hers, and the smile lines at their edges deepened. "I forgot how much I love your hair. As white as an angel's."

Those last words brought her to her senses. She was no angel—she'd proved that fact irrefutably.

"That's what first made me suspect it was you." Jean-Jacques's words tugged her focus back to his face. He was still smiling. "Your hair so pale. It's the same color your father's was, just a shade darker than when you were little. I'd never seen another man with hair that fair. Even though you were all covered up"—he motioned toward her clothing—"your hair started me thinking. The longer I thought, the more I had to know for sure if it was you."

Disappointment pressed through her. She'd not thought to try to color her hair. But how could she? Rub soot into it? That would make her a mess for sure. Maybe she should simply pull her collar higher when they met strangers on the trail. Or perhaps she could sew a hood onto her coat to wear underneath the hat.

Silence settled between them, and Jean-Jacques was watching her. She worked for a smile. Something natural.

He didn't return the look. Instead, his eyes turned sober. "How is your father, Colette? And your mama? Do they know where you are?"

She let herself drop the smile and pulled her gaze away from him. "Papa has been gone five years now. He died of a wound that festered. Not long after, mama sailed to old France to see my sister. Her ship went down on the voyage over." She'd not let herself think about her parents often. That all seemed like another lifetime. The life before Raphael.

Maybe the ache surging up her throat, stinging her eyes, came from telling Jean-Jacques the news. He'd known her parents well, had eaten more meals around their table than she could ever count.

She focused on the river that could barely be seen through

the tree branches. The flowing current shifted and swayed, but never ceased.

"I'm sorry." Jean-Jacques's voice held much more than sympathy. Pain clouded his tone.

Silence stretched again as memories tried to press in. Probably, he was remembering. But she couldn't let herself do the same. Sinking into happier times would only weaken her ability to face the present.

Straightening, she turned to him and strengthened her voice. "Now you see why it's important for me to keep my disguise as a man out here."

He studied her as though trying to work something out in his mind. "I *don't* see. But on that topic, it would help if you tell me everything our companions know about you. That way I can be careful not to let on more than you want." His brows drew together. "They call you Mignon?"

She nodded. She'd taken that name from a trader in one of the forts she'd skirted. "They really don't know much more than that. I'm a young man who wants to earn some money trapping. I'm willing to do my part in the group. I have a better gun than theirs and a small gunsmithing kit with extra parts. I've been working on Hawk Wing's fusee as a little extra payment for allowing me to come along."

His brows shot up. "You're a gunsmith now too?" His tone held surprise and maybe a little admiration.

She certainly didn't deserve the latter. She shook her head. "Not a gunsmith. I learned by working on them. Not hard to do once you understand the mechanics. The fusee is a simple weapon."

"And trapping? You learned that by doing it too? You taught yourself how to find the animal trails and where to place your bait? And how to skin an animal to leave the fur intact, then scrape and work the furs to make them the finest quality?"

Now he was pressing too far. And that might have been a hint of derision in his tone.

She shrugged. "Young Bear let me follow him the first few times he set his traps. Hawk Wing too. They've all given me helpful advice here and there."

Jean-Jacques nodded and turned his gaze forward, toward the trees and the river beyond. "Those are nice traps you have. One of the best designs I've seen. They look like they were made by a blacksmith who specializes in snares. Must have cost you a pretty penny."

What was he insinuating now? That she'd stolen them? She hadn't. Not really. "They were..." She stopped herself before *my husband's* slipped out. "...a gift from a friend."

Raphael hadn't made them for her, but they'd been stock he was building up in preparation for the rendezvous. What was his had lawfully become hers at his death, right? Or maybe they should have passed along to his brothers. No way to change that now. Hugh and Louis would have taken everything else.

"A fine gift." The tension in his tone eased, his voice sounding more like his old self. "Whoever made them must have been a talented blacksmith indeed."

She nodded but couldn't trust herself to speak. Raphael had been talented with his work, his traps sought after by men all up and down the Hudson Bay line. If his drinking hadn't gotten in the way, he might have earned the riches he'd dreamed of.

Silence settled again between them. She should go work some of her older furs.

But Jean-Jacques straightened before she managed to. "I came out here to look for onion grass to add flavor to a stew. Guess I'd better get moving."

He pushed to his feet, and she did too, but so much clumsier than he. The baby made it hard to bend as easily. "You volunteered to cook the evening meal?" If he knew what to add in the stew pot to soften the taste of wild game, she'd be happy to learn from him.

"Volunteered to be the camp keeper. That means every meal." He bent down and scooped up her hat. Thankfully, he didn't step near her to place it on her head. Just held it out.

"You really meant that? Have you spoken to Young Bear?"

He dipped his chin in a nod. "Right before I came out here." Then that familiar smile tipped one side of his mouth. "Had to do something to sweeten the idea of me sticking around. If you can mend guns, I can do the cooking."

A smile tickled her own mouth, but she pressed her lips to hold back. "Well then, far be it from me to stop you."

But keeping her secrets from Jean-Jacques would prove much harder the longer he stayed.

CHAPTER 6

Colette's belly roiled as she sat up in the early morning light. Would this nausea never end?

She reached for a bite of meat from the pack behind her. Elk Runs, Hawk Wing, and Cross the River had already left to check their traps, and Left Standing slipped the strap of his carrying pouch over his head as he prepared to follow them.

Young Bear sat on his pallet with a buffalo robe wrapped around his shoulders. The night had been colder than other recent ones, and the chill still lingered, clouding her breath in front of her.

Jean-Jacques had risen with the other men and knelt over the fire. He'd already retrieved a pot of water from the river, and it sat nestled among the flames. Hopefully he was planning something warm to break their fast. What she wouldn't give for a hearty batch of Johnny cakes. Or even better, a freshly baked breton galette or croissant. The thought knotted a pain in her belly, and she tugged another bite of meat from the chunk with her teeth. At least roasted beaver had flavor, though she was sick to death of the taste.

Or maybe just sick. The familiar nausea churned again in

her middle, and she inhaled a deep gulp of chilly air. That usually made the sensation subside.

After a few more minutes to fill her belly with meat, she reached for her hat. Without water, the dried meat was enough to choke a body. She rose and grabbed her cup from her pack, then stepped to the fire.

Jean-Jacques turned a warm smile up at her. "Morning." His voice held an extra rumble from sleep, and its intimacy drew her nearer. As much as she wanted to crouch beside him, that wasn't such an easy task these days. Not with the way her balance shifted more each week. So she settled for returning his smile with her own "Good morning."

Having him bedded down at the head of her pallet had been a comfort last night—just knowing he was near. She'd been a little worried he might pull out a flask during the evening meal, but he didn't. And he showed no signs of carrying whiskey. That didn't mean he wouldn't drink when the opportunity arose, but at least she wouldn't have to worry about it every night. Jean-Jacques's father had been an awful drunk, which was one of the main reasons they'd spent so much time together early on—Jean-Jacques trying to escape the misery that consumed his home.

He reached for her cup, and she handed it over. "I couldn't find coffee beans in the food pack. I'll keep an eye out for sassafras leaves for tea, but all I have to drink for now is warm water."

She should've also been watching for some kind of leaves or bark to use for a tea. But she'd been more focused on survival than comfort. "Water is fine."

As she sipped, she peeked over his shoulder at what he was working with on the flat rock. Some kind of batter.

"I found some parched corn in a little bag at the bottom of the pack, so I ground it up for cornmeal. It won't make many corn cakes, but at least it'll be hearty. Thought we'd have a bit of fresh meat with it."

Just the thought of some form of bread curled through her belly, tightening the ache of hunger. "That sounds wonderful."

Her tone must've been a bit too dreamy—or maybe desperate—for Jean-Jacques tipped a smile up at her before focusing again on his work. "I hope it is. I guess we'll see."

It would be several minutes before his fare was ready, and her morning needs pressed. She'd eaten enough meat from her pack to hold her a little while, so she headed toward the woods. After seeing to her ministrations, men's loud voices drew her toward the river.

Angry voices—at least one of them. The other seemed calmer.

When she stepped through the brush to the water's edge, the four men who'd gone to check their traps stood in a loose circle. Hawk Wing spoke in angry tones, waving his hand toward his traps across the river. His Blackfoot words cascaded in a fierce ripple, so quick she had no chance of deciphering any sounds.

A figure stepped through trees from the trail leading toward camp. Young Bear. Probably coming to see what the ruckus was about. Jean-Jacques followed him and cast a glance toward Colette. Was that relief in his expression? Maybe he thought the men were speaking so loudly to her.

He raised his brows and shot a glance toward Hawk Wing, as if asking what the problem was.

She shrugged, then turned her focus back to the braves.

Young Bear asked a question, his tone commanding and calm. Always the voice of reason. He was one of the reasons she'd decided to join with this group. Men who were ruled by a calm leader would be easier to get along with. And the others seemed to respect him well.

Hawk Wing answered his elder in a tone that held a little less anger, though indignation still rose off him.

Left Standing noticed her then and took a step away from the group toward her. He sometimes translated when the others were speaking their native tongue. She closed the distance between them. Jean-Jacques drew near too, and Left Standing spoke to them both.

"Three of his traps had the catch stolen from them. He says we should leave this place. Go to where predators are not so hungry."

Leave again? They'd ridden for two days solid before finding this valley. And before that, they'd barely stayed in one location more than a day, or two at the most. So long in the saddle made her bones ache. Finding new places for traps took time. The thought of more travel, then starting all over again, made the strength seep from her bones.

"How does he know the catch was stolen? Does he suspect what animal might've taken it?" Jean-Jacques's tone stayed calm. Inquisitive. Would he mention her own trap where the catch had been taken? He'd even found the kill site, so maybe he had a suspicion what animal it was. But if he spoke of this, it would add more reason for the group to move on.

Left Standing glanced at the others for a minute. Hawk Wing was still spluttering on, motioning across the river again. "He says there were bits of hair by the traps, proof the prey was taken. He found places where the catch was eaten. He says he lost three good beaver this night."

Young Bear finally began speaking, and they all quieted to listen. Colette could pick out a few words, but nothing that made sense together.

After a moment, the leader glanced their way. Maybe he was realizing they had no idea what he said. He switched to broken English. It seemed most of these men knew more English than French, so that was the mutual tongue they mostly used.

"We have found good trapping here in this valley, better than any camp in the last moon. If we leave this place, we may not find so good again."

"What good are full traps if we are not allowed to empty them ourselves?" Hawk Wing must have recovered control of his temper enough to speak English also.

"We all will choose. Go or stay?" Young Bear pointed first to Elk Runs, who seemed to hold the position of second in command sometimes.

"Stay and see if this bad thing continues."

Young Bear nodded, then pointed to Cross the River.

"Stay for now."

The older man pointed to Hawk Wing, who'd done an admirable job holding his tongue until his turn. "Go. As soon as we dress our morning catch. We should find a new place to set our traps before dark."

Young Bear turned and pointed to Left Standing.

"I wish to stay here for now."

Then Young Bear looked at her, and warmth slipped through her. They were giving her a voice, as an equal. Or...mostly so. She was being asked last, which would be the place of the youngest of the group.

She adjusted her voice to the deeper tone. "Stay for now." She always tried to use as few words as necessary when speaking.

The vote was confirmed then. But instead of stating that fact, Young Bear turned to Jean-Jacques. Was he being asked his opinion as well?

Jean-Jacques gave a nod of acknowledgement. "I will be content with what you all choose. If I am given a voice, I would wish to stay here until we see whether this predator lingers." Well spoken.

Young Bear seemed to think so too. With a nod, he turned back to the braves in front of him. "We will stay here for now. If this stealing continues, we will leave this place."

Relief swept through her. *Let the varmint leave us, Lord. Please.*

~

French slid a glance at the gray clouds edging toward them as he used his knife to flesh a muskrat hide. Most of the group had already finished with their morning catch. Only he, Colette, and Left Standing still worked by the river.

The air smelled of rain, but hopefully they could finish these last tasks before taking cover. There wouldn't be much shelter out here—only trees. He should have taken time to stretch an oilskin, but he hadn't.

For his part, he didn't mind a little wet. He'd already draped furs over everyone's packs so no water could soak them. But it would be nice to give Colette a place to stay dry.

He sent a glance toward her. She wore that twisted grimace he was becoming accustomed to as she scraped her hides. The expression would be cute if it weren't for how hard she had to work at the job.

Even if he made a shelter, she probably wouldn't take cover in it. Would probably think that made her look unmanly.

The thought went down like sour milk. She didn't need to be out here suffering, not when he could take care of her. Not when he *wanted* to take care of her.

Maybe he should simply tell her that. Tell her he still felt the same way about her as when they'd promised themselves to each other at thirteen. She didn't have to pretend to be a man and do such distasteful work. They could head north again, find the first town with a preacher, and get married.

Or better yet, they could ride west across the mountains and catch up with his friends. Let Caleb perform the ceremony, since he was an ordained minister. Then go wherever Colette's heart desired.

Certainty grew inside him with every stroke. That's exactly what he would do. Why hadn't he already done it? Maybe

Colette didn't think he felt the same. Perhaps she didn't want to hold him to their childhood promise.

To his right, Left Standing straightened from his work and eyed the darkening sky. "Rain comes soon." The man placed the bundle he'd been working on with his others from today and stood.

As the fellow started down the trail to the camp, French glanced at Colette, but she hadn't lifted her focus from her work. "Want to head back to camp before we get wet out here?"

She shook her head and didn't stop working. "We'll get wet there too. Need to finish this last one."

Stubborn, as he'd suspected.

He'd only made two more swipes on his hide before fat drops began peppering his face. "There it comes." He scooped up his hides and the meat that needed cooked. "Let's get under the trees."

The drops fell faster now, turning into a deluge.

When he shifted to help Colette, she was folding up the hide she'd been working on. He scooped up the stack of furs at her feet, and she grabbed her bundle of meat and her pack.

Raindrops pounded in a thick curtain, as though a dam had broken in the sky. They ran toward the trees, moving into the densest part where the shelter would be best.

By the time they reached decent tree cover, he was panting. So was she.

Rain battered the new spring leaves on the trees above them, with some drops breaking through to pellet their heads. He lowered his bundles to the ground, then grabbed the largest fur he'd worked that morning, turning it hair side down.

"Here, move closer." He held one end over his head, leaving a spot for her to tuck beside him under the shelter.

She set her bundles on the ground. "I'm already drenched."

Her hat had protected a little circle around her collar, but the rest of her buckskin outfit had turned dark. Clearly sodden.

He shifted to widen the spot for her. "This is better than nothing."

She stopped arguing and moved in close to his side under the fur. The leather of her sleeve brushed his own buckskin tunic, but she didn't press in beside him.

He didn't bother with such carefulness. Just leaned over so the covering sheltered her more fully. His arm that held the fur looped behind her, and he let his elbow rest lightly on her shoulder. He had no idea how long this downpour would last, and it wouldn't be easy to hold the fur overhead longer than a few minutes.

She must have realized that, for she reached up and gripped the hide near his hand. "I can hold this side."

The brim of her hat blocked her face from his view, and with the noise from the rain pattering around them, he couldn't hear whether there was tension in her voice from their nearness, or if she was simply being considerate.

He dropped his hand from the fur but cupped the curve of her waist and shifted her a little in front of him, so they'd both be better protected. The rain was pounding fiercely, even under these trees. If she wanted to resist his touch, she would have to step into the torrent to do it.

Though she didn't give in to his guiding easily, she didn't push him away. He kept his hand at her waist. Not a firm press. Light enough that maybe she didn't even feel it through her thick wet leathers.

Still, with her warmth under his fingers, every one of his senses came alive and blazing. That confounded hat was in his face, but he could ignore it with the sheer pleasure of having Colette so close to him. Her shoulder pressed his chest. Barely a brush, but his heart pounded double time.

The rain didn't last nearly long enough. Though his arm holding up the fur on his side complained, he would've gladly stayed in his wet clothes for hours to have her so near. If the rain weren't pounding so loudly, this would be a good time to speak to her about the promise they'd made all those years ago. But something in her manner gave him pause. She didn't seem ready quite yet.

He breathed in a deep breath. He'd gotten used to the scent of trail grime a long time ago, but Colette's flavor was sweeter than most. Everything about this woman drew him in. How long could he keep pretending she wasn't a woman?

CHAPTER 7

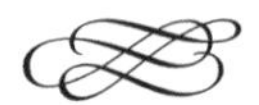

As French had feared, the moment the rain trickled to a steady dripping, Colette stepped away from him. Far too quickly for his liking.

She didn't look at him, just bent to gather her things. That hat still blocked his view of her face. Had she so hated being near him? What disease had he contracted that she no longer seemed drawn to him as she had when they were young? Why wouldn't she trust him?

With a sigh, he gathered his own belongings. Colette had already started toward camp, so he lengthened his stride to catch up to her. He'd love to change out of these clingy wet leathers, but he'd have to go someplace private to do that. He certainly wasn't subjecting Colette to such an embarrassment, even if he rigged a changing screen.

He caught up with her as they stepped through the trees to the campsite clearing. Colette stopped short, and his bundles slammed into her back before he could stop himself. She didn't stumble forward—something had her rooted too deeply to the ground.

He moved beside her to see what she was staring at, tensing

to drop his load and grab his knife if danger threatened. The braves should be here though. Surely they wouldn't allow a threat to linger.

The sight before them made laughter rise up in his belly, but he clamped his jaw before the sound tumbled out. He was helpless to stop the grin though.

Left Standing, Hawk Wing, Elk Runs, and Cross the River had all stripped off their tunics and leggings—leaving only breach clout—and were in the process of hanging the garments on tree branches. Young Bear had removed his tunic and was bent over to pull off a moccasin. He carried a small middle-age paunch, and the way he was leaning revealed more than was seemly beneath his breach clout.

French stepped in front of Colette to shield her from the view, but another belly laugh pressed up. He should be appalled…really he should.

And he *was* for Colette's sake. She was probably mortified, even in her manly garments. But these men were doing nothing untoward for their culture, especially since they thought the company was all male. Or…maybe they saw through Colette's disguise.

Either way, Colette had planted herself squarely in this position through her own devices.

But he had to do his best to protect her from anything more than she'd already witnessed. He glanced back at her, and relief slipped in when he saw she'd already turned away. "Why don't you head back to the river? The rain's mostly stopped, but take this fur to shelter yourself." He spoke French and kept his voice low so the others didn't question why he was sending her away.

"Will you hand me my pack beside my bedroll?" Colette, too, kept her voice low, but it held a bit of growl. Her face had flared bright red, at least the part he could see.

He strode toward their covered bedding, dropped his load beside his other things, then lifted the fur atop her belongings.

Hopefully, her pack contained other clothing she could change into. Else, she'd be as miserable as him in these wet buckskins.

When he handed the satchel to her, she jerked it from his grip and nearly ran back through the trees.

He finally let his chuckle slip out as he watched her go. Then he turned back to put his things away.

But when he glanced at the Indians, Young Bear was watching him. The man's expression gave away nothing of his thoughts, but he was definitely considering something.

Did he think Colette's sudden shyness strange? What else had he noticed?

~

Jean-Jacques had settled into their group so seamlessly, Colette finally stopped letting worry tie her insides in knots. He wouldn't tell her secret. At least, not the one he knew—the fact that she was a woman.

Jean-Jacques had always kept her confidences. The only thing that kept her from telling him more now was the fact that anything could slip out when a man put himself under the influence of that demon they all seemed to love—alcohol and all its forms. She'd seen it happen more times than she cared to remember, especially with the man she'd married.

Raphael had told her things she didn't want to know during his binges. About the men he'd cheated in his work. The times he'd sought out other women after a few drinks too many. He cried and begged for forgiveness, all while sloppy drunk. She'd learned well that no man could be trusted when whiskey took over.

And with the way Jean-Jacques's father had overindulged so often, he was probably more susceptible to the power of strong drink than most men. She'd heard more than one person say tendency toward drunkenness ran in the bloodline.

So she couldn't tell Jean-Jacques her secrets. Besides, part of her couldn't stand the thought of him hating her for what she'd done. She despised herself enough, even though she'd not intended that awful act. She'd only been protecting her babe.

But that didn't change the outcome.

This was the third day since Jean-Jacques joined their camp, and now he was off searching for fodder to add to their meals. That was another thing she'd quickly come to appreciate about his presence. He actually spent time thinking about the food he would cook, about ways to do his work better, no matter how humble the task. He went out of his way to find more variety and plants to use for seasonings. He'd become a better cook than she'd thought a man could be.

Raphael had certainly never cooked, and neither had her father. She'd not spent much time around the other men at Fort Pike, save for trips to the trade store and occasional passings outside of fort walls.

But Jean-Jacques didn't mind doing what she'd always considered women's work. He did it well, with pride.

He'd ridden his horse on this trek away from camp, so perhaps he planned to go far. She'd use the opportunity to seek out her hidden spot for a nap. The baby was seeping even more of her energy, for at times she could barely keep her eyes open.

The sun shone brightly, and though she didn't fall asleep, she could lie here and enjoy her thoughts.

A nicker sounded in the distance from the direction where the horses were hobbled to graze. Had Jean-Jacques returned already? Perhaps he'd found a plentiful gathering of the plants he sought and harvested them quickly.

She'd better rise and head back to camp. If he caught her sleeping, he would wonder why. Even being worn out from scraping hides all morning wouldn't cause this much exhaustion in a healthy person.

Another whinny sounded, and this time an answer came

from farther in the distance. That must be Jean-Jacques's mount.

She sat up and dusted the grass from her hands, then took up her rifle and the blanket she'd brought to lay on. After fixing her hat atop her head, she stood the easiest way she'd found—by moving to her hands and knees first, then working up to standing. She still had at least four months to go, maybe closer to five. Moving about would only get harder…and then everything would change completely.

She gave herself a quick moment to rest her hand atop her belly as she started through the trees toward camp. *Are you happy in there, little one? Grow strong and healthy for me. I can't wait to meet you.*

It didn't seem real, the fact that she would finally have her own babe to snuggle. She'd dreamed of it in her early days with Raphael. But this wasn't at all the way she'd imagined.

Voices sounded from the direction of the horses, and she strained to pick out Jean-Jacques's. One of the other braves might be with the animals too.

The words were spoken in French, but not Jean-Jacques's smooth cadence. The voice was gruffer, as though the man smoked tobacco often. None of the braves could speak the French language so fluently…at least they hadn't in her presence. Had a stranger come?

Fear clutched her, and she stilled.

Had Hugh and Louis found her? The voice didn't sound like either of theirs, but maybe they traveled with others. Perhaps they'd brought a whole posse to help their chase.

Her entire body tensed with the urge to bolt. But she needed to be wise about this. First, she had to know for sure who the newcomers were. Maybe these were other strangers she should be wary of. If she looked too spooked, she might draw unwanted attention. She couldn't give up her current protected situation unless Hugh and Louis really had found her.

She stepped toward the voices, walking softly so she didn't make noise, and doing her best not to look like she was creeping, in case someone caught sight of her.

The voices continued, and she made out a few words. The man was saying they'd been riding down to a lake they'd heard about past the Rocky Mountains. They planned to spend some time trapping there and would it be all right if they bedded down here this night?

She paused and strained to hear the response. Was Young Bear there to answer?

The senior brave's voice rumbled deep and steady, and the sound swept a bit of relief through her. If what the stranger said was true, Hugh and Louis weren't with him. She'd only have to keep her distance from these men for a night, then they'd be gone.

But she had to make certain the men spoke truth—that her brothers-in-law weren't part of the group.

As Young Bear used his halting French to tell the men they could share the campfire, she crept closer, shifting from tree to tree.

The forms of men and horses could barely be seen through the trunks, and the bright sunshine in the clearing where they stood made their faces blurry. Hopefully she was deep enough in the shadows no one would spot her as she scooted from one pine to another.

At a sturdy trunk wider than those around it, she paused and peered around the side. Now she could make out features on the men.

They were dismounting, three that she could see, with six horses, counting their pack animals.

None of their grizzled faces matched that of Hugh or Louis. It'd been a while since she'd seen Hugh, the elder, but there was no way he could have aged as much as any of these men.

She stayed behind the tree, bile still churning inside her as the men unloaded. They removed pack saddles and riding saddles but didn't unstrap supplies from the pack saddles. Hopefully that meant they planned to ride out first thing in the morning.

Soon, they'd walk toward the camp. Did she want to be there first? No, better to watch from a distance to make sure they weren't hiding anything.

There was always a chance they'd met Hugh and Louis along the way and been given her description to watch out for. Her hair had given away her disguise to Jean-Jacques. It would likely do the same for these men too.

She should make herself scarce until closer to nightfall. Then maybe she could find a way to cover her hair before joining the others at the campsite.

From everything she could see, the men were hiding no secrets. She stayed in the shadows long enough to watch them drag their things into the clearing next to the rock cliff, then she moved away from the sound of their voices as they spoke to Left Standing and Young Bear.

Maybe she could keep an eye out for Jean-Jacques and let him know of their guests before he was surprised in camp. She could also let him know she wouldn't be coming back until dark. That way he wouldn't worry, and hopefully he would cover for her.

That plan helped ease the knot in her belly, and she started toward the river. Maybe she should even saddle her horse and ride to find Jean-Jacques. The thought of sitting on that hard saddle again when she didn't have to made her calluses ache where they'd formed over blisters. Besides, the men might return to the horses and find her there while she saddled her mare.

She strolled upriver instead.

She'd not explored beyond their area. Hadn't had the energy

to, in truth. But there was no way she could nap now with strangers wandering around.

As she walked, she surprised a covey of birds, which flew up in front of her. A little farther along, a group of three mule deer grazed in the tall grass. Their long ears always made their bodies look small, so it was hard to tell the ages of these for sure. But they looked like a full-grown doe and two yearlings.

The animals eyed her as she stopped to watch them. A real trapper might use this opportunity to bring in another hide, but their camp didn't need meat, and she had no desire to disturb this group. They were beautiful and showed their trust in her by not darting away at her presence.

After several minutes, the deer perked their ears in the opposite direction. She strained to see what they saw. Grassland stretched beyond them for about thirty strides, then a cluster of trees. Something must be coming through the woods.

Whatever was approaching appeared to be more threatening than they'd found her to be. In another heartbeat, the animals darted away, leaping in fluid bounds. She'd never thought them as pretty as the white-tailed deer, but this graceful show proved her wrong.

She refocused her attention on the distant trees, raising her rifle and pressing the butt to her shoulder so she could aim and fire quickly if needed. As the men had said, bear should be out of hibernation by now.

A moment later, a figure on horseback appeared through the shadows. She dropped to her knees to make herself smaller, not as obvious. This grass was low enough that she couldn't fully hide even if she lay flat, but from this position, she could shoot easier.

If this was one of Raphael's brothers, she would only wound him, and only if it came down to it. She wouldn't take another life, no matter what. She already had enough guilt to last a lifetime.

CHAPTER 8

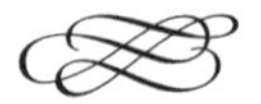

As the horse and rider stepped into the sunlight, relief swept through Colette.

Jean-Jacques. Of course it was him...she'd been waiting for his return. The strangers at camp simply had her on edge. With her arms full of blanket and rifle, she pushed to her feet and waited for him to reach her.

He arrived with a grin, that old familiar Jean-Jacques smile that brightened every day, no matter the weather or how badly things had been going before. She tried to keep her own grin tucked inside—better this man not know how he affected her—but it was no easy thing, and her face might have betrayed her a bit.

Reining in right in front of her, he jumped to the ground. "Came out to meet me?" He sounded pleased with himself.

"Sort of. I needed to stay out of camp, so thought I'd explore this area."

He pulled the reins over his horse's neck and turned to her with raised brows. "What's happening at camp?" A glimmer slipped into his eyes. No doubt he was remembering the scene yesterday where they'd come upon the braves nearly exposed.

She pushed the memory away, but not before heat surged up to her ears.

To cover her embarrassment, she scowled at him. "We have visitors."

His face lost all hint of pleasure. "Who? People you know? Indian or white?" His voice took on more tension with each question. Then his expression brightened. "Did my friends follow me here?"

She replayed the men's voices in her mind, then shook her head. "I don't think so. It's three white men. Frenchmen. They're heading to a lake south of us, and Young Bear said they could camp with us overnight."

His mouth pressed in thought. Then he nodded. "Well then. Let's go meet them."

She stepped to the side and motioned for him to pass in front of her. "You go on. I'll be back to camp around nightfall."

His brows lowered, and his voice took on a hesitation. "Are you hiding from someone, Colette?"

Her heart thundered in her ears. She hadn't expected him to jump to that conclusion, only that she wouldn't want her gender to be discovered. She couldn't let him know the awful thing she'd done. Better to redirect him. Of course, that might be a challenge without actually lying.

She shrugged. "I thought it might be easier to appear as a man after dark. Better not to chance their suspicion in daylight."

He rolled his lips as he seemed to be considering something. What if he pressed more? She should send him on his way before he had the chance.

She motioned toward the path back to camp. "I don't mean to stop you though. Go meet the newcomers. See what you think of them. Maybe you've even seen them before." He'd said he'd spent quite a while trapping and traveling.

After a beat, Jean-Jacques nodded. "All right. Signal me if you need anything. An owl hoot or..." A grin broke over his features. "Do you remember our secret sign?"

Warm memories soaked through her. She couldn't help an answering grin. "A crow's caw." She'd lived for that sound. Its shrill cry always meant hope and pleasure in her younger days.

He nodded, then opened his mouth and made a soft *caw, caw* sound.

A giggle slipped out, more from his pleased expression after the noise than anything.

Her laugh turned his smile a bit silly, as though she'd brightened his day. He reached up and tweaked the brim of her hat. "Call me if you need anything. Anything at all." His voice became tender with those last words, making her want to lean into him.

Instead, she simply nodded. "I will."

Watching Jean-Jacques walk away left an aching knot in her throat. If only she could be free to come and go as she wanted. Not always fearing discovery or the threat of who might suspect what.

Eventually this would change. She just had to press on through these hard months ahead. She would make it. For her child, she would summon the strength to build a new life.

There wasn't much to do now. She couldn't go back to camp yet, and strolling farther away no longer held a draw now that Jean-Jacques had returned. And she was still so weary, her eyes longed to close.

She had her blanket and rifle, so she moved forward to the patch of trees Jean-Jacques had ridden through and found a smooth place near the shelter of the branches. Her hungry belly would wake her by nightfall if nothing else did.

She must have needed that sleep, for by the time she awoke, dusk was settling over the landscape. Jerking upright, she scanned the area around her for any sign of movement. Any threat. Nothing stirred save a gentle breeze in the grass and the steady flow of the river.

Her belly gnawed at her insides, reminding her it had been far too long since the meat she ate at noontime. She should have brought her possibles satchel that contained more food, but she'd only planned a short nap in her hiding spot near camp.

A few more minutes and she would start back toward their fire. This would be a good time to check her traps, but she had no way to reset them without her pack that contained the bait. Still, maybe she could at least retrieve the catch. Or better yet, she could call Jean-Jacques to bring her pack and knife.

Pushing up to her feet, she blinked against the dredges of sleep that still clung. Straightening so quickly made her vision darken, but after a moment of stillness, her sight returned to normal. With her rifle in one hand and her blanket in the other, she started downstream.

Men's voices sounded as she neared the stretch of traps belonging to Hawk Wing and Elk Runs. She skirted them with a wide berth to reach her own sets. The catch had been stolen from one of her traps, and another still sat open and empty. The other four had snared three beavers and a badger. Not bad for a half day.

Darkness had closed in by the time she turned back toward the creek crossing. All the others appeared to be finished checking their lines. Hopefully all would be around the campfire indulging in another of Jean-Jacques's good meals. Maybe they could even trade with the strangers for more foodstuffs. A better variety would be nice.

Laying her catch at the edge of the trees, she lifted her chin and made the call of a crow. Her skills had diminished, more so than Jean-Jacques's ability. But the sound was still discernible.

Would the Indians question the noise? They seemed to have accepted her as part of the group, but she still wasn't certain whether they'd seen through her disguise. These were savvy men. If Jean-Jacques hadn't been fooled by her cover, would these braves?

But they hadn't said anything. They hadn't done anything untoward—at least not intentionally. That undressing after the rain hadn't been indecent for their culture.

Though she couldn't help wondering, she'd better not borrow trouble.

Footsteps sounded through the trees, and she tucked behind a trunk to see who it would be.

Jean-Jacques's form came clear, easing the tension in her shoulders. She shifted enough that he would see her, and he moved her direction.

"Are you all right?" His face wore concern in his gathered brows.

She nodded. "What have you learned of the men? Do you know them?"

He shook his head. "I've never met them before today, but they seem a good sort. Canadians as we are. We're eating beaver dumplings and drinking coffee." His eyes sparkled. "Real coffee, Colette. You have to come."

Though his pleasure brought a smile, the thought of coffee twisted her belly. The dumplings would be good, but such a strong brew wouldn't settle well.

"I need my trapping pack. Can you bring it? Once I reset my snares, I'll come to camp."

Disappointment eased his smile, but he nodded. "I'll get it."

He was true to his word, and after taking the pack, she made quick work of rebaiting her traps. She should have drawn the task out, but Jean-Jacques's good word about the strangers made her eager to return to camp.

And food. If she had to wait out here another hour, she might well skin one of those beavers and eat the meat fresh.

Her belly turned at that thought. If it couldn't manage strong coffee, she'd never be able to force down raw meat.

After field dressing her catch and securing it high in a tree where it should be safe for the night, she finally set her steps toward camp.

Her body was ready to collapse on her bed pallet. Company or not, she'd eat enough to fill her belly, then settle in for the night. Did every expectant mother suffer this exhaustion?

Lord, don't let there be anything wrong with the baby.

She pushed the worries away and focused on the voices ahead of her. The strangers were louder than their group. Their voices had been strong even when she first caught sight of them on horseback, but now the men seemed to be belting out each word they spoke. And was that a slur in one man's speech? Maybe that was his natural cadence, but she'd heard such sluggish tendencies before. Knew the telltale sign well.

Her entire body tightened as she paused in the trees a few steps from the camp clearing. It hadn't occurred to her that these men might've brought whiskey with them. Had all the men overindulged?

This could be awful. Almost as bad as if Raphael's brothers had come looking for her. Panic pounded through her chest.

She had her gun. Raising the weapon, she positioned it so she could easily aim and shoot.

But she couldn't do that. She couldn't kill another man, not even if he came at her in a drunken rage.

But her baby. That other time flared fresh in her mind, mixing with this moment in an awful distortion of past and present.

Did she dare enter that clearing? Once she made her presence known, it would be so much harder to sneak away again.

She couldn't do this. Couldn't willingly step into a den of drunken sots. Some men only turned sloppy when they consumed. But you never knew when the rage would take hold. She couldn't put herself in that position again.

Before she could move, one of the men spoke clearly enough

to grab her attention. "So French. You said she was traveling with her papa up the Missouri River? What's his name?"

"Wilkins. Thad Wilkins." Jean-Jacques's level voice barely reached her. She strained to hear his words. "Her name is Susanna. Unfortunately, Mr. Wilkins passed away a few weeks after we first met them. But I'm grateful he brought Susanna to us."

Susanna. Pain pressed through her, cutting off her breath. Was he speaking of his wife? Who else would he be grateful for? The warmth in his tone had been impossible to miss as he said her name. And the *us* must be him and the friends he'd mentioned. Why hadn't she thought of that earlier? When he spoke of his comrades, she'd assumed he meant fellow trappers. But his wife must be among them.

Tears blurred her vision as she eased backward, away from the firelight filtering through the trees. She raised a sleeve to swipe the moisture away. She'd known he was married. This wasn't a surprise to her. Only a painful reminder.

Her back bumped a trunk, and she nearly cried out at the unexpected jolt.

Settle down, Colette. She had to get away from here—without them knowing. She couldn't walk into that camp and face—not only men who'd been drinking, but a very married Jean-Jacques.

There might be questions later, but she'd find another place to spend the night.

With a glance behind her, she shifted sideways and eased backward so the tree separated her from the camp. She scanned a path toward the river, a route free of branches and anything else that might signal her presence if she stepped wrong.

She followed that route, one tiptoed step at a time.

At last, she arrived in the open stretch along the creek's bank. She eased out a breath and gulped in fresh air. Her legs shook, and she gripped a tree to keep herself upright. Maybe this would be a good time to skin her catch from the evening.

The thought tasted foul. She didn't have the nerve to do that awful job right now. She'd need to find a place to spend the night. The hideaway where she sometimes took naps would do. With any luck, the men would drink themselves to sleep and not even realize she didn't return for the night.

At least, they wouldn't know until morning, when they found her bedroll as she'd left it today. She could come up with some excuse then.

Now that she had a plan, some of the strength returned to her legs. She'd have to go the night without eating, which meant it might be a while before her hungry belly finally conceded to let her sleep. She might as well start trying now.

With her rifle in a position to fire easily, she started toward her private sleeping spot. The hunger would be nothing close to the misery she'd experience if she were forced to spend the night around a group of drunken fools.

CHAPTER 9

French padded through the trees as quietly as he could so he didn't frighten Colette or draw attention from the others. There was so much drinking and wild storytelling back at camp, he doubted anyone had seen him slip away.

Where was Colette? She should've returned a half hour ago at the latest. In truth, he'd expected her long before that. It shouldn't have taken her that long to reset her traps. Had she decided to skin the catch as well?

Why was she so hesitant to meet the strangers? It had to be more than concern for her disguise. Every one of his instincts confirmed that suspicion.

What was she running from?

Surely the threat couldn't be as bad as she seemed to think. What would drive her into this wilderness and make her pretend to be a man, to live with Indians and skin animals all day? None of that sounded like the Colette he knew. Yet something had forced her to this life. He needed to make quicker progress in getting her to trust him enough to tell.

There was no sign of her on the riverbank where they

skinned the animals and scraped hides. Maybe she was working on her traps for some reason. He walked all the way down her line and even to his own sets.

No Colette. All six of her snares were open and ready for an animal. Had she gone back upstream for some reason? Surely, she didn't plan to spend the entire night out. If so, where?

Near the horses? Maybe she'd gone there to check them, but she probably wouldn't linger in that place. One of the newcomers might go out to check their animals. Although, from the bottles being passed around back at camp, he doubted any of them would think of it this night.

Still, he should check the horses himself. And maybe he'd find Colette along the way.

When he stepped into the open grassy area, he found that the animals all seemed fine. Resting in the darkness, most of them, though a couple still grazed. No person lingered around that he could see.

After patting his mare a final time, he stepped away from the herd and paused to listen. "Colette?" He kept his voice low so it wouldn't carry back to camp. But if she were nearby, hopefully she would hear him and make her presence known.

Surely she wasn't hiding from *him*. After all, she'd called him earlier when she needed her trapping pack.

What about the place he'd found her sitting the other day? The grass had been flat like she'd been lying there, maybe napping in the warm spring sun. Maybe she'd decided to spend tonight there.

Finding the spot took some work in the darkness, but he finally located it. A tiny area of grass surrounded by thick trees. An excellent place to hide away.

Sure enough, a body lay in the grass there, covered by a blanket. Her hat rested beside her, and the white of her hair shone in the faint moonlight. Even in sleep, her brow wrinkled with worry. What made her fear these newcomers so much she would hide out here? The question was enough to drive him mad.

Should he stay here with her? The night was warm and she had a blanket, so she didn't look like she needed more. Her rifle lay beside her, only a handbreadth away.

It might be better if he returned to camp, where he could keep an eye on the men. With most of them intoxicated, hopefully they would sleep well through the night. But one never knew for sure.

Guarding the strangers. That was where he could serve Colette best. And he'd sleep with one eye open.

~

Pain shot through Colette's shoulder as she scraped her eyes open and pushed herself upright. Dawn had already penetrated the eastern sky with reds and oranges. A few minutes later than she normally slept, but at least she'd made it through the night. The little clearing around her looked the same as when she'd lain down the night before.

She strained for sounds from camp. She couldn't hear anything, but that area was far enough away that she didn't normally hear the men when they spoke in regular voices. Only a shout or louder noise.

Her belly grumbled from hunger almost as much as her neck did from the position she'd slept in. Nausea churned, rising up into her chest. She had to get food, or she'd be sick for sure.

Pushing to her feet, she stumbled a step, then caught her footing. One would think she'd been the one with the bottle the night before.

She had to prepare herself for what she might face in camp this morning. Questions from Young Bear and the others probably. Hopefully the visitors would sleep off their head pains, then be on their way.

After taking care of morning needs, she gathered her rifle and blanket, then started toward camp. As she stepped into the open area along the creek's bank, Elk Runs and Hawk Wing were trudging toward their trap lines. Both paused when they saw her and waited for her to reach them. Hawk Wing's eyes held a rim of red, and Elk Runs seemed a little sleep dazed still. Or maybe dazed by the lingering remnants of whatever he'd imbibed.

"You did not come for strong drink." Hawk Wing eyed her.

She shook her head. "I don't like that drink." She might have said something about how these two and the others probably drank her portion, but better not to be sarcastic.

Hawk Wing nodded, then turned toward the river as though he needed no other explanation. Maybe his own roiling belly made him think her stance would have been better for him as well.

She moved on toward camp, glancing up to see that her catch she'd hung the night before was still safe. They'd not had trouble with mountain cats—a blessing indeed.

As she neared the edge of camp, she slowed to determine what she would find before making her presence obvious.

Jean-Jacques knelt by the fire, his usual position as he prepared the morning's meal. Young Bear sat by the blaze, smoking a pipe. He didn't usually do so in the morning, but maybe he was also nursing an aching head. A few bodies littered the open area, and she took a step forward to better see them.

Three forms, all tucked inside fur coverings. Their visitors must still be sleeping off the festivities.

Jean-Jacques had turned and was watching her. No surprise shone in his eyes. Did he even know she hadn't slept in camp? He simply studied her. At last, he offered a "Morning."

"Good morning." She stepped into the clearing and moved toward her bed pallet. She'd pretend she'd just been out to check her traps early.

Jean-Jacques turned back to his work. "I have corn mush ready. We traded for more cornmeal, so there should be plenty to last a week or so. Longer if we conserve it, but I thought something warm and filling would help this morning."

Her belly growled at the words, but the nausea churned thicker. She was going to cast up her accounts—what little accounts she had left—if she didn't get food quickly.

She sank down to sit on her bed pallet and inhaled a deep, slow breath through her nose. Out through her mouth. In through her nose. She kept her chin up, focusing on each breath as she struggled to keep her insides from heaving.

Maybe she should make a run for the trees now. She couldn't chance losing her dignity in front of these others. But she was managing to keep her roiling nausea down, and standing might put her feeble control at risk.

Jean-Jacques appeared in front of her, crouching with a cup in his hands. "Here, eat. You don't look well."

He was studying her again, but she couldn't take time to focus on him. She grabbed the cup and raised it to her mouth.

The gruel was hot—almost scalding—so she took only a small sip to start. She would have to down the food slowly or it would all come back up. Once her belly had enough to ease its gnawing, the nausea would die away.

After sipping half the cup, her insides had finally settled enough to let her focus on Jean-Jacques. He still crouched in front of her, watching her. His eyes cataloging.

She didn't have the strength to feign a smile. "I'm well. Just a little too hungry."

Twin lines formed across his brow, as though her comment didn't make sense. He was probably fighting an aching head from the drink too.

His father's anger had always burned worse the morning after a binge. Or so Jean-Jacques had said. He'd never let her near his house during his father's overindulgences or their aftermath. He usually tried to keep himself far away too.

Those last few years, when he'd been a little older, he hadn't stayed away as long. Sometimes he would mention his mother, enough for her to realize he worried over her. And sometimes he wouldn't come to find Colette until he was certain his mother had left the house for town or gone to work in their garden.

Those latter times, the two of them never strayed farther than earshot from his home. She'd been aware of it all back then, but the seriousness had never settled in her young mind. Her world had been so very different. Safe.

Not until Raphael's father passed had she understood what Jean-Jacques must've gone through.

The memories brought up another surge of nausea. She needed to get out of this place. Away from the stench of whiskey and the sight of those who'd indulged in the poison.

She turned away from Jean-Jacques's stare, reaching for her gun and her possibles sack. "I'm going out to do some exploring today. I'll probably be gone several hours." The words slipped out before she had time to fully contemplate the idea.

But that was what she needed. Time away from these people. This place. All these memories that wouldn't stay suppressed.

Jean-Jacques stood, yet he didn't step back. The burn of his gaze pressed into her, but she didn't offer him a glance. Did she have everything she needed? There was food to snack on in her sack, although she might need a bit more. She wouldn't let herself get so hungry again if she could help it. She should take her Bible...she needed some quiet time with the Lord's words. She'd not been consistent about that lately. Maybe that was part of the reason her mind felt so muddled.

By the time she'd tucked everything in her bag, Jean-Jacques had stepped back to his place by the fire, but he still watched her. Young Bear did as well.

She stood and turned to them both. "I'll be back after noon. Don't worry if I'm a little later. I just want to see the area around us." She sent a glance toward the stew pot. "I'll try to find more seasonings for you too."

Jean-Jacques still didn't say anything, so she finally dared to lift her gaze to his face. Those lines across his brow had deepened. Concern and...hurt?...showed in his eyes. "Collette, I'd like to come with you."

Tensing, she tried not to focus on the fact that he'd used her given name in front of Young Bear. Hopefully the man wouldn't realize it was a female's name. She had to address the rest of his comment though.

She shook her head. "I want to go by myself." Then she jerked her gaze from him. No need to give him a chance to say anything more. Instead, she focused on Young Bear, waiting for acknowledgment that he understood. That he didn't think anything amiss.

He gave a slow nod. Whether he thought her behavior strange or not, he didn't say. That nod was all she needed.

She turned and started down the path toward the horses. She hadn't yet checked her traps that morning, but she couldn't stay long enough to do it. They'd have to wait. The urgency pressing through her drove her forward.

Faster. She'd keep going until she finally found peace.

~

French lifted his gaze again to stare in the direction Colette had ridden. Noon had passed several hours ago. When would she return? He should've followed her as his gut had told him to.

He couldn't make sense of this new Colette. She wouldn't let him in. She was hiding something big, troubled by something that must be of great significance. But she wouldn't trust him with it.

He forced his focus back to the hide draped over his fleshing beam and scraped with his knife a few more times. He'd emptied her traps that morning and processed both her catch and his, as well as what she'd tied up in the tree the night before. The work had kept his hands busy but left his mind to wander far too long. He still had one more raccoon pelt to scrape after this beaver fur.

Then maybe he should start a pot of stew for the evening meal. He glanced up in the distance again, straining for any movement that might signal a horse and rider. Maybe she wouldn't return from that direction, but he couldn't stop himself from searching there any way. She'd ridden out the same way he'd gone the day before to get the stewpot seasonings. There was plenty of open land along the river's edge to ride, probably for hours. If she followed the water, she wouldn't get lost. Did she know that? Had she been in her right mind enough to think through details like those?

When he'd handed her the corn mush, she'd seemed to be in the middle of some kind of…attack. Maybe panic, or some bout of pain.

He straightened. Was she hurt? Sick? Was that her big secret?

Fear sluiced through him. If Colette was ill, she shouldn't be wandering off into the wilderness alone.

Then a new fear slammed against him, nearly knocking him backward. Surely she hadn't gone to…die.

He dropped his tools and sprinted to the river to clean his hands and arms. He had to find her. Had to fix whatever this was. Why hadn't he seen the problem earlier? Her secrecy… The fact that she wouldn't come around the strangers…

A new thought pressed in. Was she contagious? Was that why she'd hesitated to let him near? It didn't matter. He had to get to her.

He passed Left Standing coming from the camp. "I'm going to find Mignon." He barely remembered to use that foreign name. "I'll be back as soon as I find him." He didn't wait for more than a nod from the man.

In camp, French grabbed up his food pack and bedroll, then an extra supply of roasted meat. What else would he need? His extra powder and shot were in his pack.

He scanned Colette's things. She'd left her bedroll, but the edge of a blanket had shown from the bag she carried. Along with his things, hopefully that would be enough to keep her warm. He didn't have much by way of medicine, only a salve for wounds. That wouldn't be enough if what ailed her was an internal sickness. Susanna and Elan had carried all the herbs and other medicinals for their group. Were there some in the pack Colette took? He could only hope so.

He couldn't waste any more time. With his things loading him down, he sprinted toward the horses.

CHAPTER 10

Tracking Colette in this vast mountain wilderness proved harder than he'd expected. At least he knew which direction she'd gone. He'd watched her horse pick its way alongside the creek, moving upriver.

The area abounded with such plentiful grass, much of it tall brown winter growth, with new green shoots rising up between the taller stalks. The thickness made it even harder to find hoof prints, especially since he'd let so much time pass that the grass was no longer bent over from where the horse had pressed it down.

He studied the ground as his mare plodded along. Surely there would be tracks somewhere. Once he picked up one print, he could find others much easier. He'd have a better idea how they would appear in this terrain. He rode at least five minutes, worry needling him as he strained for any sign.

There. A few broken winter-brown stalks, and the outline of a hoof pressed into the new growth beneath. He slipped from his horse and studied the print, memorizing its shape. This must be the hind left hoof, a little smaller and deeper than one of the front prints would be. Almost toed in.

Mounting up again, he nudged Giselle forward. Now that his eye was trained, he spotted another print a few strides farther. This one was barely more than a couple taller stalks bent over, but the fresh breaks meant a rider had come through that day.

Onward he rode, and in half an hour, he spotted clear horse tracks in the mud on the creek's bank at a likely crossing spot. Across the water, the valley stretched in an open area that would be a good place for a canter. Maybe Colette had needed the freedom of the wind in her hair.

He didn't allow himself that pleasure but kept his mare to a walk as he examined the ground. This lower grass showed signs of recent disturbance better than the other had. He pushed his horse into a trot as Colette's path showed clearly before him.

Lifting his focus to the distance, he strained for any sign of movement to signal an oncoming rider. How far had she gone before turning around? *Had* she turned around?

Surely she hadn't gone somewhere to die. Surely her sickness hadn't progressed that far. She would have told him, wouldn't she? Not left him in such turmoil, with so many questions. Even if the telling would be hard, the Colette he knew would have done at least that for him.

In times like this, he wished he still believed praying helped. If only there were a God who cared to step in when the people He'd created needed him.

God had never been there for him in the past, and he couldn't expect Him to help now.

As the valley ended in the base of a mountain, with two more peaks rising on either side, he searched for the route she'd taken. She'd tracked to the left, and it looked like she'd been hoping to find a path between the two mountains.

The ground grew rockier as the trail began to climb. But there was still enough dirt for an occasional print to show him he was on the right path.

He rode on for at least an hour, following the route she'd picked out between the peaks. His horse had to maneuver over several boulders, much harder riding than the valley land below. Colette must have been determined to keep going this far.

The tracks skirted around the center mountain and turned onto a game trail. The ground was so rocky, he couldn't be sure he would find the prints if Colette had turned her horse off this path. But there wasn't really another place to go except straight up the cliff. Surely she wouldn't have done that. Her horse could likely make it, but there would be danger to them both. And why risk such a feat?

The ground sloped on the other side of the mountain. In the distance, the winding growth of shrubby trees and bushes must be a sign of water.

As the path widened, possibilities appeared for places Colette might have turned off. He had to move slower, seeking out hoof prints in the dirt. At least the rain from two days before had kept the land from being too hard to hold a track.

Finally, he found a faint mark pressed into the ground. Only a quarter of a hoof, but the same shape and size as what he'd been following before. Probably the right rear inside toe. Relief slipped through him. He hadn't lost her trail, but where was she? He could find no sign of a horse and rider as far as he could see. Mountains spanned along the left side of the valley before him, and the right side stretched out in openness.

He kept his horse slow to spot her trail. At last, he found another track, then a few strides forward another. Now that he had a better feel for which direction she was taking down the slope, he could move a little faster.

Yet not much faster than a loose-reined walk. Surely Colette had turned around and started back by now. If she was still moving away from camp, he'd never catch up to her at this speed.

She said she'd return a little after noon, but the sun would begin to set in an hour or two. Why hadn't he found her yet? Did she know of a path that circled back to camp? Her comment about exploring when she'd left didn't lead him to believe she knew the area that well.

Fear pressed hard inside him. If only he knew what she'd been thinking. Why she'd been so desperate to escape camp. Why she wasn't doing what she said she would. She must not have found the peace she sought.

Or maybe she hadn't planned to return.

A new wave of pain slipped through him. He couldn't lose Colette again. Not after finally finding her. He wouldn't let her slip away so easily.

~

Colette only had the strength to lie curled around her belly. She sucked in a slow breath, let it out, then pulled another in. Bile churned in her belly, rising up into her chest. Another breath in.

Maybe she should just let the heaving come again. Purging would make her feel better for a few minutes, but then this awful feeling would come back. How could she have anything left inside her to expel?

The sour taste rose up her throat, triggering her body's internal panic. The first heave jerked through her, and she pressed up enough to keep from spewing on herself. She hated this. All of it. And why was it happening? Was something wrong with the baby?

The convulsions came, over and over. They were little more than clear bile at this point, but her body seemed determined to wrench every last drop out of her.

At last, her belly's heaving subsided. Her energy had been spent, but she possessed just enough strength to scoot back to keep from lying in her vomit.

Was this the end? She was ready for it. As much as she'd tried to live for her baby—to give her child life and health—maybe they would both see the Lord today. So be it.

Her eyes drifted shut, the darkness within even stronger than the dark of night around her. Sleep tugged her, and she gave in to its call. Unless the Lord took her now, she would only have a few minutes before the convulsions started again.

The churning in her middle awakened her, though it felt as if she'd not slept more than a few heartbeats. Inhaling a deep breath, she squeezed her eyes against the awful sensations within.

Lord, take this from me. Please. How in the world had Jesus managed to add on those words—*not My will but Yours be done*? Faced with torment like this, she would do almost anything to make it pass.

The bile churned harder inside her, rising up to her chest. Would this never end?

A sound in the darkness tried to press through her attention, but she had no focus to spare. The noise was probably only her horse, come to see why she hadn't been unsaddled and led to water. Those first pains had come on so quickly, Colette had thought only to rest a minute to let the nausea subside. But here she lay, hours later, her horse still unattended. It felt like days, but this was only the first night.

A long, awful night that would never end.

That bitter taste filled her mouth, and the first heave pressed through her. She'd never been so helpless to stop something. Not even Raphael's advances when the liquor consumed him. Was this her punishment for that metal bar to him when his attentions turned dangerous? For dealing that life-ending blow?

As she braced herself on her forearms, barely keeping her mouth above the ground with each convulsion, her heart cried out. *I'm sorry, Lord. I didn't mean it. Take me. You know I'm Yours.*

You promised forgiveness. Please, take me. And have mercy on the babe.

"Colette?"

The voice came from behind her, but she had no energy to turn. Her body gave a final heave, leaving her with nothing left. Her head sank to the ground, barely missing the tiny puddle of bile she'd expelled. She had strength to do nothing but lie there.

"Colette, what's wrong?"

A hand touched her shoulder, finally breaking through her fog to make her aware of the voice. Jean-Jacques? She must be dreaming. She must have finally lost her mind. *Please, God. Take me home to be with You. Save me from any more of this torment.*

The voice murmured over her, but she couldn't find enough strength to clear her mind to understand. Warm hands brushed the hair from her face. Those hands eased her onto her side.

She could only manage breaths, in...out. Her belly no longer complained. She would have a few minutes before the churning started again.

She needed rest. Had to...rest.

~

Panic surged through French. It was his worst fear come true. Colette was dying.

Right here on the side of this mountain, the woman he loved more than life itself had come to die. He'd found her in time, but could he help her?

He bent closer to her ear. "Colette, can you hear me?"

She'd been moving when he arrived. He'd heard sounds like retching, but when he reached her side, she'd only released a few moans. Now nothing. No movement at all, except breathing.

At least she was breathing.

He stroked the hair away from her temple. There was no

fever that he could feel. Should he turn her on her back? Would that make her breathing harder or easier? The last thing he wanted was to affect this last critical function of life.

What would Elan and Susanna do if they were here? He scanned the recesses of his memory for what they'd done with other sicknesses in the group. Most had involved fevers. They'd kept the ill person warm, used wet cloths to soothe sweat-dampened brows. They spooned bits of water at first, then meat broth when the patient grew stronger.

He raised his focus to take in the area around him. The night was warm, but Colette would probably still appreciate a blanket. Maybe the one from her pack? It would be a familiar comfort.

He scrambled to his feet and moved toward her horse. He might have never found Colette if he hadn't heard the mare's nicker of greeting to his own mount. Maybe God played a hand in that, leading him to this place. Or maybe it had only been the natural instinct of the horses. Herd animals at heart, after all.

His fingers fumbled with the tie on Colette's pack. Maybe he should get his own furs. They would be easier to retrieve, but the night didn't seem cold enough for such thick coverings. He didn't want to make her more uncomfortable.

At last, his stubby fingertips worked the knot loose, and he flipped open the pack. The blanket was near the top, but when he jerked the cloth out, something else tried to come with it. He pressed the leather-wrapped bundle back in, then spun back toward Colette.

Dropping to his knees by her side, he spread the blanket over her. She hadn't moved even a finger from the position she'd been in before. There was still only the faint shift of her shoulders with each breath.

God in heaven, if you care at all, keep this woman alive. Please. For Colette's sake.

He rested his hand on her back, letting the steady rhythm of her breathing soothe his frantic thoughts. What else should he do? Wet cloths across her brow? She still didn't feel feverish. If anything, her brow was cool, though a little clammy. There had been a creek at the base of this mountain, so he could get water, but wet cloths seemed like they would only make her colder.

He could spoon the water into her mouth, though. That might be helpful. Either way, he should bring up water from the creek. He would probably have need of it before this was over.

But dare he leave Colette long enough to retrieve some? If he took his horse, he might get there and back in ten minutes. He only had his drinking flask to carry the water. Did she have something in her pack so he could bring more in one trip?

He leaned low over her ear. "I need to leave for a minute to get you water, *mon amour*. I'll be back soon. Wait for me. All right?" No response, but at least the breathing continued.

She seemed completely unconscious. Had she fallen from the horse and hit her head?

He ran his hand over her hair, stroking with gentle motions over each part of her scalp. There were no bumps that he could feel. Perhaps underneath, where her head touched the ground. He should ease her fully on her back so he could check that side.

"I'm going to lay you onto your back." He spoke as he performed the action, as gently as he could manage. Her head flopped as though she had no control over its motion. The sight of her lying so still, her face as pale as her white hair in the moonlight, squeezed his chest with a new wave of fear.

You can't let her die, Lord. You can't. Please. He shouldn't be commanding the Almighty. But his desperation spoke before he could question the prayer.

He smoothed his hand over Colette's head to check the new area. Still no bumps. What caused the unconsciousness then?

He had to get her water. That was the only thing he knew to do. And he should go after it now, before she awoke. *Please let her wake, God.* He sent up the prayer as he stood and strode to the horses.

CHAPTER 11

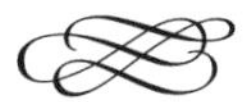

Colette did have a water skin hanging from her saddle, so French grabbed it and mounted Giselle. Then he spun his horse back the way they'd come. He pushed her harder than was probably safe in the night over the boulder-strewn trail.

But Giselle seemed to feel his fear. She maneuvered like the excellent mount she was, and they finally reached the gurgling creek. He leapt to the ground and dropped to his knees at the water's edge. The canteens took forever to fill, and his hands shook as he re-corked each one.

Would Colette still be alive by the time he returned? The thought sent another sluice of fear through him. He was breathing hard as he remounted Giselle and dug in his heels for the return trip. The mare matched his determination, maneuvering the rocky hillside with steady footing. She slid to a stop by Colette's horse, and he vaulted to the ground. Finally, he reached Colette's side and dropped to his knees. "I'm here, mon amour. Are you well?"

She stirred as he bent over her. Was that his imagination? He brushed his hand over her hair, letting her feel his presence. "I brought water. Can you drink a little?"

A groan slipped from her. He definitely hadn't imagined the sound.

"I'm here, Colette. Let's give you a drink." He had no spoon to dribble the liquid between her lips, but he could do it carefully with the canteen.

As he reached for one of the flasks, her hands moved. She strained, like she was trying to turn onto her side.

"Easy there. Let me help you." Maybe she was having trouble breathing on her back, as he'd worried about.

Desperation seemed to awaken her, and her eyes flickered open. Then widened. Her hand clutched at the ground, and he helped her turn onto her side.

Then under his palm, her shoulder jerked. Something like a convulsion shook her. She lifted from the ground just in time for her shoulders to heave.

Realization swept through him. She was vomiting. A new wave of panic stirred inside him. What should he do? Was there any way to stop this? To help her?

She seemed barely able to keep her face above the ground. She must be impossibly weak.

He leaned over and slipped his hands under both her shoulders, lifting her a little and taking the weight off her arms. Another convulsion pushed up from her core. He shifted his hands to make sure he wasn't hindering the flow of whatever was coming out of her. But was anything actually purging? This was not a normal vomit. Her body seemed determined to rid itself of some poison, but nothing would come. Did she have anything left inside?

At last, she drooped in his arms. He eased her backward, then laid her on her back again. Every part of him ached for her. Ached to draw her against him and cradle her. To soothe away the pain, the exhaustion, and whatever malady was tormenting her.

He settled for stroking her brow. Her eyelids flickered, then lifted to reveal tiny slits.

"I'm here, *ma cherie*." He cradled her cheek with his hand. "What can I do to help you?"

He couldn't see her eyes well enough to read them, but her mouth parted the smallest bit. He couldn't tell if she meant to speak or not, but the movement shifted his gaze to her lips—cracked and bright red. She needed water, especially if she'd purged everything from inside her. But would drinking make things worse? Bring on another vomiting episode? He would start with a little. She had to have something.

"Let's see if you can drink a sip." He reached for the flask and pulled off the cork with his teeth. He couldn't bring himself to pull his hand from Colette's cheek. He needed the connection, and maybe she did too.

He slipped his hand behind her head. "I'm going to lift your head a little so you can drink."

Her eyes slipped shut, but her lips parted more. He only lifted her head a small bit off the ground, enough to keep the water from choking her on its way down. He dribbled some into her mouth.

When she swallowed, her face contorted in a grimace. Was her throat that dry? She parted her lips again to receive more, and he did his best not to pour too much.

This time, the grimace was replaced with a slight pursing of her lips. Her eyes stayed closed, but her breathing seemed a little louder in the quiet. Was he exhausting her? "One more time, then you can rest."

She opened her mouth again, just enough for him to pour in more liquid. She swallowed, then eased out a breath.

"There now." Lowering her head to the ground, he let out his own breath. If that small amount of water stayed down, he'd try more in a few minutes.

How often was the vomiting coming? And how long had it been going on? Only today, or had she been hiding this from them all for days? Maybe even weeks. In his mind, he ran through the time he'd been with her at the camp. She'd worked around him and the others for long spells as they skinned the catches and scraped hides. She looked a little pale after a skinning sometimes, but he'd expected worse than that.

That morning though, when she'd sat in camp and he brought her the cup of corn gruel, she'd been fighting something.

Realization swept through him. Maybe this vomiting was a sign of the end of whatever illness she had. Maybe she realized it this morning, and that was why she'd fled.

No. God, you can't take her. Not yet. Everyone had their time to die, but this wasn't Colette's. They were supposed to have years and years together. There was so much to catch up on, and so much left of their dreams to fulfill. *You can't take her.*

He forced his focus back to the woman before him. She was lying perfectly still again, no movement except her breathing. How could she slip back into unconsciousness so quickly? This must be another symptom of the disease.

After recorking the water flask, he straightened the blanket that had twisted when her convulsions had started. What else could he do?

He stroked her brow again, running his fingers through the softness of her feathery hair. So many times he'd wanted to do this since he'd found her again, and even back when they were little. But this wasn't how he'd planned it.

"Colette, you can't leave me." His voice trembled with the emotion clogging his throat.

She moved, her hand sliding along her leg, just a little. She didn't seem to have strength to lift it. Did her body need to purge again?

But this didn't seem to be the desperate reaching from before. She appeared to be reaching for something. He moved his free hand to help her, slipping his fingers around her palm to lift it wherever she wanted to reach.

She closed her fingers around his, then her hand stilled. Was that it? She wanted to hold his hand?

A new flood of emotion eased through him, and he firmed his hold around Colette's. Maybe she simply wanted to know that someone was there. That help had come.

But he would do more than merely nurse her. He would strengthen the connection they'd always had. He would do everything he could to renew her. To bring her through this sickness to the life they both wanted. He had to believe she still wanted it, even a tiny bit as much as he did. And he would find a way to fulfill the dream for both of them.

~

The rosy blush of dawn lightened the distant eastern horizon, and if French hadn't been so exhausted, he would have soaked in the hope of the new day. He dropped his gaze to Colette's face. She slept again. That was good, right? Surely her body needed rest to recover.

She'd suffered three more vomiting episodes in the night, with more time spread between those last two. She'd managed to drink a little in between each, and anytime he wasn't forcing her to drink or the convulsions weren't racking her body, she lay so lifeless she might have been dead.

Except for the steady breathing.

He should wake her to drink more water. Her lips still seemed chapped—a bright red that stood out against her impossibly pale skin—pale except for the bruising under her eyes.

Maybe those were only shadows, but the sight made his chest squeeze even tighter.

He readied the canteen, then stroked a hand across her brow, running his fingers down her temple. "Colette, honey. Can you wake and drink again?" Her body must be desperate for water. It was hard to believe she had any left inside.

Her eyelids fluttered but didn't open. At least she was awake.

He slipped his hand behind her head and lifted it a little, as he had before. She parted her lips and received the water he drizzled in.

The first swallow always seemed painful, and this time was no different. He pulled the flask away as she suffered through, then returned the nozzle to her mouth for more. After the third drink, she opened her lips, as if for another. This was good. She'd only been able to manage three sips at a time before.

After she swallowed the fourth, her body sagged into his hand, and he lowered her head to the ground. "Sleep again, mon amour. I'll be here when you need me."

While she rested, he moved around the camp, accomplishing everything he could. He'd already unsaddled the horses in the night and hobbled them nearby. Now, he led them down to the creek, taking the canteen he'd been using with Colette to refill.

This valley had better grazing than up on the mountain where Colette lay, but he hesitated to leave the animals so far from them. What if he needed to take Colette away quickly? He would have to carry her, for she wasn't even strong enough to sit up by herself. Better to have the animals nearby in case they needed to ride. He could move the horses every few hours to fresh grass. He certainly had little else to do while Colette slept.

On his way back to her, he gathered up what dry tree limbs he could find. He should start a fire and see if he could make a broth from the meat they had with them. Surely her body needed sustenance as well as water.

As long as the vomiting didn't start again.

Hopefully, she would soon be rested enough to open her eyes fully and speak to him. To tell him what was wrong with her. Maybe she knew of other ways to treat the condition.

Or maybe she even carried medicine with her. Why hadn't he thought of that sooner?

He tugged the horses faster, and as soon as he reached the little camp he'd made around Colette, he dropped to his knees by her saddle. Now that he had daylight, he went through her pack meticulously. The leather-wrapped bundle he'd pushed back in during the night held food. Dried meat.

The rest of her pack held the usual supplies, including a set of cloth trousers and shirt. The ones she'd changed into after the rainstorm, if he wasn't mistaken. She'd only worn them the rest of that day, then had change back into her buckskins. Maybe she preferred the warmth of the leathers, or maybe she thought they made her look more like a man.

A Bible caught his notice, pressing his conscience. Did Colette still cling to the faith they'd shared in their younger days? She must, since she carried a Bible with her. There was precious little else in the pack, so this must be one of her prize possessions.

But he could find no sign of any medicine inside the pack. Not even leaves or roots that might be medicinal. Had she not tried to treat this condition? She'd probably run out of whatever remedy she'd brought with her. Maybe that was why she suffered so much now.

A seed of hope rose up inside him. Maybe if he got her back to civilization, they could get what care she needed to cure her illness. But why had she left a doctor's care to begin with?

So many questions, and it was about time he received some answers.

CHAPTER 12

After untying the pack from Colette's saddle, French carried it and the water flask over to her. He figured he'd better hobble the horses again before he settled in.

After finishing that task, he took his place beside Colette. She shifted, then slitted one eye. He managed a smile for her. This was good that she was waking on her own.

She parted her lips and looked to be trying to speak. He leaned close as hope rose within him.

"Water." The word rasped in little more than a croak.

Of course. If the stomach ailment really had subsided, she would need a great deal more water than she'd been able to drink thus far. He reached for the canteen, removed the cork, and helped her drink again. She managed larger sips this time, then settled back after four swallows.

He resettled her on the ground and recorked the flask. Both her eyes were still somewhat open. She seemed to be watching him, though he couldn't see much in the dark blue shadows between her lashes.

He turned to her fully and took her hand in his. He'd done this often through the night after she'd reached for him that first time. She didn't always seem to realize he was there, but the connection helped him. "I'm glad you seem to be feeling better."

She didn't answer, but maybe that was because he'd not really asked a question. Perhaps he should keep saying simple comments like that, enough to start conversation, but not anything that required answers. That way she could reserve her strength for his real questions.

He reached up and brushed the hair from her forehead again. The fine tendrils tended to slip over her brow when he helped her drink, and brushing them back gave him another excuse to touch her. "I thought I'd make a fire soon and cook some meat broth."

Those words finally brought a shift in her expression. Something like a grimace. Her mouth parted, and again the single word slipped out. "Water."

He studied her face for a sign of what she meant. Did she want another drink already? Or maybe she simply wasn't ready for broth. Perhaps she suspected she could only keep down water.

He was tired of guessing, and since he planned for this to be a reckoning, it was time he start asking his questions instead of keeping them festering inside him. "You mean you're not ready for meat broth yet? You only want to drink water for now?"

Her chin dipped in the slightest of nods.

Relief swept through him. That wasn't so hard. Now he had a clear answer and didn't have to read her mind. Perhaps he could try another question.

He brushed his thumb over the back of her hand. "Colette, what's wrong with you? What ailment is this that's made you so sick?"

She didn't answer, not with words or with the shake of her head to show she didn't want to respond. Maybe she was simply trying to find the words. Or deciding how much to tell him.

He waited, and at last, her mouth parted again. "Not...sick."

He barely held in his frustration. "Of course you're sick. I watched you vomit four times last night. You can hardly open your eyes now." How could she possibly think he would believe that lie?

Maybe he should get straight to the real question. Giving her hand a gentle squeeze to show he was still on her side, he gentled his voice. "Are you dying, Colette? Please tell me. I need to know."

She hesitated, and he couldn't tell if she was gathering strength to speak or debating how to answer his question.

Please tell me the truth. He held his breath until she finally spoke.

"I thought I might die…last night. But then…you came." She squeezed his hand with the slightest grip.

What did she mean by that? Could her illness be passing? Could the worst possibly be behind her? "Tell me what sickness this is, Colette. Please. Why were you casting up your accounts all night?"

Her mouth parted again. Her eyes had closed. Maybe she was reserving her strength to speak. "Must have eaten some bad meat."

Frustration sluiced through him. "You can't expect me to believe that. You've been secretive ever since I found you again. You're hiding something. Some kind of illness, I think." He tried to soften his voice, but taking away the edge of anger only made his tone crack with the emotion underneath. "Tell me what it is, Colette. I won't make things worse. I promise."

Again, she was quiet. But her lips stayed parted, as though she would speak again. He waited.

At last, her voice came out a whisper. "I'm with child."

The words didn't penetrate at first. His mind tried to morph them into some kind of ailment. Then their full meaning splashed in.

She was… A babe grew inside her?

How and...?

What had...?

Who?

He grasped frantically for the fraying edges of his control, struggled to rein in the whirlwind of his thoughts.

"Jean." Colette's tiny voice broke through his turmoil, and he forced his focus onto her.

Her brows were lowered in a grimace, something like pain. He scanned the length of her, and only then did he realize how tightly he was squeezing her hand.

Releasing his clench, he stroked his thumb over her fingers. Whatever had happened to her, he would see her through this. He would be whatever she needed him to be. But he had to have some answers.

"Who, Colette?" His voice cracked even on those two words.

Please respond. If she didn't, he would go mad, his mind churning with every awful possibility.

Colette's eyes opened a little. "My husband."

Another blow, this one like a solid punch to his gut by a man twice his size. He might have sucked in a breath, but it did nothing to block the pain.

She was married? His Colette had married another? How could she? Had she given up on him so easily? Did she not believe he would go to the ends of the earth to find her, just as he said he would when they last parted?

Then she spoke again, her words stilling his questions. "He's gone...died."

How many blows could a man take in the space of a few minutes? Yet he was so numb from the other, this one felt like little more than a punch to the shoulder. Enough to spin him until he was disoriented, but nothing more.

How long ago had the man died? A few months, at the most, for he'd been around recently enough to leave her a babe. A new thought washed in. Were there other children? Did she have other wee ones somewhere, or maybe lost? What had killed her husband? If sickness, had the disease also taken her other children?

He had to rein in his mind and find out the truth.

He forced in a deep breath. If only there was a stiff icy wind to clear his head. These balmy spring days didn't hold the punch of winter temperatures. He pushed the breath out, then focused on what to ask first.

When he finally honed his gaze on her face, she was watching him. He had no idea what his expression had told her, but he didn't care. He'd never hidden things from Colette. Not anything she *wanted* to know anyway. He'd not spoken of his father or the challenges at home unless she asked. But that had been his cross to bear, not hers.

Now, he would take the weight of this burden from her, as much as he could.

Best to focus on the facts. The things he needed to know to help her. "How long have you been alone?"

Her eyes drifted shut again. "About…eight weeks." Her voice sounded exhausted. He needed to make the most of the few questions he would be able to ask. He couldn't overtire her. Not only was her own health at risk, but a precious life inside her needed everything she could give it.

He stroked her hand again. "How did your husband die?" If his illness had been catching, that might give him insight into what was wrong with Colette.

The lines creased her brow, and her lips closed. Would she refuse to answer any more questions? *Just this last one, my love. Please.*

Maybe he didn't have the right to call her that anymore. Not if she'd given herself to another. But she would always be his love, no matter what. And if her husband had passed away, perhaps it wasn't so wrong for him to think of her that way now.

But he could contemplate that line of thought later. For now, he had to think clearly about what Colette needed. And how he might get this one answer before she fell back asleep.

Her lips parted again, and he stilled, straining for any response she might give.

"He was...killed."

Her husband had been murdered? Was that why Colette was hiding? Did the man seek her life too? He grabbed a firm hold of his thoughts before they raced off to form new scenarios. Better he simply ask.

"Why? Are you afraid of the murderer? Is that why you're disguised as a man?"

Her mouth worked, but no sound came out. Her lips weren't as bright red as they had been in the night. In fact, nearly all the color had leaked out of them. Her face was as pale as it had been when he found her.

He was pushing her too far. The next words she spoke confirmed it.

"No...more." Her voice was faint. So weak.

With his free hand, he reached up to run his fingers down her temple. "Rest now. Do you want water before you sleep?"

She parted her lips wider in confirmation, and he obliged. Lifting her head, pouring in a sip. Then another. She managed a third drink, then closed her mouth.

He eased her head back down, pulled the blanket up around her shoulders, then brushed her forehead once more. "Sleep now. I'll be here when you need me."

And in the meantime, he had much to work out in his mind. By the time she woke again, he needed to have a plan.

~

French had plenty of time to work out his plan. Colette slept all morning and didn't wake again until the sun had nearly reached its noon zenith.

By then, he'd sorted through most of his thoughts. And taken the horses to water again, then hobbled them with new grass. He'd also started a fire and figured out a way to make a stew of sorts. He had no metal dishware, so he'd had to be creative to make the water simmer.

After placing two rocks about a handbreadth apart, he moved a stoked fire between them. He found the best of his meat and broke it into pieces small enough to fit inside one of the water skins. Colette had mentioned eating bad meat, but these chunks were from his own supply, food he'd roasted himself just the day before. They'd been cooked well and salted enough to last for weeks without turning rancid.

After putting the meat and water in the canteen, he placed it across the rocks where the flame almost reached the leather casing. The heat would definitely warm the liquid inside, and if he was lucky, it would be enough heat to simmer the water into broth.

In the meantime, he found some good healthy cedar and started carving out a bowl.

Colette didn't make a sound when she awoke, but something drew his attention to her. Perhaps the flicker of her eyelids. Or maybe just the awareness of her he'd always possessed.

He worked for a smile—not a hard effort when even a glance at her brought happiness. "Thirsty again?"

In answer, she parted her mouth, her usual sign she was ready to drink. After giving her a few sips of water, he reached for the canteen with the meat inside. "I'm trying to make some broth, but I don't know how it's worked without a pan. Let's see."

The leather was almost too hot to touch. Maybe he should

have pulled it away from the flame earlier so the liquid could cool. When he touched a drop to his finger, he had to bite back a wince. "We'd better let this cool a minute."

He kept the conversation light while they waited. It wasn't a conversation exactly, just him filling the air with words. But he told her of all he'd done that morning. About the creek at the bottom of the mountain, the bowl he was carving, and how her mare was enjoying the new grass.

Colette moved her hand, lifting it a little off the ground. Reaching for him. He slipped his fingers around hers, pressing their palms together to seal the connection.

A knot clogged his throat. He couldn't lose this woman. *God, don't let me lose her.* She'd definitely brought him back to prayer, a feat no one else could've accomplished. He hadn't quite had a heart-to-heart with the Almighty, but maybe he would get there. Maybe.

Finally, the stew cooled enough for him to pour a little into her mouth. The liquid wasn't very dark, but hopefully she would get at least a few nutrients.

She drank more than he'd expected her to. When he lay her head back on the ground, a noise sounded near her belly.

A smile tickled his mouth. "Still hungry, are you?"

She parted her lips, but this time it was to speak. "Do you have…meat?"

Hope nudged inside him. "I'll give you a piece that's been boiling in the broth. That should be softer."

Getting the chunk out of the flask wasn't easy, but he finally pulled out a small bit and placed in her mouth. The act of feeding her seemed intimate, leaving his focus on her lips long after she took the meat between her teeth. He forced his gaze away, down the length of her to see whether there was something else he could do to make her comfortable.

His attention stalled on her belly. There was a tiny swell

there, not large enough that he would have noticed it if he hadn't known the truth.

Yet he *did* know. The wonder of new life was growing and forming inside her. Part of him longed to reach out and touch the place, though he never would. He shouldn't even think it. But something inside him yearned for that connection with a baby he didn't even know.

Once again, he tore his gaze away, but this time he made himself look away from Colette altogether.

He had to focus on his plan. On giving her the care she needed to grow strong again. Healthy enough to get back to their group. Young Bear and the others seemed like good men, what little he knew of them. At least when strong drink hadn't affected their senses.

Their camp would be a safe place for Colette to recover completely. Especially since French would be there to protect her, to help with whatever she needed—whether that be safety or care while she recovered.

Eventually, he'd like to take her to the Nimiipuu village to catch up with his friends. Elan, Susanna, and the other women would dote on her. Susanna was with child herself, maybe only a little farther along than Colette. He'd need to learn the exact date from Colette when he could, but that question could wait until later.

And no matter what, he wouldn't be letting her skin any more animals, not unless their need grew dire. Perhaps he should tell the braves that she was a woman. He was fairly certain they'd guessed it anyway.

If they hadn't, would the knowledge put her in danger? He would give his life to protect her, but he might have to do that very thing if he were forced to fight five braves at once.

He didn't think it would come to that, though. Everything he'd seen of Young Bear made him think well of the man—except for the drunkenness the other night, but the braves hadn't partaken nearly as much as their visitors. Still, better not to chance things. As hard as it was to fathom, she'd probably been smart to attempt to disguise herself as a man.

For now, he had to focus on getting her well. She definitely wouldn't be ready to return to the others today, so he needed to start thinking about what they would need in order to spend another night here.

A much more comfortable night than the last one.

CHAPTER 13

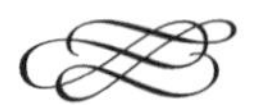

Colette's belly ached, drawing her from sleep again. She squinted to measure the daylight. The sunlight seemed dim, like early morning or dusky evening. Was this still the same day, or had she slept through another night? Jean-Jacques sat beside her, as he'd been every other time she'd awakened.

He'd saved her life.

She'd become so weak by the time he appeared, she would never have made it to her horse and the drinking flask hanging from the saddle. She'd already felt her body shutting down for want of water.

But he'd brought her back, little by little. God had used him to keep her here for a reason—for the young life growing inside her. *You'll do great things, little one. Your Heavenly Father is already preparing you.*

As if in answer, her belly gnawed again. That must be the babe crying out for food.

French uncorked the canteen and reached to lift her head for a drink. She obeyed, gulping down the refreshment.

She needed food too. Maybe with sustenance in her, she could manage more than a few words. Though she'd said everything she could about Raphael's death. There wasn't a single other detail about that ordeal that would be safe to share.

She'd needed to tell Jean-Jacques as much as she had, though. The questions in his eyes had grown too numerous to hold him off much longer. With what she'd revealed, his curiosity seemed satisfied.

Determination had taken its place, and that might be a good thing. Jean-Jacques had always been her champion, and she had no doubt he would do what he could to help her now. It hadn't seemed safe to let him before. But now…

At least for a while, she couldn't manage without him. *Don't let me have made the wrong choice, Lord. Protect this man.* A memory flashed of his father, eyes bloodshot from his last drunken binge. *And protect me, too, from him.*

If things turned bad—if the worst happened and Hugh and Louis found her—she would flee. And this time, she would do a better job of hiding herself.

She prayed it wouldn't come to that.

~

French awoke that night to a tingle running down his spine. His nerves stood at alert, straining.

Colette?

He studied her face, still and quiet beside him. Had she groaned? Her lips were parted to let air pass through. He shifted his focus to her chest, which rose and fell in steady rhythm.

An eerie howl sounded from the night. A shiver swept through him.

Wolves. That was what had awakened him. They weren't far away. How many?

He sat up, reaching for his rifle. He'd not laid it beside him when he bedded down but had left the weapon with the packs at his feet. He'd been more focused on making sure the canteen was full and having food nearby in case she woke hungry.

He couldn't let himself lose sight of protecting her, though. Colette wasn't safe—whether it was man or beast seeking her.

Another howl sounded, this one from the opposite direction.

And close. As he cocked his rifle, he strained to see into the darkness. No eyes glittered back at him, but they must be just outside of the firelight.

He glanced toward the horses. The animals stood at attention, their ears flicked backward in worry. He'd brought them near enough the firelight to see them well. The wolves would probably attack the animals first.

He pushed up to his feet, fixing the weapon against his shoulder so he could fire when needed.

Another howl pierced the night, this one on the other side of the horses. He strode that direction. He didn't want to shout and wake Colette, but a wolf attack would wake her anyway. Better to scare the creatures off before they hurt something.

He positioned himself by the horses in a place where he could still see Colette. "Get away!" He barked out the command, but his words seemed to only fade into the darkness.

Another howl rose from the other side of Colette. The predators had surrounded their camp.

He charged toward the sound and yelled, "Get away!"

Colette was stirring, but he kept his focus on the darkness around them, straining for the sound of movement.

There. Was that a pair of beady eyes in the shadows beyond Colette?

"Get away!" He stomped toward the animal, making himself as big as he could manage. He kept his rifle pointed toward the creature.

Another howl echoed to his left, releasing a burst of panic inside him. Shouting wasn't sending the creatures away. He had to make more noise. Spinning toward the sound, he tucked his chin to aim the rifle.

With the shift of his finger, a blast filled the air, gunpowder puffing around him. He whirled and dropped to his knees by his shot pouch to reload. In less than a minute, he'd recharged the gun and jumped to his feet, aiming in the direction he'd seen the eyes.

The beady circles were gone.

He strained for sign of movement.

Nothing.

For long moments he stayed like that, listening. His nerves on edge. Senses strained.

No more howling. Had the single bullet scared them away? Better send out another just in case.

This time, he moved around Colette so he wasn't shooting over her and aimed at the exact place he'd seen the beady eyes. The blast ricocheted in his ears, and the gunpower stung his nose.

He reloaded just as quickly as before, but there was still no sound of movement except the shifting of the horses. They'd dropped their heads down again, though, so maybe the danger truly was gone.

He finally lowered his focus to Colette, keeping part of his attention tuned to sounds around them.

Her eyes were wider than he'd seen them since he found her the night before. The fear in her gaze twisted his chest.

"I think the wolves are gone. A gunshot has always scared them off before."

Her shoulders twitched like a shiver ran through them. Fear? Or cold?

He dropped to his knees by her side, though he still held his gun in his shooting hand. "Are you cold?" He pulled the blanket up over her shoulders.

"Just...glad you're here."

The words slipped through him with enough warmth to stir his soul. He met her gaze. He could drown in those blue depths. "I am too."

One of the horses shifted, and he jerked his focus back toward the animal. Then into the shadows beyond. He strained to hear any movement, to see the glow of predator eyes.

Nothing.

The horses weren't standing alert. They would smell wolves long before he heard or saw them.

He eased out a breath, then pushed to his feet. Better put more wood on the fire to build up the blaze. He wouldn't be sleeping anymore this night.

~

Colette opened her eyes to a new day. Her belly was hungry enough to eat her insides, and she finally had strength to sit up and reach for the food herself. It was about time.

She should have made herself get up and ride back to camp today, even if she didn't feel up to it. Surely Jean-Jacques would help her with her mare.

This burst of energy was exactly what she needed to manage on her own. Well...mostly.

Jean-Jacques was bent down on the other side of his mount, working on the hobble that held the mare secure. The horses had eaten all the grass around their camp, so he must be moving them farther away. At least none of them had become wolf fodder last night.

He straightened and glanced her way, and when he saw her sitting up, a wide grin spread across his mouth. That Jean-Jacques grin—unrestrained and boyish enough to recapture her heart every time.

She returned his smile. Yes, she was feeling that good.

He patted his mare on the shoulder, then strode toward Colette with long intentional steps. "You look like you're feeling much better."

She reached into her pouch and pulled out another bite of meat. "I am."

He stooped by the fire and picked up the wooden bowl he'd carved the day before, holding it carefully as he rose and moved to her side. "I've had this stew simmering. Hopefully it will taste better than what I made in the canteen."

"Anything will be good, as hungry as I am." She reached for the bowl, and he helped her settle it onto her lap.

"It's hot."

She nodded even as she raised the bowl to her mouth for a sip.

He knelt beside her, watching. "I'll go hunting in a bit. We're getting low on meat, so better to stock up now."

She swallowed the first sip of scalding broth, then shook her head. "We can ride back today. I'm better now." Though that steaming stew had seared her throat.

He was studying her, concern on his face. Refusal on his tongue most likely. Better she speak first.

She turned a smile on him. "I feel like myself again this morning. I'm sure I'll feel even better once I eat. I'm sure the others wonder where we've gone." Or maybe he'd told them something to keep them from worrying. She raised her brows at him. "When do they expect you back?"

He shook his head. "I didn't say much when I left. Just told them I was headed out to find you." He studied her again. The refusal had lessened in his eyes.

She sipped another bit of broth. It was cooler now. "Are they checking our traps, do you think?"

His brows lowered. "I hope so."

She took a longer swallow this time, the warm liquid gradually filling her insides. "I only need a half hour, then I'll be ready to ride."

He hesitated. His face said he would relent soon though.

But then he dipped his chin and raised his brows in a stern expression. "I think you should get up and move around a little before we decide. I won't let you wear yourself out. Getting back isn't worth endangering your health."

This protective side of him was new. As a boy, he'd always kept her safe, but he hadn't been so stern about it. Back then, if she pushed, she could wear down his concerns.

But this Jean-Jacques was different. And though she shouldn't like the fact that she couldn't sway him so easily, the care behind his protectiveness wrapped around her like a warm blanket on a cool morning. It didn't hurt that he looked so attractive in the doing.

He went back to finish his work with the horses while she ate the rest of her stew and more of the meat from her pack. With her belly no longer aching from hunger, other needs pressed in.

After pushing the blanket aside, she moved to her hands and knees in preparation to stand. But she had to pause there as her vision went black. This was happening more often of late. From weakness? Lack of enough food? She was tired of trying to guess at all the causes for her body's changes.

She would never again take for granted having another woman near. Especially one wiser and more experienced in matters like these. She had to get settled in Young Bear's camp before she grew too heavy with child.

She sent a glance toward Jean-Jacques. Now that he knew the truth, how would she make him leave? Did she really need to? He was a man, grown and able to live his own life. If he still had a wife somewhere, he would need to go back to her soon.

The thought pressed hard in her chest. Surely he didn't have a wife anymore, not with the way he looked at her. *Lord, don't let me lose my heart to him again.*

She forced that line of thinking away and pushed up to standing.

The world swayed around her, finally fading to a dark gray. She took in a deep breath, reaching out to catch her balance. She couldn't fall. If she fainted, Jean-Jacques would insist they wait another day.

But as she inhaled more steady breaths, her vision cleared. She had to focus on moving her feet, but her body finally found its balance as she stepped toward the trees opposite where Jean-Jacques worked.

She desperately needed a creek to give herself a good cleaning. From what Jean-Jacques had said, the nearest one was down the mountain. She vaguely remembered passing it but didn't have a very good idea how far down it was. She probably couldn't walk that distance. Perhaps once they started out, they could stop a while there. Perhaps she could find some trees to shield her while she accomplished a sponge bath.

Jean-Jacques was kneeling by the fire when she returned to camp, but he stood at her approach. His eyes studied her, and she managed a smile for him. Just walking the short distance made her breathe hard, but she did her best to quiet her inhales and act stronger than she felt. "I'm ready to ride out when you are."

His gaze turned earnest as he studied her face. "Colette." His voice had softened into that tone that gripped her heart. "We don't have to rush your recovery. We can stay here as long as you need. You and the baby both."

Heat swept up her neck at the comment. She'd not talked of the baby with anyone, at least not in such a casual tone. The words sounded so intimate spoken aloud, especially when she wasn't on her deathbed.

Her hand wandered to her belly. Was she pushing the little

one too hard? Surely a few hours' ride wouldn't be too much. The horse would be doing most of the work.

She lifted her gaze to Jean-Jacques's again. This time she softened her voice to match his. "I really do think I'm strong enough. My horse is gentle, and the ride is only a few hours."

His expression turned skeptical at her last comment. "We'll need to keep the horses to a walk, so we'll be lucky to make it by nightfall."

She turned toward her bedroll. "Let's get packing then."

"*You.*" The way he emphasized the word stopped her short. "Sit down and rest while I pack and saddle the horses."

That might be the better choice to conserve what little strength she had. But she wouldn't say that thought aloud.

CHAPTER 14

French eyed Colette's swaying form as the horses maneuvered up the mountain trail. They'd been riding a couple hours now, and he'd kept his mount beside her most of the time, except when the trail grew too narrow. She'd maintained a brave face, but the dark circles under her eyes deepened the longer they rode.

And now, this view from behind had him even more worried. Her side-to-side swaying was far more than what would result from normal shifting with the horse's stride. She clutched her saddle tight. If she grew so weak she fell off the horse, the tumble could do real damage to the baby. And if she hit her head on a rock… He couldn't let that happen.

At the first section where the trail widened enough for two horses to walk abreast, he called up to Colette. "Stop here a minute."

She reined in. As he rode alongside her, she was still clutching the saddle and hunching low, as though it took all her strength to hold on. Exhaustion dimmed her eyes.

He scooted back in his saddle, then tapped the seat in front of him. "Ride with me a while. That way you don't have to use energy to sit upright."

Her eyes shifted to the spot in front of him. She must have been as exhausted as she appeared, for she didn't hesitate. Simply leaned toward him and tried to lift her leg over his saddle to slide from her mount onto his. She didn't even have energy for that.

He reached out and gripped under her arms, then hoisted her onto his saddle. She finally managed to move her leg up over his mare's neck.

The fit was tight, and at first she seemed to be trying to hold herself upright—away from him. Her hair tickled his face as he breathed in the familiar scent of her. He'd strapped her hat on her bed roll, so it didn't serve as a barrier between them now. Her shorter hair was free to blow in the breeze, and now that it wasn't constrained, the strands looked longer than he'd thought before.

Having her so near made his heart hammer so hard he could barely breathe. He did his best to shake himself free from the spell. "Just give me a minute to tie your mare behind mine, then you can lean back against me."

Once they were moving again, Colette sank back against his chest. He could ride forever like this, having her so near. Cradled in his arms.

Hopefully soon, she'd agree to marry him, and he could hold her like this even when she wasn't too exhausted to keep herself upright.

By the time they reached the next valley, the sun had peaked in the sky. They stopped by another creek to let the horses drink and to refill their canteens. They'd both been eating as they rode, but the chance to stretch their legs and attend to personal needs was welcome.

After returning from a patch of trees, Colette sank to the ground and waited for him to finish tending the animals. She didn't look quite as spent as when he'd moved her to his saddle earlier, but she would definitely need to ride with him again for the second half of the journey.

She must have felt the same, for she waited for him to help her mount his horse. Within minutes, he climbed up behind her and they settled into their earlier rhythm. Her head tucked perfectly into the crook of his neck.

About an hour into the afternoon, her body had gone completely limp against him. The one time he leaned forward to glimpse her face, her eyes were closed, her mouth parted in steady breathing.

She was so beautiful. And even more so when she trusted him this fully. His heart ached with the love growing stronger every day. There was nothing he wouldn't do for this woman. And now, he was quickly feeling the same way about the babe who grew inside of her. That child was part of *her*—the Colette he loved.

French had been pushing to arrive back in camp before dark, but stars had just begun to twinkle in the darkness when they crossed the familiar creek. He guided the horses to where the other animals were hobbled to graze, then reined in at the edge of the trees.

Colette straightened in front of him. The last few hours, he'd not been sure if she was awake or dozing. Now, she looked around as though trying to place her surroundings.

"We're back. I'll get you to camp, then come see to the horses." He eased down from his saddle, then reached up to help Colette down.

When he placed her on her feet, her legs didn't hold her at first, and she would have gone to her knees if he hadn't been gripping her upper arms.

Gradually, she stood without his help, but she still clutched the saddle.

He kept his hands hovering nearby just in case she needed

him. "Do you want to try to walk, or would you rather I carry you?"

"I can walk." Her voice came quiet, drained of energy.

"Let me tie the horses, then I'll go with you."

While Colette still clung to the saddle, he quickly secured both mares and unfastened her pack, tossing it over his shoulder so he could have both hands free to help her.

He gripped her arm to support her, and they started toward camp. They'd barely stepped into the woods when a figure appeared through the trees ahead.

French's heart stuttered, even though he was expecting one of the men to come see who'd arrived. Still, the brave's stealthy appearance might've taken a year off of French's life. He cleared his throat. "Left Standing."

The man took them in and must have seen Colette's condition. "Come to the fire. There is food, though not so good as what you cook."

He turned and led the way toward camp. The glowing fire called to them through the trees, and the other braves were sitting in their usual positions, most with bark slabs for plates in front of them. Young Bear held his pipe. All looked their way as they stepped into the clearing.

French offered a tight smile of greeting. "Sorry we were gone so long. Mignon took sick and needed a few days before he was strong enough to ride back."

He hated the lie of calling Colette a man. Especially when everyone here likely saw through it. He glanced at her. With her white-blonde hair ruffled and no hat in sight, she looked even more like a woman. She also looked weak and exhausted and in need of a soft bed and gentle care.

He motioned toward Colette's bedroll, still exactly where she'd left it two days before. "Lie down and we'll get you some food."

She didn't argue or even try to explain their absence to the others. One more sign she was spent beyond herself.

As he helped Colette onto her bedding, Hawk Wing's voice sounded from near the fire. "We began to think you meant to leave us. But with these nice furs waiting, we thought you would return."

With Colette settled, French turned to the man and summoned a grin. "If anything ever happened to us, you all are welcome to split our furs among you. You've been good companions. But we aren't planning to go anywhere. Didn't expect to be gone so long this time."

As French stepped to the fire, Elk Runs lifted two bark plates of meat to him. The man must have cooking duty for the day. They might all be relieved to have their camp keeper back.

French nodded his thanks. "Looks good."

After laying the food beside Colette and watching her take the first bite, her eyes almost too heavy-lidded to keep open as she chewed, he turned back and settled in the empty spot between Hawk Wing and Young Bear.

While the men caught him up on the happenings over the last few days, several of them sent occasional glances toward Colette. Were they simply curious? Worried about her? Or did they suspect something?

It wasn't right to lie to them any longer. These men had shown themselves to be friendly, fair, and hard-working. They'd shared willingly and never given cause for alarm with him and Colette, except maybe the other night when strong drink had been involved.

His instincts told him it was time to come clean. Or at least ask questions that might tell him how much they'd guessed.

Tomorrow. He'd find Young Bear when the man was alone and start the conversation. Should he ask Colette first? No, he'd find out how much the man knew and tell her what he learned. Then she could choose how much more to reveal.

~

Colette slept hard through the night and was still breathing the steady rhythm of deep sleep when French checked on her the next morning. He'd already emptied both of their trap lines and now laid a bundle of wrapped meat beside her so she could eat when she woke. He also had ground cornmeal set aside to make gruel.

But perhaps the corn gruel had been the cause of her sickness the other night. The thought gave him pause as he stared at the stew pot.

She'd said she thought it was bad meat, so he'd thrown out the few pieces in her pack that looked questionable. Then he'd re-cooked the rest of their meat supply up on the mountain. He'd intentionally eaten her stock himself and fed her from his, so she wouldn't be affected if the food was tainted in some other way. Neither of them had suffered stomach ailment after that, so he'd assumed the problem had been put behind them.

But might the corn be tainted? That was the last thing she'd eaten before leaving camp.

He was fairly certain it wasn't possible to undercook dried corn. In fact, people sometimes ate the stuff without grinding and cooking it. Neither he nor the other men had suffered ill effects from the corn. So maybe there was nothing wrong with it.

Either way, he'd get Colette's thoughts on the matter before he fed her any. If she felt comfortable eating corn gruel, he'd make sure he boiled it plenty long.

With a final glance to make sure Colette still slept, he started out to the skinning area to process that morning's take.

He worked with all five of the other men for a while. Then one by one, the others finished with their catch and left for other duties, leaving only Young Bear and him. The older man worked slower than the younger braves. Maybe this was the right time to see what Young Bear knew.

French hadn't been able to talk with Colette yet to decide how much to share, but he simply wouldn't give away anything the fellow hadn't already guessed.

Young Bear kept his pipe nearby, something he didn't do often when he worked. When he finished with a hide—and once or twice in the midst of working on it—he would pause and reach for the pipe, then puff for several minutes.

During one of those breaks, French straightened from the beaver skin he was scraping and stretched to work out the aches in his back. He'd certainly strengthened some muscles during this time with the braves. The couple days off had made things more challenging this morning.

He sent Young Bear a glance. How to begin? He should have given more thought to what he would say to prod details from the man. He could usually start a conversation with a story, but what tale would be right to lead off this questioning?

Before he could find an answer, Young Bear spoke. "Mignon is better this morning?" He took another puff from the pipe as he waited for French's answer.

That was the right topic. Maybe this conversation would flow easier than he'd thought.

"Still sleeping." He was careful not to use the word *he*. "When I came upon the mare up in the mountains, Mignon was in rough shape. Not conscious and barely breathing. Thought bad meat might've been the cause."

Young Bear nodded. "Is weak still." Was he also being careful not to use anything that would show Colette's gender? Or maybe that was simply the extent of his skill speaking English.

French nodded. "Yes. Very." He needed to find a question to lead into how much Young Bear knew about her. "Have you known Mignon long?" That might make the man wonder, for he must expect that Colette had told French already.

Young Bear inhaled from his pipe, watching French with an indecipherable expression. He exhaled a long puff. The scent of tobacco lingered, even across the half-dozen strides between them. The man still didn't answer but took another puff, then another long exhale. Was he deciding how much to tell?

At last, he seemed to make up his mind. "Mignon joined us a few days after we left the rendezvous. I knew all was not as told to us. But I have three daughters, too, and I would want others to give them help when needed."

French's pulse leapt, and he studied the man. Was he saying…? He had to be. *Three daughters,* he'd said.

He had to make sure. "You knew?" He wasn't giving away Colette's secret, simply asking a question.

The man puffed out a stream of smoke. "She must have need of protection. I would want the same for my daughters."

Relief sagged through French. He inhaled a deep breath, then nearly choked on the tobacco stench. But the relief was too strong for anything to bother him.

He met Young Bear's gaze. "Thank you. You're a good man, as I had already come to believe."

French took in another breath as he worked to gather his thoughts. His gaze slipped toward the camp. Toward Colette. Should he say anything about her plight? Her condition? Or even who French was to her?

That last thought was laughable. *He* still wasn't sure what he was to Colette. Though he planned to make that clear soon enough.

Better to keep the rest to himself. The story was Colette's, however much she felt comfortable sharing.

In the meantime, he should find out a bit more about what they knew. He turned back to Young Bear. "The others?"

The man nodded. "They are good men, though some young. She is a sister to them."

Another wave of relief. A sister. The kind a man protected. He sharpened his gaze on Young Bear and made sure the truth of his words thickened his voice. "I'm so glad she found you."

CHAPTER 15

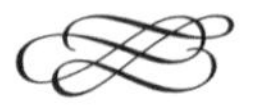

Sleep still weighed heavily on Colette, stealing the strength from her muscles. But she forced herself to sit upright.

They'd made it back to camp. Clearly they had, for she was sitting on her own bedroll in the area beside the cliff wall. But the ride here was so hazy in her mind, she couldn't recall more than vague impressions. The security of Jean-Jacques's arms around her as she leaned back against him. The desperate thirst that assaulted her as they rode. The way her belly constantly grumbled for food. More meat. Did the baby really require so much? She might have to use up all her time simply eating and drinking. All her energy too.

Even now, her middle grumbled, and other needs made themselves known too. Better start with the food though, lest the nausea raise its voice again.

Jean-Jacques must have placed the leather-wrapped bundle of meat beside her blankets. If only he'd left her canteen there too. A glance at her pack showed it laid on top, so she only had to reach for it.

That simple stretch left her breathing harder. She sat upright and gave herself the leisure of eating and drinking as much as her body needed while she gathered strength to stand.

Once her insides had finally stopped complaining—except for that other need which was becoming more urgent—she corked the canteen and set the food aside. Now she had to summon the energy to retreat to her private spot.

She worked herself up to standing. But then the darkness closed in, blocking out her vision. She threw out her arms for balance, but everything around her spun. *Don't let me fall, Lord.*

She *was* falling—backward. But maybe that was a trick of her senses?

She bent forward to shift her balance and right herself, but her vision darkened even more. Panic washed through her, and she tensed for impact, flailing her arms to stop herself no matter which way she toppled.

A hand clenched her upper arm, and another supported her back. Catching her. Lifting her.

She reached out for the arm, for something secure to grab onto. Her hand closed around solid buckskin. Jean-Jacques must have saved her again. She grabbed hold with both hands as she squeezed her eyes shut, willing her body to settle.

Finally, the sensation of spinning stilled, and she eased open her eyes.

The face studying her was not Jean-Jacques's dear one, but another she'd come to appreciate too. "Hawk Wing."

She was clutching him tight, and maybe her weakness would expose the fact she was a woman. But her vision hadn't quite stabilized. If she let go, she might topple again. At least this time she could aim better toward her sleeping pallet.

After a few breaths, her vision brightened to normal, and her spinning head settled. Now if she could only hide the embarrassment flooding her neck. She eased away from him and tried to tame her blush with a solemn expression. "Thank you. I guess I'm still weak from the sickness."

He was studying her, scrutinizing, but his face gave no hint of his thoughts. Finally, he stepped back and nodded. "You were very sick."

"I was." She couldn't deny the truth of his words.

He motioned toward her bed pallet. "Good to lie down."

Yes, it would be much safer to lie down, but she desperately needed to find a bush to take care of other matters first.

Yet Hawk Wing didn't look like he would leave until he knew she was safely seated. So, she eased herself down, moving slowly enough to keep her head from spinning again.

Once she was seated, he nodded once more, then moved to his packs. After scooping up a leather satchel and his hunting knife, he turned toward the path to the river.

When he sent another glance her way, she offered a weak smile. "Thanks for saving me."

His expression softened, then he slipped into the shadows of the woods.

With a sigh, she reached for the bundle containing the meat and pulled out another slice. Hawk Wing really had saved her from more pain. Hopefully, her hands would've kept the fall from injuring the baby, but better not to risk it. Maybe with a little more meat inside her, the dizziness would ebb.

After eating for a few more minutes, she wrapped the food back up and prepared to stand again. This time she only made it to her knees before footsteps sounded through the trees. A sigh slipped out.

Should she sit back down now? Wait for this person to leave before she attempted to stand? Her body may not let her wait that long. Better she move forward now and pray that eating more had helped.

A glance over her shoulder showed Jean-Jacques stepping into camp. Relief eased some of the pressure from her chest.

When he saw her on hands and knees, concern gathered in his brows, and he darted forward. "You need help?"

She gritted her teeth and raised her upper body. Only a bit of gray crept into her vision.

His hand slipped around her arm in a loose hold. "Do you want to stand up?"

"Yes." The word slipped out almost as a growl, since she was straining to push up to her feet. Even with all her effort, she teetered halfway through rising.

Jean-Jacques's grip tightened on her arm, lifting her the rest of the way up. Holding her secure even when the blackness threatened to close in again. "Colette, are you sure you should be up? Rest a little longer. I have corn gruel if you're hungry."

A new flood of embarrassment rose up within her. "Need… to find…a tree."

Though she couldn't focus on his face, his silence probably meant he understood. Then his voice came hesitantly. "I'll walk you there. Then leave you alone until…"

Another dose of relief eased through her. She pointed toward the path she usually took to the private spot. "That way."

By the time she finished, the haze and spinning in her vision had left completely. She started back to camp without calling for Jean-Jacques. When she came in sight of the clearing, he was standing at the edge of camp, looking her direction with as much anxiety as a pup locked behind a fence, waiting for its master to return.

He strode toward her the moment he saw her, and she let him take her arm, though she couldn't help adding, "I'm better now."

She could no longer trust her body, so it might be good to have him by her side. If only she weren't always so weak in his presence. She wanted him to know the version of her that could be strong and capable. Wanted him to love that person as much as she'd always loved him.

But that was a dangerous line of thinking, a desire that could only end in a new round of heartbreak.

She pulled away from his hold. They were inside the clearing now, and only a few steps from her bedding.

He stood nearby as she took those last strides and eased down onto her blankets. Maybe *plopped* was the better word. With her treacherous balance and the weight now beginning to bulge in her belly, there was nothing graceful about the way she sat.

He turned toward the fire and added more logs. "I have corn meal ready to make a warm gruel for you. I thought you might like something other than meat, and it would be good for the baby. Something to fill you both up." He didn't look her way as he spoke of her unborn child, but he said the words so casually, as if the babe were a normal part of his thoughts and conversation.

"I started to wonder though," he continued, "do you think the corn gruel made you sick before?" This time he did glance her way with brows raised. "You said you thought it was bad meat, but you'd eaten mush that morning, so I wasn't certain."

She shook her head. "I think I know what meat it was. My belly started to complain not long after I ate it on the trail. I threw it out then."

He raised his brows with a slow nod. "I see. Do you and the little one feel up to corn mush then? Wish I had some fresh milk to pour into it." He shrugged in that boyish way he used to.

The memories that gesture brought back slipped through her, lightening her mood and tugging a smile over her face. "Sounds perfect."

While he worked, she took the opportunity to watch him. To soak in this man she'd loved for so long—as far back as she could remember. Maybe even from that first day they'd met, when he found her working in the garden. And now as a grown man, he stirred her insides in a way no one else ever had. Not even Raphael.

Maybe she had loved her husband once, or maybe it had

been only infatuation. When she met Raphael, she'd given up on ever having Jean-Jacques, though it had taken her two years after mama shared the news of his marriage. Raphael had seemed like a good second choice. Funny and attentive—and recently come from France. That point had been a strong one in his favor for Mama. And her parents' approval had been a strong point in his favor for Colette.

The early days of their marriage had been trying sometimes, but that was always the case when two people learned to make a home together. They'd finally settled in and found a rhythm. Maybe if she'd been able to stop missing Jean-Jacques, she could've given her heart completely to Raphael.

But then Raphael's father had died. At first, he'd grieved in a way that seemed normal. He'd not been on good terms with his father in several years—none of the brothers had, since the man often let his temper guide his words. But after his death, Raphael mourned the fact that they'd never reconciled. She'd not realized about his drinking at first. Looking back, she could see it had started much earlier than she'd thought.

By the time his personality began to change, she had no idea how to stop it. She tried everything she could to help him.

She prayed. First, for the Lord to help him stop drinking. For the Heavenly Father to bring peace to his grieving heart. She prayed for God to amend their marriage. For Him to make her forget Jean-Jacques. For her love for her old friend to fade. For her heart to want to love Raphael, no matter what he said to her. No matter how hard he made their lives.

And then when she learned of the baby, she'd cried out for God to give her wisdom. So much of her feared raising a child with the man her husband had become. But what could she do? She'd wed him in God's sight, taking holy vows.

Then on that life-altering night, the decision had been made for her.

But not really. Surely, she could have found a way to stop

Raphael's manic advance without striking him with that metal bar.

Or, if she'd just hit him in a different place.

Or not so hard.

"Here you go." Jean-Jacques's words drew her from the dark thoughts. He crouched before her, a bowl of corn mush in his hands.

A burn crept into her eyes as she took in his earnest face. The concern tugging at his expression. Jean-Jacques was there. And looking at her the way he always had, with earnest affection in his eyes. The way he did in her dreams, both the waking ones and the night dreams that had come so often. Her Jean-Jacques.

She wanted to reach out and touch him. He was near enough that she could pull him closer—close enough for their lips to meet.

The thought splashed through her like icy water, bringing with it a deluge of eye-opening fear. There was one very important reason why she and Jean-Jacques could never be together. Not *just* because of what she'd done. Not *just* because she carried a child that wasn't his, a babe sired by the man she'd killed.

It was more than both of those good reasons. She wouldn't make the same mistake again. She simply had to guard herself with the most important reason. To brace it in front of her like a shield against this man. She raised the shield now. "The other night, when those men were here. They gave you whiskey?"

His expression shifted, and he seemed to draw away. Just a little, but at least he was moving in the right direction. "I…think it was whiskey. Some kind of strong drink."

As she'd known. But the confirmation helped strengthen her defenses. "And you drank it?" How could he *not* have? His father had been a drunkard, even more openly than Raphael, even at the end. That weakness would be in Jean-Jacques's veins too.

CHAPTER 16

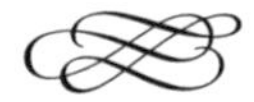

Colette watched Jean-Jacques's expression as she waited for his answer.

His look turned guarded, then he shook his head. "I didn't. I think most of the others did, but I'm not certain about Left Standing."

Liar.

Raphael had lied, especially at the beginning. Later on, she didn't waste time asking if he'd been drinking. She knew all the signs.

Jean-Jacques was watching her, and maybe he saw the disbelief in her eyes.

His brow lowered, then his tone gained an edge of frustration. "I waited with the others for you to come to camp after dark. I kept stew ready for you, then planned to make sure you weren't bothered by the newcomers and could bed down in peace.

"When you didn't come for so long, I went looking for you. I searched all the way down our snare lines, then back up the river. I checked with the horses, but you weren't there either. I remembered that place where I'd found you resting before, and when I found the spot again, there you were.

"You were sleeping and even had a blanket and your gun. I decided the best way I could help was by keeping an eye on the men at camp." His jaw grew solid. As though her lack of belief angered him. "I stayed up until the others had all bedded down or drunk themselves to sleep. Then I made sure I was up with the first riser."

That was anger on his face, but there seemed something more. Something deeper in his eyes—not at all like rage. Hurt? The last thing she wanted was to hurt this good friend.

Could he be telling the truth? His moment-by-moment recounting matched what she knew to be true. He could only have known where she slept if at least that part was real.

She studied his face for a long moment. *God give me wisdom. Help me discern truth from lie.*

As she ran her gaze over the nuances of his expression, his sincerity settled inside her. No inner voice warned against believing his story. *Are You sure, Lord?*

A deeper peace pressed through her.

This was only one instance, but maybe he wasn't as drawn toward vile drink as she'd assumed.

She nodded. "Thank you for watching out for me." Those words sounded paltry considering all he'd done these past few days, so she tried for more. "And for everything else. For finding me, staying with me, and helping me ride back." Heat crept up her neck unbidden at her few memories of him on the return journey. She couldn't seem to stop blushing this morning.

The wariness and that hint of anger slipped from his expression, and the smile lines at his eyes deepened. "I'm glad I was able to." He nodded toward the bowl in her hands. "Eat up. That little one needs everything he or she can get to grow strong and healthy."

She lifted the bowl to drink from it like a cup, even as

another smile curved her lips. Yes, she loved the way he brought the baby into everything. Especially with the warmth that slipped into his voice when he spoke of the child.

Jean-Jacques moved to his pack, and she closed her eyes as the warm gruel slid through her, filling her insides with its soothing goodness. As the sound of his steps came near again, she opened her eyes.

His gaze twinkled as he moved past her and eased down to sit on the blankets beside her. That was just like him, to intrude into her life without an invitation. Yet she was always so glad he did.

As he settled in, she glanced at what he held. A block of red cedar and a small carving knife. "What are you doing?"

He flipped the wood over to show an arc he'd been scraping. "Working on a spoon." He nodded toward the bowl in her hands. "To go with that fancy dishware."

A laugh bubbled through her. "You always have been more cultured than me."

Now was his turn to chuckle, but his didn't hold as much merriment. "Not hardly."

Comfortable silence slipped over them as she swallowed another bite of corn mush and he chipped slivers off the cedar. A spoon really would make eating easier. She should've thought of making one earlier. She'd never attempted to carve, but it might be fun to try, if she had a blade as small as Jean-Jacques's.

"I spoke with Young Bear this morning." His voice broke the quiet, crashing through the peacefulness with words that clenched in her belly.

"You spoke with him? About what?" Surely he wouldn't tell her secrets. But what else could he mean?

He glanced at her. "I didn't tell him anything. I just... Well, I've been thinking for a while that these men must have seen through your disguise. I wanted to get an idea of how much he knew. I asked him how long he'd known you, and he started talking from there."

Thoughts swirled through her, churning with the fear that rose up from her belly. "Started talking about what? What did he say?" If her cover no longer held up, she'd have to leave these men. She wouldn't be safe here.

Where else could she go? Strike out on her own? The thought made the nausea rise up to her chest. The corn gruel she'd just eaten might soon reappear.

"Colette, it's all right." Jean-Jacques raised a staying hand. "He said he realized when you asked to join with them that something wasn't right. He has three daughters of his own, and he would want someone to help them if they were in need. He said that's why they let you come along. The other braves think of you as a sister and want to help you too."

His words were slow to penetrate, but her mind clung to the one—*sister*. Could that really be true? They all knew the truth and wanted to protect her?

It seemed too good. Too unlikely for a group of men. But maybe God had led her to these very people for protection. She'd sensed that from the beginning, but she'd thought her disguise was an important part of her safety among them. Had the Father truly managed it all?

He certainly was capable of it. The Almighty didn't need her help to manage the world and weave all things together according to His plan. *I'm sorry, Father. How could I have been so prideful?* She'd not seen it that way before, but the entire picture came clear now.

She took a moment to soak in the sweet presence of the Lord. He was so good to her. Why did she work so hard sometimes to override His blessings?

Finally, she turned to Jean-Jacques. "Do you trust them?" She was pretty sure *she* did, especially Young Bear. And his word seemed to go far with the others. But she valued Jean-Jacques's opinion.

He gave a slow nod. "I do."

Good. "I think I do too." She inhaled a calming breath, then released it in a puff. "Now...since everyone knows the truth, I suppose I don't need to pretend anymore. At least with them." Her mind raced through possible scenarios. "I should probably still dress as I have in case we meet others."

The moment the words slipped out, she replayed them in her head to see if she'd given away anything about her trouble. About Hugh and Louis. Would her need to hide from strangers make Jean-Jacques suspicious as it had before?

She slid her gaze toward him to see if his face showed signs that his thoughts had gone that direction. But a smile was tickling the corners of his mouth.

He saw her looking, and his grin widened. "Those clothes didn't stop me from noticing you're a woman."

Another flush swept up her neck. "That's because you knew me before." She hoped that was the only reason he'd seen past her disguise. At least his mind hadn't gone the other direction.

But then his expression sobered. "If you're worried that you're in danger, Colette, you don't need to fear. I promise to protect you. Dress like a man if you want to, but I won't let you be hurt. You have my word on it."

Nausea swirled in her belly again. He had no idea what he was saying. If Hugh and Louis found her, they would kill her. She had no doubt. Hugh had killed before, and for far less reason than the need to avenge his brother's death. If Jean-Jacques got in their way, he would be in as much danger as she was.

She would have to make sure he wasn't around if they found her. At the first sign of Raphael's brothers, she would run—far and fast.

But for now, she needed to focus on this conversation and

her next steps with the others. "I guess I need to say something to the men. To thank them for helping me."

Jean-Jacques gave a thoughtful nod. "I'm sure they would appreciate that. Might be a good way to clear the air. We all want to help you, and the more we know of what's going on, the better we can prepare."

She couldn't tell him anything more, but better to make him think he knew everything. As for the others, it wouldn't be safe for them to know about the baby yet...would it? Men tended to be uneasy around a woman with child. They might make her leave or try to send her back to one of the northern forts. She couldn't risk it.

She leveled a firm gaze on Jean-Jacques. "I will thank them. But I don't want them to know of the baby yet. I want life to go along as before."

His mouth straightened in a thin line, but he nodded. "If that's what you prefer." He might be thinking her condition would become obvious soon. He was right. But until then, this was her decision.

She poured the last bite of gruel into her mouth, then set the bowl aside.

Jean-Jacques reached for it. "I'll let you sleep now. Anything I can get you before I go?"

He was looking at her with that earnest Jean-Jacques expression again, the one that always drew her in.

She shook her head. "I'm full and content. Thank you." *For everything.*

But as he gathered the pot and bowl and started toward the river, a feeling settled over her that was far from comfortable. Did she dread the coming conversation with the men? Or was this sensation a harbinger of much worse to come?

~

Colette was still hiding something from him.

As French pushed harder on the scraping knife, bits of flesh and sinew flew off the fur. Whatever secret she still kept had her clutched in a tight grip of fear. What could it possibly be? Did she know her husband's murderer? Had the man attempted to take her life too?

His fists clutched the knife tighter, and he thrust harder with the blade.

Too hard. He penetrated the hide with a jerk.

Hotheaded idiot. He straightened and inspected the tear. He hadn't damaged a hide in years. Not this badly anyway.

Now this pelt wouldn't bring enough in trade to justify all the labor he'd put into it. He'd have to stitch the hole and keep it for himself. Unfortunately, the badger skin wasn't big enough for a blanket, not unless he sewed several more to it. And he didn't need another blanket anyway. Maybe he could get a pair of moccasins from the piece—or one moccasin anyway.

He forced himself to ease the pressure of his stroke as he started again. He'd have to take extra care around the tear.

A rustle sounded in the trees, and he glanced up as Colette stepped into the sunshine from the path to camp.

Just the sight of her lightened the weight of his frustration. She still hadn't put that awful hat back on, and she was walking with a much gentler step than normal. More like an angel than ever, with her sleep-tousled white-gold hair.

He straightened again and smiled. "You must be feeling better." He'd checked on her often through the afternoon, but she'd been lying on her bed pallet each time. She didn't look strong yet, but at least she had enough energy to rise and walk around.

She offered a gentle smile. "Much. Where are the others?"

He glanced in the direction of the animals. "Young Bear and Elk Runs are with the horses, I think. Left Standing and Hawk

Wing went for a hunt. And I thought Cross the River was back at camp?" He swung his gaze to her in question.

She nodded. "Doing something with his furs."

Her brow furrowed as her gaze dropped to the hide in front of him. "You're dressing the catch from my traps too?"

He nodded. "They fill up quickly."

The line in her brow didn't ease. "I'm sorry you're having to do my work. You can have the hides, of course."

He shook his head. "I don't want your furs, Colette. And I don't mind the work. Gives me something to keep busy." If only it could occupy his mind as much as it did his hands.

Her expression finally eased into a smile. "Thank you. Seems I'm saying that a lot these days."

He dropped his focus back to the fur and began scraping again. "I'm glad to do it." He didn't want her furs. He simply wanted her trust.

"Can I help you?"

He shook his head but didn't look up from his work. "I'm almost done. Why don't you sit by the river and enjoy the sunshine?"

She took his advice, and his body tracked her every movement as she stepped softly past him and eased down at the water's edge.

With her sitting behind him, his mind stayed very focused. Not on his work, as it should, but circling around Colette and what she might be doing or thinking. How much he wanted to sit beside her and talk. Or better yet, pull her closer and finally get the chance to—

He snapped the lid closed on those thoughts and forced his focus back to the hide under his knife.

Finally, he finished the work, then gathered his tools and turned to Colette. "I need to start the evening meal. Do you want to walk back to camp with me?"

She sat with her feet in the water that must be icy, her face turned up to the sun, her eyes closed. No angel had ever looked as beautiful.

She kept her eyes closed as she spoke. "No, this feels so good, I think I'll stay here a little longer." Her voice held a whimsical quality, reminding him so much of the little girl she'd once been.

His body ached to cradle her in his arms, to pull her onto his lap and hold her close.

He turned himself away before he did something he would regret. He couldn't rush her. He'd have to be patient. He'd be available when she was ready.

If there was one thing he knew about Colette, it was that she wouldn't do anything until she'd made up her own mind about it. That was one of the things he loved about her, but right now that was making him crazy.

CHAPTER 17

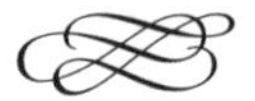

She had to do this now.

Colette accepted the bowl and spoon Jean-Jacques handed her and took her seat with the others around the fire. Elk Runs and Young Bear already sat with their cups of stew, and the other three waited to fill theirs.

Hopefully, Jean-Jacques planned to carve more spoons and bowls so she wouldn't be the only one with the special dishware. But then, the Indians may not be accustomed to using spoons. He should at least make one for himself, though.

She sent a glance around the group as they all settled in with their food. She'd give them a few minutes to eat, then speak up about her secret.

Jean-Jacques sent her a smile before raising his own cup to his mouth. Did he know that she was planning to speak to the braves after the meal? He probably suspected it.

She only managed two swallows of her stew while the others finished theirs off.

As Young Bear reached for his pipe, she cleared her throat and prepared to start. "I, um, think you all might have guessed my secret." Every eye turned toward her, curiosity sparking in most of their gazes.

Pretending to speak to them as one man to another was one thing. But addressing this group of virile men as a woman nearly had her hands trembling.

She pressed down her fear and raised her chin. "I thought it would be safer if I pretended to be a man while I travel through these mountains, but I think most of you have seen through my disguise. I'm sorry for attempting to deceive you. But I need to thank you for keeping my secret and for all your help." Her mouth had gone dry, and she swallowed to moisten it again.

She motioned toward her stack of furs. "You taught me to trap. You taught me some of your language. Thank you. For everything." How many times had she said those words lately? It wasn't enough.

As she looked around the group, her gaze caught on Jean-Jacques first. He gave her an encouraging nod. Then she looked to Young Bear. He, too, dipped his chin. The expression in his eyes was so fatherly, a burn rose up to her throat. If Papa had lived, would things have become so bad with Raphael? Maybe he would have seen the warning signs.

Her mother wouldn't have gone back to the old country to visit her sister. Papa always disliked the idea of crossing the ocean. And in the end, he'd been right. That journey had been her mother's last.

She forced her thoughts back to the present and swallowed down the sting in her throat. She continued to shift her gaze around the group, meeting the eyes of every man.

"It is good you stay with us." Hawk Wing broke the men's silence. "Trap with us. As long as you can."

She met his gaze with a nod. "Thank you. I would like that." By *as long as you can,* did he mean until she grew too large with child? Surely he hadn't guessed that secret also. She wasn't showing enough for anyone to notice.

The others murmured words of agreement, then silence again slipped over the group.

Jean-Jacques straightened. "I'm going to water the horses one last time. Tomorrow, I think I'll see if I can rig a corral so they can reach the water anytime they want."

He stood, then turned to her. "Want to come along and watch? You can stretch your legs."

If she could have sprung to her feet, she would have. Now that she'd said her piece, she needed time away from these men and their heavy stares. Her actual standing was so slow, the men would likely think her still dizzy and weak. That was true, but she felt more cumbersome than anything.

Jean-Jacques led the way down the path through the trees, since most of the trail was narrow enough to require them to walk single file. When they stepped into the meadow where the horses grazed, his mare lifted her head and nickered in greeting. One of the other horses did the same.

He gave a low whistle, and his horse started toward them. Even the animal had fallen under his charms. Maybe she'd seen what a good man he was and longed for his attention. Colette could relate well.

When the horse reached him, he stroked her while she nuzzled his hand. Colette stepped forward, too, and rubbed the mare's neck on her other side. "Have you named her?"

Jean-Jacques's white teeth flashed in the moonlight as he smiled. "Giselle. I traded for her at a Nimiipuu camp."

"She seems to be happy with the match."

A soft chuckle came from the man opposite her. "She's a good girl."

With a final pat, he started toward the rest of the herd. "I need to untie the hobbles on the two spotted mares, then we'll take them to the creek."

She followed him, and when he bent beside one of the horses to untie the ropes at her ankles, Colette moved to the other.

He waved her away. "I'll do it. She kicks sometimes. Better not to risk the baby."

As much as she hated to concede, she couldn't chance a hoof hitting her belly. So, she simply stroked the mare's neck. "Why are you only hobbling these two now?"

Jean-Jacques stood and patted the horse he'd been working on, then moved around to hers and crouched by her hooves. "I found if I just hobble a couple of the horses, the rest stay nearby. Horses are such herd animals, and these all get along well together. Each day, I pick a different pair to hobble, that way they all get equal chance to move around. If I can rig a corral, though, I'll just keep the two inside it each day and let the others wander nearby. At least those two won't be held to one spot, and they can have access to water anytime they want."

"Good idea." His method of managing the horses proved his wisdom and his savvy with animals, as well as his kindness. So many men wouldn't have taken the time to find the perfect number of animals they had to confine so the rest could run free and still stay nearby.

He stood and patted the horse's neck. "Go get a drink, girl."

The mare obliged, sauntering toward the water as the other had done when he loosed her. The mare's absence removed the barrier between them, and Jean-Jacques moved to stand beside Colette. They were both facing the horses and the creek, but her awareness honed on the man at her side.

"You did well, what you said to the others back there." His voice had quieted, deepening to a luscious baritone that rumbled through her. The old Jean-Jacques hadn't possessed that tone, only this new man. And she liked it—too much.

"It was just a thank-you. I owe them much more than that."

He chuckled again. "If they weren't in love with you before, I suspect they are now."

She jerked her gaze to his face. "What? No." *No, no, no*. "You said they thought of me as a sister."

His brows rose, and his look turned rueful. "They'll protect you as they would a sister. But it's hard *not* to love you, Colette." His voice rumbled low again with those last words, even more intimate than before.

And his eyes... The moon was bright enough to shimmer in his gaze, melting her with its intensity.

"I know I do." His eyes held her so steady, she couldn't be sure if he'd actually spoken those last words or if his gaze had planted them in her heart.

She couldn't give in to this aching need for him. No matter how much his presence, and the yearning in his eyes that matched her own, raised the longing within her. She should pull back, but as his gaze dipped to her mouth, as his head moved nearer, she rose up to meet him.

His breath warmed her face, and her eyelids dipped closed, drawing her deeper into his hold, the power of his nearness.

This man. His hand slipped around her back, easing her closer as his lips brushed hers.

Sweet macaroons. His mouth caressed hers, his touch sending a tingle all the way through her. She pressed her hands to his chest, as much for support as to touch him, to keep him close.

His lips pressed deeper, connecting with hers in a heart-rending, breath-stealing caress that made her press for more. She needed so much more of him.

He returned the kiss with a hunger she'd never experienced, as if he'd longed for this as much as she had. Yet even as his touch drew her in, tugging her into its passion, there was a restraint in his manner. A gentleness that made her feel safe.

She didn't have to protect herself from this man. Not from Jean-Jacques.

Her hands roamed upward, slipping around his neck, her fingers threading through his hair. He pulled back with a groan that seemed to wrench from his core. He was breathing as hard as she was, a ragged heave that urged her to pull him close again.

He pressed his forehead against hers, their breaths mingling in a warm dance. "Colette. You have no idea how long I've wanted that."

She pulled in a breath that came much shakier than it should have. "Me too." Those words slipped out against her better judgment.

With another groan, he took her lips again, stealing her breath and stirring the longing inside her so high, she needed to pull back. Jean-Jacques would protect her, but her desire was fast overshadowing every other thought.

She forced herself to slow her kiss, though her body fought against her control.

Jean-Jacques sensed her change, and he softened his caress, his mouth easing to a final, gentle brush of his lips.

Then he drew away completely, his feet moving back a step, his hand sliding off her back. Both his hands cupped her elbows, then he ran his fingers down her arms to take her hands in his. Lifting them both, he pressed a kiss to each set of fingers, then finally raised his gaze to hers.

A smile shimmered in his eyes. "You stole my heart with your kiss when you were thirteen, but I never imagined the control you would have over me now that you're a woman."

A laugh bubbled out from her chest. A little too loud, too bright for the quiet around them. But her heart couldn't hold back the joy reverberating through her.

She shouldn't have kissed him, shouldn't have returned his kiss so strongly. She couldn't hurt him. And she might have to in the long run.

And what of his wife? The thought pressed, evaporating her happiness in a swift blow. Susanna. Was she waiting for him somewhere? Or had she passed away?

Colette needed to ask him. It wasn't right to kiss him the

way she had without knowing for sure. But surely Jean-Jacques wouldn't have begun the kiss if he was wed to another.

She pulled her hands from his, severing their connection completely. But as she dared a glance at his face, she couldn't bring herself to ask about Susanna. Maybe not knowing for sure was better. She couldn't let herself get caught up in an emotional tangle that would distract her from the watchfulness she had to maintain. Her baby depended on her to keep them both safe.

No distractions allowed.

Turning away from him, she started back toward camp.

CHAPTER 18

At last.

French pounded in the last sapling pole with the rock he'd been using as a hammer. He wrapped the loop of the rope around the pole and fitted it into the notch he'd cut to hold the cord secure from slipping down.

Stepping back, he eyed the pen for signs of weakness. With his first try, he'd spaced the poles too far apart, letting the rope sag so much the horses would have little trouble walking out. But with these extra saplings he'd added, the corral should be more secure. If the animals really wanted to leave, they could push through it, but the grass in this area was thick enough that they should be content here a few days. He could move the corral as needed, as long as Young Bear and the others wanted to remain camped here.

As soon as that badger fur he'd accidentally sliced yesterday was dry, he could scrape off the hair and cut the hide in small strips to braid for more rope. The more length he added, the bigger this pen could be.

As he removed the hobbles and led the two horses into the corral, a faint scent pricked his nose. Woodsmoke always soothed him. One of the others must have added more wood to the campfire. Maybe that was a hint for him to start on the evening meal.

As he patted the gelding's neck and closed off the rope gate to the corral, his gaze swept around the area.

Something in the distance caught his attention—a stream of smoke rising up above the trees to the north. Opposite the direction of their camp. Was another group staying nearby?

His belly tightened at the thought. Strangers didn't always mean danger. But one never knew if they were a war party out to gain any plunder they could find or a friendly group of hunters and trappers. Or, it could be the man who murdered Colette's deceased husband, now hunting her to finish his dirty deeds.

French scooped up his tools and strode back to the edge of the woods, where he'd left his gun and canteen. The smoke appeared to be a little distance from their camp, but probably only a quarter hour's hike. It seemed odd the strangers hadn't noticed their own trail of fire smoke, or the sound of his hammering stakes into the ground, and come to announce their presence.

Best he did some reconnaissance and see what these newcomers were about.

With his rifle in hand and his shot bag slung across his chest, French touched the hunting knife strapped at his side to make sure it held secure. Should he let the others know where he was going?

No. He'd only sneak close enough to investigate, then return. He wouldn't alert the strangers to his presence at all, even if they looked safe. Once he'd seen them, he would come tell the others, and then they could decide as a group if anything should be done about them.

He followed the creek upriver in the general direction of the smoke. It made sense the newcomers would camp near water, and probably at the edge of trees so they would have access to firewood and a break from the wind that sometimes swept through.

Once he passed the first patch of trees, the land along the creek's edge stretched in open grass. It looked like the smoke was coming from just beyond another group of trees in the distance. He'd do best to skirt this open area, even though it would require him to take a roundabout path to follow the tree line—an extra five or ten minutes.

He turned left to begin traveling around the edge of the clearing, closer to the base of a low mountain. Striding at a swift walk, he kept an eye on the distant trees that were his target and the smoke rising just beyond them. There was no sign of figures moving among the trunks.

At last, he reached those woods and stepped into them, keeping his path aimed toward the smoke. The scent was stronger now. They must've use leaves to help start their fire.

A man's voice drifted to him, and he stilled to listen. The rolling cadence of the words had to be the French language, but he couldn't make out what was being said. The man spoke in a normal volume for casual conversation, not a shout or command.

The talking ceased, and French listened another long moment for any other sounds. Only normal forest noises met his ears, so he started forward again, keeping his footfalls light in the toe-to-heel rolling motion Beaver Tail had taught him.

He'd traveled a dozen steps when a motion through the trees ahead stopped him again. There was more daylight there, like at the edge of the woods, and a figure moved across the light. From the shape of the body, it must be a man, but the movement had stilled. One of the trees might be blocking him.

French worked hard to steady his breathing as he debated his next move. He had to get closer, but he needed to stay behind the trees as much as he could. Should he duck lower? No. That would make it harder for him to move quietly.

With his gaze, he traced out his path to another tree wide enough to hide him, then darted forward on quiet feet to duck behind that trunk.

He peered around the tree to check for movement where he'd seen it before. Smoke rose up in a column, which must be the location of their camp. No other movement showed, nor any sounds from the men. Had they left camp? Gone to the river, or maybe to their horses?

He sought out his next hiding spot behind a wide pine, then slipped to it.

One by one, he shifted from tree to tree, checking for movement or sounds from the camp after each advance.

At last, he was only ten strides from the fire, and from this position he could see the area around it fairly well. At least two saddles were stacked beside a tree trunk, with several packs next to them. That meant the men had mounts, either horses or mules. No bedrolls had been laid out yet, nor were there any other signs that they'd made themselves comfortable. They must have arrived recently and only taken time to build a fire before they'd gone…to do what?

He'd have to wait for them to return. Surely they would be back soon, since their things and a blazing fire were all here.

Time passed—maybe a quarter of an hour?—and he strained for any sounds that might signal the men's return. Nothing.

Would Colette wonder where he was? Indeed, he should've started the evening meal before now. Would she worry? Maybe he should have told one of them where he was going. But they might have tried to come with him, and the more people traipsing through these woods, the harder it would be to stay quiet.

At last, the sound of a horse's nicker drifted from farther

upriver. That was the opposite direction from where French's and the rest of their group's animals grazed.

Then another whinny sounded from downriver. French cringed. That was one of their own animals, returning the greeting. If the men didn't already know of their presence by the smoke from their fire, that whinny would alert them.

He gripped his gun and tensed for action. He really wanted to get a glimpse of these strangers, but maybe he should go back and warn the others first.

The sound of voices made his decision.

Two men came into view, striding toward the camp with rifles held loosely. They both wore buckskin coats and wide-brimmed hats—somewhat similar to the one Colette wore. The color of their cloth shirts under the leather was the first difference he noted.

The man on the right wore a neutral gray, nearly blending into his buckskin trousers. Much of his face was covered with a thick light-brown beard, revealing the lines of hard living on his face above. He was definitely the older of the two, though maybe not more than thirty or so.

The other fellow sported a much brighter red tunic, and his trousers appeared to be cloth—and new enough that he must have obtained them recently. He also wore dark scruff on his young face—almost black to match his dark hair—though not a full beard like the other man.

When they first came into view, the elder had been speaking, but both fell into silence as they approached camp. Neither appeared to be in a hurry, nor did their gazes turn in the direction of the horse's whinny. Maybe they hadn't heard it.

The two seemed to be going about the process of setting up camp, one man pulling food out of a pack, the other scooping up loose branches for firewood.

French honed his focus on the guns they'd placed near their packs. Both appeared to be quality rifles. Not the older fusees many of the Indians carried—one more sign these men must have come from the east. Or maybe the northeast in Rupert's Land or the Canadas farther east.

Both men finally settled in beside the fire and appeared to be cooking fresh meat. From their position, he could only see the back of the bearded man and a little of his side profile. A scar at the fellow's temple was shaped like a half circle, like perhaps he'd been cut with the broken round base of a glass bottle. The wound looked to be several years old though, not raised and angry, but not so pale to signal it was from his childhood.

French had a much better view of the other, enough to see how young the fellow really was. Somewhere around twenty years, maybe less.

They only spoke occasionally, and then they said simple things like "Hand me that stick, will you?" and "Getting cold." They both spoke the French language fluently. It must've been their mother tongue. And they seemed at great ease with each other, as if the two had traveled together a long time. Or maybe they'd known each other before venturing into this untamed land.

Since the men had settled in, French needed to get back to the others. Maybe these two really didn't mean any harm. Perhaps they simply hadn't noticed the smoke from his fire, as they didn't seem to have heard the horse's call. These must simply be trappers or explorers, recently traveled from the east and out to make their fortunes in the vast mountain country.

After a final glance, he turned his focus to retracing his footsteps. Better he focus on caring for the woman God had finally brought back to him.

~

As Colette stirred the stew, she sent another glance toward the two paths leading out of camp. First the one pointing north, toward the horses. Then the trail to the creek. Where had Jean-Jacques gone, and why hadn't he returned in time to start their evening meal? Not that she minded cooking, not at all. But it wasn't like him to shirk what he considered his duties.

Her gaze landed on Young Bear, who'd settled into his usual place by the fire. Elk Runs and Left Standing had also finished checking their snare lines for the evening and now lounged in camp, waiting for their meal.

Maybe Jean-Jacques was checking their own traps. She'd already done that and secured their catch for the night. Just as she'd told him she would so he could finish the fence for the horses. Maybe he'd forgotten her words.

"You want me to look for him?" Left Standing's voice pulled her focus from the path to the horses, and she glanced at the man.

Should she ask him to? "I don't know where he would've gone. Maybe to check our traps? I told him I would do it, but perhaps he forgot."

The man's attention jerked toward the trail to the horses, and Colette turned her focus there too.

A few heartbeats later, Jean-Jacques appeared through the trees. He carried his gun and the other things he'd left with earlier that day, and the corners of his eyes tugged downward with weariness. Had he still been working on the fence, and she'd simply missed him when she went to check?

She offered him a smile. "Food's ready. I hope you don't mind that I did the cooking."

Fatigue slid from his gaze as his eyes turned warm. "Not at all. Sorry I left you with the chore though."

As the men scooped out their cups of stew, Cross the River and Hawk Wing padded into camp and joined them at the fire.

She lifted her bowl of warm soup to her face and soaked in the steamy aroma for a long minute before spooning her first bite. She'd cooked corn with the meat to add flavor and texture and hopefully fill their empty bellies a little better than meat alone did.

"We have neighbors." Jean-Jacques's voice rang above the sounds of eating.

The food in her belly soured as apprehension tightened inside her. She turned her focus to him just as the others did.

"I saw smoke from a campfire a little way upstream and went to see who was there." He met the gaze of each man in turn, then slid his focus to her. "That's why I was gone so long."

Every part of her itched to grip his shoulders and drag the identity of the men out of him, but she forced herself to stay perfectly still and wait.

He shifted his gaze back around the group. "It's two men—Frenchmen, I think. They have horses and carry rifles, but they seem peaceful enough. I didn't make my presence known, and I don't think they saw our camp smoke or heard our horses."

Her insides balled tighter. "What did they look like? Did you hear them speak?"

Jean-Jacques turned to her, his brows dipping in thought. "One was young, maybe around twenty. The other a little older and with a full beard. The older one had a scar on his right temple." He made a motion with his finger in the shape of a half circle.

Dread coursed through her. "A scar?" She managed to make her voice strong, despite the knot in her throat.

Jean-Jacques nodded. "Looked like it came from something round, maybe a broken bottle or a tin can."

Colette couldn't breathe. Her mind flashed an image—of Hugh with stitches forming a half circle to close the skin of his temple. It'd been only a few months after she and Raphael were married. Her husband had gone to retrieve his brother from one of the outlying forts after he killed a man in a drunken brawl.

She'd been so thankful at the time that Raphael hadn't taken after his elder brother's drinking and wild ways. If only he'd stayed that way.

"Colette? Do you know them?"

The call barely pulled her from the memory, but Jean-Jacques's other question sent a spear of panic through her.

The time had come. Raphael's brothers had found her—or they would by tomorrow morning. She couldn't be here when they came upon this camp.

But this time when she ran, she had to do a better job of covering her tracks.

She schooled her features to cover her fear. She couldn't let him guess what she was planning. Somehow, she'd have to sneak away without any of these men suspecting she was running. She would need time to cover enough ground before they discovered her absence. After she was gone, maybe Jean-Jacques would return to his wife. Did Susanna still live? Colette was a weakling for not asking. She certainly couldn't ask him now. She would never know for sure.

He was still watching her, waiting for her answer to his question. A glance around showed all the men were. She'd been silent too long.

Jean-Jacques knew Raphael had been murdered. He'd asked once if she worried that the murderer would come after her. She'd let him think she was, though she'd not lied outright.

Now, he would guess she was afraid of these men. Her silence would make him suspicious. Maybe she could find a way to make him think she didn't really know them.

She forced a thoughtful look onto her face. "You said one of the men was younger? Was his hair light colored, only a little darker than mine?"

The deception burned like bile down her throat. Raphael's younger brother's hair was as black as hers was fair, and Raphael's had been almost as dark. Hugh's was a lighter brown with a reddish tint, a difference her husband had joked about, saying their eldest brother must have been an orphan their parents took in.

Jean-Jacques shook his head, a frown tightening his features again. "It was dark, maybe black."

She forced her expression to ease. "And the other man, you said he was older? About Young Bear's age?" She hated this deception. Hated the way his features relaxed as he shook his head again.

She'd convinced him she didn't know these men. That they weren't the ones she feared. *I'm sorry, Lord. Please forgive me.*

None of the burden lifted from her heart. Was it hypocritical to beg forgiveness while continuing with the lie? Of course it was.

But she had to protect these men around her. Had to protect her baby. The only way to do that was to get far away from Hugh and Louis.

Far enough away this time that she couldn't be tracked. Then she would start over…again.

CHAPTER 19

Colette focused on the steady breathing around her and counted each different sound. Cross the River and Young Bear both snored lightly, so she could discern theirs easily. But she had to strain to pick out each of the others. It must be after midnight by now, and all the men had been breathing steadily for almost two hours.

This was as good a time as any. These men slept so lightly, especially the younger braves, she wouldn't be able to make a single sound.

Lord, help me.

Before going to bed, she'd stuffed her pack full of as much meat as she could carry, as well as her horse's bridle and the possessions most valuable to her. She would have to leave her fur bedding behind, but the one cloth blanket fit in her satchel. Now that the weather was warming into full spring, hopefully that blanket would be enough.

The worst thing would be leaving her saddle, but there was no way she could pick it up and carry it out of camp without awakening the others. The squeaks of the leather would be too loud. As hard as it was to ride for days on end in a hard leather seat, riding bareback—especially at faster gaits—would be awful.

But if one of these special men was killed because of her, that would be so much worse.

Moving more slowly than she ever had in her life, she eased up to sitting. Then—one tiny shift at a time—she pushed up to her feet. Such slow actions were almost painful as her heart pounded in her ears, her instincts screaming for her to run.

But the only way to stay perfectly silent and keep from waking the braves was to ease along no faster than a turtle.

It must have taken her five minutes to pick up her pack and cross the few steps to the first trees. She'd already planned out where she would place each foot on the barren ground. Thankfully, no leaves sounded her presence. Once she walked into the woods, silence would be even harder. She would have to keep moving at this achingly slow speed.

She didn't increase her pace until she'd nearly reached the clearing where the horses stayed. But even then, she kept to a walk. The horses might make sounds if she startled them. Better not wake them until she reached her mare, if possible.

The animals stood in a group, two inside the rope corral Jean-Jacques had made and the others resting nearby, heads lowered in sleep.

As unlikely as it seemed, none of the horses nickered or even made a sound until she ran her hand down her mare's neck. The horse breathed a gentle hello and sniffed into Colette's hand. *Sorry to wake you girl, but this is important.*

The mare took the bridle easily, and Colette led her down into the creek. The braves were excellent trackers, especially Elk Runs, so the only safe place to walk without leaving prints would be the water.

The mare stepped into the creek willingly, and Colette eased in beside her. The icy water stung as it penetrated her moccasins, but she ignored the pain. Beside her, the horse's hooves splashed with each step.

Colette jerked the horse to halt. This noise would never do. Even with the trees between them, some of the braves might hear the loud sloshing. The men seemed to sleep with one eye open and one ear straining.

She scanned the area in every direction. Could she cover her tracks any other way? They might see the grass trampled down, and the mare would leave an occasional print.

She planned to go southward, opposite the direction where Jean-Jacques said Hugh and Louis were camped. Since she'd had to go north to retrieve her horse, moving south now would take her past their own camp again. So she couldn't go either direction through the creek without passing by one group or the other.

Panic surged up to her chest. *Lord, I don't know what to do.*

Did she risk the men being able to track her? Or would it be better to keep the mare walking slowly through the creek and try to get past the braves without waking them?

Maybe traveling over land would be best. There was always the chance they wouldn't pick up her tracks, and if they did, perhaps they would choose not to come after her. That possibility didn't ring true in her chest, at least not about Jean-Jacques.

She could cross the creek and ride through the grass until she made it well past where the braves would hear the water. Then she could move back into the creek again so they would lose her tracks completely.

Thank you, Father. That plan would work.

After leading the mare up the far bank, she took three tries to pull herself up on the horse's bare back. As she settled onto the slippery coat, she missed the security of the leather seat. But she would do without. Taking a tight hold on the mane with one hand and the reins with the other, she nudged the horse forward.

The plan worked well, and when they were well past the camp and moved back into the creek, the crescent moon allowed enough light for her to rein her horse around the larger rocks she might've stumbled over.

The only downfall was how slowly they had to move. With so many stones in the water, her horse had to keep to a walk, and the hours dragged by. Was she making enough progress that the others wouldn't find her?

She'd been riding beside a range of mountains on her right—the same range that included the cliff that had marked one side of their camp.

Riding up into the mountains over rocky terrain would be best, for the stone would help them leave no tracks, but the grassy stretch between the creek and the mountains had kept her from crossing over.

Finally, up ahead, the mountains stretched down to touch the water's edge, making the bank rise much higher along that section, almost like a cliff wall. Maybe they could leave the water at last, if she could find a place her horse could maneuver up.

After riding with the cliff on her right for several minutes, a steep stone path rose to climb diagonally up the mountainside. The faint trail looked to be an animal trace, maybe traveled by mountain goats or sheep.

Her horse could probably manage it. Maybe the mare would do better if Colette dismounted though. The extra weight might make balancing up the steep path precarious.

She slipped off her horse onto the stones, stepping from one to the next so she wouldn't get her feet wet. Of course, her moccasins were still damp from the first few steps through the water before. But she could feel her toes, and it wasn't cold enough to worry about her appendages freezing.

The mare balked about climbing the steep path at first, but Colette encouraged her onward. Once they were both climbing, she focused on the trail and staying far enough ahead of the horse that she wouldn't be trampled.

This really was an excellent animal. Colette had traded for her at a fort south of Pike, when she realized she wouldn't be able to cover enough ground on foot to escape Raphael's brothers. Maybe she should give the horse a name, but part of her had hesitated to do so. Naming the animal created a bond between them, and what if something happened that required her to leave the horse behind? Colette had already lost so many people she loved. Better to keep from becoming too attached to this horse.

At last, they reached a place where the path leveled enough for them to stop and rest. She was breathing hard, yet no matter how much air she drew in, her body still cried out for more. The chill in the air had dried out her throat. She needed a drink, but her canteen was inside her pack, and she couldn't yet manage the effort to pull it out.

Finally, she caught her breath enough to take in her surroundings.

It wasn't a big mountain, and she'd climbed nearly halfway up, from what she could see in the dim moonlight. Boulders covered most of the slope, which would make finding a path challenging. The animal trail they'd been traversing climbed over a large boulder in front of her. It must surely have been made by smaller animals, creatures nimble enough to leap up and down the slick rocks. Her mare wouldn't be able to climb up onto this taller, massive stone.

God, what do I do? She strained to see farther in each direction. The way the boulders cast shadows, it was hard to tell if any of the crags might be maneuvered.

Turning to her horse, she patted the mare's neck. "Stay here, girl. I'll find a way and come back for you." The animal stood with heaving sides, still catching her breath. Hopefully, the horse wouldn't shift around when Colette stepped away. The wrong step on the mountain in the dark could send the animal plummeting down the slope.

Colette moved to the boulder where pressed mud showed prints from tiny hooves. She'd been right about the height of the stone. It wasn't fair to ask her horse to jump up onto the rock. If she slipped, there was too much chance of a fall.

Easing around from that rock to the next, Colette found a series of lower stones that could act as a staircase to move higher up the mountain. She couldn't tell how much farther they would be able to go that way, but she hated to move out of sight of her horse to find out.

They might need to travel like this for a while, with Colette scouting ahead each leg of their path. The main downside to traversing this route was that the direction wove back around the mountain toward the north—the direction she'd come from. But they were moving up, so that was progress.

After stepping back to her mount, she turned the horse in the tight quarters, then led the way up the series of stone steps.

The mare hesitated, but with a little coaxing, she climbed upward. Once the horse was moving easily, Colette turned her focus to peering ahead through the darkness. As they ascended up and around, there was rarely more than one possible route. The farther they climbed, the rougher the terrain grew, and the more fear pressed in her chest. What would she do if they reached a point where there was no possible path? Would the horse be able to climb back down the mountain the way they'd come? In so many places, a single misstep would send the animal tumbling down the rocks.

Perhaps she should've come alone. In these mountains, was it foolishness to try to bring a horse? Was the mare holding her back from the speed she needed to escape?

Lord, have I made a disastrous error? It had seemed absurd to leave the horse behind when having a mount would help her run much farther and last much longer. But she'd not planned to scale stony cliffs.

The moon no longer shone overhead to light the way. Clouds must have covered the thin crescent. Maybe this was God's punishment for her sin.

She gave herself a mental shake. She'd asked the Lord's forgiveness for what she'd done to Raphael. God had promised that forgiveness. The Lord didn't take back His mercy. But maybe this was what came from putting others in danger. Should she have run before now?

I will lead them in paths that they have not known. I will make darkness light before them, and crooked things straight. The words from a verse she'd long ago memorized slipped through her memory. She nearly laughed at the irony compared to her current situation. *Yes, Lord. Turn this darkness to light and make this crooked trail straight.*

Then she sobered. *Please, Father. Take us to safety. Give me wisdom.*

They were nearing the peak now, and the slope had eased into a more gradual incline, though the mountain still seemed made up of boulders stacked on boulders. They had to maneuver massive stones in some places.

As she led the mare around one such rock, a large dark area appeared in the mountainside. Colette jerked the horse to a halt as she strained to see deeper into the darkness. A cave? A stone covered in black moss? The murky shadow seemed deeper than that.

She edged closer, leading the mare a slow step at a time.

At last, she came near enough to reach out and touch the blackness. Her hand brushed nothing. Would a cave be so inky and completely devoid of light?

"Stay here, girl," she murmured to the mare as she released

the reins and shifted sideways to touch the side of the rock light enough to see.

She groped along the stone, reaching into the darkness—deeper, deeper. She could no longer see her hand, but her fingers crawled along solid stone. This must be a cave, but how deep did it go? Would any animals enter into such blackness?

Perhaps it was only so dark inside because of the night. A wild animal might venture in during the daytime and sleep through the dark hours.

Could this cave be a good hiding place for her and the horse? If only she had a torch. She had flint and steel packed in her satchel, but she hadn't planned to light a fire. The smoke might alert others of her presence.

Perhaps she would be safe to wait here at the cave opening until morning. She couldn't quite bring herself to enter that yawning darkness at night.

Turning back to her horse, she stroked the mare's neck. "We'll settle in here until daylight, then decide what to do next." The mare's ear twitched at her whisper, but she kept her head lowered.

Colette sent a final glance around and strained to hear any movement from down the mountain. Nothing except the whistle of the wind in her ears.

Lord, let us be safe here. And send wisdom. I need it more than anything right now. If she made the wrong decision at any point, so many people would pay the price.

CHAPTER 20

Something felt off.

French opened his eyes in the early morning darkness and strained with all his senses for anything out of place. He couldn't see Colette with the packs positioned between them. A rustle of bedding sounded from the other side of camp, and he jerked his gaze that way. Elk Runs sat up on his pallet and ran a hand over his face. He was usually the first to rise.

After a moment, the brave pulled the fur off his legs and stood in a smooth motion. He didn't act as though he sensed anything wrong. Maybe French's imagination had conjured a threat that wasn't there. Or maybe the worry came from the remnants of a dream that had already slipped away.

He sat up too, sent another glance around the quiet camp, then stood. With a stretch, he pulled out some of the stiffness that came from sleeping outside, then finally let his gaze wander to Colette's pallet. He loved to watch her sleep but usually felt a twinge of guilt at taking such a liberty. It felt like she was his in so many ways...but not in that way. Not yet.

His gaze slipped over her bedding, seeking out her pale hair amidst the other shades of fur. He squinted to see better. She must have pulled one of the pelts over her head.

As his eyes made out details in the faint morning light, his breathing ceased. No blond hair. No body at all. Where was Colette?

He stepped toward her pallet, scanning the bedding once more to make sure his eyes weren't playing tricks.

Her covers were mussed as though she'd slept there, but she definitely wasn't on her bedroll now.

He lifted his focus to the path she always took first thing in the morning. Maybe she'd awakened early and gone to take care of personal matters. She would return in a few minutes.

Still, his heart raced far quicker than it had moments before. Could the men camped upriver have done anything to Colette? Surely he or one of the braves would've heard if strangers had entered the camp.

She must simply be caring for morning needs. No other possibility made sense.

He grabbed two logs and used them to stir up flames from last night's coals. As soon as the first piece caught, he stood and listened for sounds of Colette's return. All the braves had risen now except Young Bear. The older man usually stayed under his covers until the fire was roaring. Then, he would sit by the warmth for a while before heading out to his trap line.

French couldn't blame him. As achy as his own body was in the morning, Young Bear's had seen almost twice as many years as his had.

There was no sign of Colette coming through the trees, so French started down the path to meet her. He tried to keep his stride slow, more like an ambling walk and less like a worried charge. What if she'd taken sick again? What if something was wrong with the baby?

When he came within sight of the group of shrubbery cedars he'd helped her to the other day, he stopped.

"Colette?" He was pretty sure he'd spoken loudly enough for her to hear. The woods hadn't yet awakened in the dim light of morning, and he didn't want to alert the others. Not yet.

She didn't poke her head around the branches. No sounds of shuffling.

His chest tightened even more. "Colette? Are you there?" He spoke louder this time. Unless she'd been knocked unconscious, she would hear him.

Don't let her be knocked unconscious. A new series of images flashed through his mind. Could she have swooned? What if she'd hit her head?

"Colette, I'm coming to check on you." He started forward, confidently at first, then slowing as he neared. "Are you in there?"

No sound. No movement.

He peered around the scraggly needles—just enough so he would see a bit of clothing if she was there. Only the deep shadows of early dawn could be seen. He stepped all the way around.

Empty.

His heart pounded harder, and the worry pressing his chest surged to panic. Maybe nothing was wrong. Maybe she'd been at the river and was back at camp, even now.

He spun and charged through the trees. As he stepped between the last of the trunks, he scanned the clearing for her blond tresses. She wasn't there.

He stopped and scanned every place she might be tucked, seeking out each stack of furs and pile of belongings.

"She is not here." Young Bear sat on his bedding, his hair rumpled and his face looking older than usual.

French scanned his features for the deeper meaning of his words. "Where is she? Did she come back?"

The Indian shook his head. "I have not seen her."

Panic knotted in French's throat. "Have you been down to the river? Is she there?"

He shook his head. "I have not left this fire." Then he struggled to stand. "I will help look for her."

As thankful as French was for the help, he couldn't wait for the old man's slow movements. He spun toward the river path. "I'll see if she's out at her trap line. Check with the others."

There was no sign of Colette along their stretch of trapping area. He saw Elk Runs farther upriver and called out to the man, but he'd not seen her either. With every step, French's mind churned with worry…with possibilities of what had happened to her. Those two strangers must have had something to do with her disappearance. The coincidence was too strong.

When he arrived back at camp, Left Standing was bent over the fire, perhaps heating food to break his fast.

French headed for his pack and gathered up his rifle, shot bag, and hunting knife. "I'm sorry I haven't cooked, but Colette's missing. I'm going to see those strangers and find out what they know."

He glanced over at the man, but Left Standing no longer knelt by the fire. He stood beside his pack, strapping a bow and quiver on his back. "I will go with you."

French nodded. "Good." He wasn't foolish enough to turn away help when Colette might be in danger. And Left Standing's presence might garner a bit more respect than French would alone.

They strode down the path that would lead to the horses, then beyond to the strangers' camp. When they stepped into the clearing where the animals grazed, he sent the horses a glance. Though he kept moving, his mind did its usual headcount.

But as he mentally tallied, he slowed his step. Where was the sixth horse? He scanned each mount individually, identifying them to determine which was missing.

Colette's mare.

The fear inside him pounded even harder as this new twist shifted the possibilities in his mind. Why would she have left with her horse? Had the men kidnapped her and insisted she take her mount? If they'd knocked her unconscious, how would they have known which animal was hers. If she'd been alert enough to point out her mount, wouldn't she have screamed or done something to alert the rest of them to what was happening? Surely she hadn't gone with them of her own accord.

So many questions, and not an answer among them.

He strode toward the animals, Left Standing matching his pace. A glance at the man's intense expression showed he must have realized which animal was missing.

The fellow's gaze dropped to the ground, and French looked that way too. Tracks. He should've been looking for them already. But with the bevy of prints in this area, it was impossible to tell which might have come from Colette or her horse.

A call from downriver jerked his attention that way. Hawk Wing strode toward them, Cross the River not far behind. Young Bear must have alerted them.

As soon as they came near enough to hear, French called out, "Colette and her horse are missing. Have you seen her? Or anything suspicious?"

Both men sent a glance around the area before Hawk Wing answered. "Nothing." His gaze lifted up and beyond them, and French turned that direction too.

A thin stream of smoke rose into the air from the same place he'd seen it the day before. Did that mean the strangers were still in their camp? If they'd taken Colette, wouldn't they have run? Maybe they'd built up the fire to throw off suspicion.

French glanced back at his companions. Elk Runs had turned toward the creek, his gaze scanning the ground. What did he see?

French moved toward him, examining the area the man

studied. There were plenty of horse tracks here since the animals had mostly free range to the water.

Elk Runs pointed to a spot. "Mignon walk here."

French leaned over for a better view. *Yes*. There was a flattened impression that might have been Colette's marks pressing the mud smooth.

He shifted his focus to scan the area around. "Do you see any other tracks? Maybe from the men camped upriver?" The chaos of hoofprints was too much for French to decipher anything more than what Elk Runs had pointed out.

The man shook his head, his focus still on the ground. He stepped forward and lifted his gaze to the opposite bank. That side wasn't nearly as trodden, although the horses did cross over at times.

Elk Runs strode through the water without flinching, as though the liquid wasn't frigid from snow runoff. French hesitated only a second, though not from the cold. They needed to check the strangers' camp. But what Elk Runs found here might make a difference. He stepped through the water to follow.

After a few minutes, the man located more of Colette's tracks a little farther downstream. As soon as Elk Runs identified her trail, the brave moved forward like a hound that had picked up the scent of fresh meat. French had to trot to keep up. The man motioned toward a hoofprint. "Is riding now."

"She mounted the horse here? Can you tell if anyone came through with her?" The grass looked as though it had been trod upon at some point in the last day, but French couldn't tell much more.

Elk Runs took a few more steps before leaning down and motioning to a tiny divot in the ground. "Her horse steps long in the rear." Then he straightened. "Do not see others."

Elk Runs kept walking, but French hesitated. He should turn around and investigate the strangers' campsite, but if Colette really did go this way recently, they couldn't lose the trail.

Left Standing made the decision for him, calling out from across the river. "Go with Elk Runs. We will see these strange men and their camp and come find you if there is news."

French met his gaze, the determination in the other man's eyes easing his worry. "Thank you, friend."

With a nod, Left Standing turned and led Cross the River and Hawk Wing toward the strangers' camp.

French focused his attention on Elk Runs, who'd moved on without him, his stride sure and his gaze fixed on the ground as he walked.

He strode to catch up with the man. "If Colette was mounted, should we get our horses too?" If she'd pushed her mare into a run, she could be far ahead of them.

Elk Runs finally lifted his focus from the ground, training his gaze on the mountains ahead of them. "I find tracks better on foot."

The man didn't sound certain, and that lack churned a new round of worry in French. But Elk Runs's tracking skill far surpassed his own. "Whatever you think is best."

The man started off again, and French lengthened his stride to keep up.

CHAPTER 21

Colette jerked awake and cringed at the ache spearing through her body. She squinted at the bright sunlight overhead, then blinked as she lowered her gaze to her surroundings.

Nearby, her horse pawed the rocky ground. That must have been the sound that awakened her. The mare was likely hungry and tired of being restrained on the side of this mountain. Her own belly ached for food, and below that, her body complained with a different need. She pushed up to sitting, wincing at the pain in her neck. She had no time to coddle herself though.

After using the rock wall to help herself stand, she peered into the cave beside her. Daylight now allowed her to see a short distance inside. The darkness within made the cave look as though it extended deep into the mountain. But when she took a step in and her eyes adjusted to the dimmer lighting, she could make out the rear wall.

The place was deep enough to provide shelter for her and her horse, if she could get her mare to enter with the low ceiling. But that was as far as the space went. There definitely weren't any wild animals inside, as she'd worried about last night. Though some dirt along the back wall might have come from decayed droppings.

The question was, should she stay here or press on? Maybe the answer would come clear if she explored a little farther around the mountain. From this place, she could only see the boulders of this mountain on both sides of her and the slope of the neighboring cliff opposite. If she could get a glimpse of what lay around the corner of her own slope, she might learn whether she should keep going or wait here until the brothers moved along.

Either way, she had to find fodder for her horse. She almost wished she had left the animal behind.

After heading back out to the mare, she checked the hobbles she'd fastened in the dark, then patted the horse's neck. "Wait here a little longer, girl. I'll see if I can find grass for you."

She didn't intend to go far but grabbed the bundle of meat to eat as she walked. After taking care of personal needs, she set out around the mountainside.

Up and over rocks she climbed, doing her best to scout paths her horse might be able to travel.

Hopefully.

Some of the boulders might be too tall for the mare to maneuver, but this was the only way forward. As often as she could, she tried to move downhill instead of up. But no matter how far she went, she never seemed to reach the back side of the mountain. The landscape became even more treacherous, and the knot of worry pulled tighter and tighter in her belly.

Her horse would never make it this far. The only way to get the animal down the mountain would be to return the way they'd come up in the night. And she couldn't go back that way yet.

Today, Jean-Jacques would be looking for her. He'd come after her that other time, so he likely would again. And what of Hugh and Louis? If Jean-Jacques or the braves approached them and mentioned her at all, Raphael's brothers would sniff the new scent like bloodthirsty hounds. They would be looking for her tracks, too.

The cave would have to be home for a few days. She'd find fodder to take back to her horse. She'd seen a few scrubby cedar trees along her way that morning. She couldn't imagine the mare eating those prickly needles, but maybe the bark? She'd heard of Indians feeding their horses cottonwood bark all through the winter. Could the same be done with the bark of an evergreen? She could at least try. As soon as she found a few more patches of grass, she would turn back to the cave again.

When she finally found a cluster of scrubby winter-brown grass, a thick layer of clouds had covered the sun. It must be midmorning by now, and as thick as those clouds layered, rain would be coming in the afternoon. Best she get settled in the cave before then.

The one good thing about rain was that it would wash away any tracks she might have left.

That also meant Jean-Jacques would have no possible way to find her. Why did that thought create such an ache in her chest?

She shouldn't *want* him to find her. She had to keep telling herself that. Jean-Jacques needed to return to his family. His wife and friends. And she had to focus on creating a safe life for her baby.

She'd have to start over completely, a whole new name this time. Something no one who'd ever known her would recognize.

The thought left her as empty as if she'd not eaten in days. If only she'd never met Raphael. If only she'd waited for Jean-Jacques, no matter how painful the aloneness was. She'd known from the beginning, from those childhood days, that God planned for her and Jean-Jacques to be together forever. Why had she lost faith in His promise, even when she learned of Jean-Jacques's marriage?

Now, she could never have him.

~

God, don't let the rain come.

French eyed the darkening sky above, then shifted his focus back to the path in front. If there was any sign of Colette through here, he had to find it. Elk Runs was walking on the opposite side of the river, searching for tracks there. French didn't have the same ability with tracking that man did, so he had to work that much harder. If Colette had left the river on his side, he had to find the signs.

He kept a steady pace as he searched, glancing across the river at Elk Runs occasionally to make sure they were tracking at the same speed. How much time had passed since Elk Runs determined Colette's mount rode into the water? More than an hour. Maybe two? With the sun hiding behind the thick layers of clouds, he couldn't tell how long they searched.

His belly grumbled, but that need paled in comparison to the pressure in his chest as he imagined all the reasons why Colette might have run. Elk Runs hadn't seen any tracks besides those left by her and her horse, so she must have left alone. Had she recognized his description of the men? She'd not acted like she did. He'd watched her carefully, but maybe he'd missed something. Or maybe a new thought had occurred to her in the night.

Lord, help me find her. Show me the truth. Every time Colette was in danger, his desire to protect her always revealed anew his need for God. She made him feel so helpless. So desperate for the help of a Greater Power. This wasn't fair to God though. He had to be all in—or not at all. He couldn't just keep uttering these desperate prayers in times of fear.

I'm sorry, God. But I need Your help now. Desperately. Help us find Colette. Don't let her get away again. Let me help her this time.

Please. And if God didn't? Would French turn his back on the Almighty again?

His foot stumbled on a rock, bringing him back to his surroundings. The ground had changed, and he'd been so focused on spotting hoof prints and working through the turmoil in his mind, he'd not even noticed the increase in stones, or the rise of the bank just ahead so it formed a cliff that rose from the water.

Across the river, Elk Runs had also paused and was staring at the bank in front of French. A few steps ahead, the mountain on their right came all the way down to the river's edge. The slope grew so steep, French would have to either drop down into the water or cross over to Elk Runs's side. Colette and her horse wouldn't have been able to scale this mountain either.

He pointed into the river. "Guess I'll wade through the water so I can watch for the place she might have climbed out." At least the river looked shallow enough through here, maybe only knee-deep. He could endure the cold if that was what it took to find Colette.

After sliding down the bank, he sucked in his breath as he took his first steps through the icy liquid. If he stayed close to the side, the surface only came up to the top of his moccasins.

They kept moving, and his focus shifted from scrutinizing the ground to slogging through the water fast enough to keep up with Elk Runs. He finally found a rhythm with each stride, maybe because his feet had numbed enough to ease the icy sting.

A line up the bank on his right caught his eye. It wasn't more than a diagonal striation in the rock, but from the footprints and bits of caked mud, it appeared animals had used it as a trail to climb up from the water.

With his gaze, he followed the faint path up past the top of the bank, along the gentler slope of the mountain. The hill seemed made of boulders, but the animals had found a way to weave between them, climbing over the smaller stones. Could Colette and her horse have managed that climb?

He turned to get Elk Runs's attention, but the man had already stopped and was studying the path.

French turned his focus back as well. "Think she and her horse could've managed that climb?"

If she had, she must have been desperate. He couldn't tell if any of the marks on the stone were fresh. A glance at the sky revealed that the clouds had darkened even more. Rain would start any minute. If they tried this route and she wasn't up there, they might lose any other tracks farther downriver.

He turned back to Elk Runs. "Should we check it? We might lose her trail if she didn't go this way." The man nodded understanding, but his gaze had lifted farther up, searching the slope far above.

French looked the same way, but from his position closer to the mountain's base, he could only see partway up. He looked back at Elk Runs, studying him for any sign of his thoughts. *Give him wisdom, Lord. Please. Don't let us chase a false trail. Don't let us lose her this time.*

At last, Elk Runs nodded. "We go." Those words could've meant either choice, but his actions clarified the decision. He slipped into the water, then trudged across the narrow river toward the steep path.

Maybe French should go up first to make sure the terrain could be navigated. Or would it be wiser to let Elk Runs lead, since he would likely spot markings better? The latter might be the best choice, and should the man slip on the steep slope, French could catch him.

That last thought turned out to be laughable, for Elk Runs was as sure of foot as any mountain goat, scaling the cliff with hands and feet like a squirrel climbing a tree. He didn't even pause for a rest when he reached the place where the slope wasn't quite as steep.

French did his best to keep up, though not nearly as gracefully. Elk Runs finally stopped partway up. French paused and heaved in air to fill his thirsty lungs. The man was studying the ground, and French blinked to focus on the spot. He'd grown a bit lightheaded, maybe from lack of air as he climbed.

But when Elk Runs pointed to a mark in the stone, what the man saw became clear. A chip in the rock, the kind that could come from a hoof striking. "Not long before."

The white of the marking did appear fresh and would probably be washed away or at least turned dark when the rain came.

"You think it was made by her horse?" Mountain goats and bighorn sheep also had hooves, but were those animals heavy enough to cause a mark like this?

Elk Runs lifted his gaze up the hill. "Not know." And with those words, he started up again.

French gulped in a deep breath, then started after him. Though they may not know for sure, that one sign could mean they were on the right trail. *Lead us, Lord. Please.*

The first raindrops came after they'd climbed another quarter hour. They kept moving, but French sent another desperate request heavenward. *Help us find her before the rain falls in earnest.*

If the rock became wet, their path would be slippery. Even dry, the slope was already steep and treacherous.

As the drops fell in steady succession, Elk Runs paused again. French moved up beside him and glanced to where the brave was looking. The rock appeared completely wet now, but he could still see faint signs of the animal path climbing up a large boulder. Surely a horse wouldn't have been able to jump up on that stone.

He wiped the dripping moisture out of his eyes. "What now?"

Maybe this had been the wrong way to go. Perhaps Colette hadn't come this way at all. *Don't let her real trail be washed away.*

They should start back down the slope as quickly as possible so they still had a chance of finding her tracks farther downriver.

Elk Runs pointed to a large boulder. "Game trail goes that way." Then he motioned to the right. "Horse could go that way." A series of rocks made something like stair steps up and around the mountain.

"You think she did?" It didn't look like many animals took that route, but it could be manageable for a horse. A surefooted, obedient animal.

"We go both ways and see."

French jerked his gaze to Elk Runs's face. "We should split up?" That might be the best use of time. They could rule out this possibility completely, then head back down the mountain. By then, there would likely be so much rain they could simply sit on their haunches and slide down the slope.

The man nodded and pointed toward the stair steps. "Go as far as you can that way. Meet back here." Elk Runs turned the opposite direction and started to climb the boulder the smaller animals used for a path.

Wiping the water out of his eyes again, French turned toward his own assignment. The faster he moved, the faster they could get back down and find Colette's trail again.

CHAPTER 22

Colette huddled inside the cave, pulling the blanket tight around her shoulders as the rain fell in sheets outside. If she had dry firewood, she might chance building a small fire to dry herself and warm up. The rain would surely wash all hint of smoke away.

But she'd carried only grass and bark back from her hike around the mountain, and her horse had downed those as soon as she placed them before her.

The rain had started falling before Colette returned to the cave, so not only had she and her clothing become drenched, her packs had also been soaked. The leather had protected some of the contents, but the outer layer would need to be pulled out and dried. It might take days for the items to dry with the rain-dampened air.

A cold wind had moved in with the rain, and she couldn't seem to stop shivering, no matter how tight she pulled the blanket around her. If only she could have brought a fur or two with her.

At least she had this cave, which was more than her horse had for protection. No matter how she'd coaxed, the mare wouldn't come under the low ceiling. Colette had moved her as close to the opening as the horse would approach, so maybe the rock wall was stopping some of the sideways rain from hitting her. But the animal was certainly drenched. At least she had a thick hide to protect herself.

Another shiver swept through Colette, and she tucked tighter into herself, wrapping the blanket around even more. Her spare shirt was one of the things drenched, so she had nothing dry to change into.

Her teeth began to chatter, and she clenched her jaw to still them. But the quiver merely pushed from her jaw into her body again, racking her shoulders with shivers that wouldn't stop.

Why is this happening, God? Why would the Lord bring her to this place of utter misery? He loved her…she knew that without a doubt. He had a plan for her. But why was His path leading through all these struggles? Had she made a wrong turn somewhere? At what point had she gone astray? Was this misery God's chastisement? Or His way of pushing her in a different direction? Maybe she hadn't yet learned the lesson he was trying to teach her.

She replayed the verse from the night before in her mind. *I will lead them in paths that they have not known. I will make darkness light before them, and crooked things straight.* She desperately longed for those straight paths and the light in the darkness. Was she not trusting Him enough? *Show me, Lord. Peel away the stubborn determination from my heart and show me where I need to rely on You more.*

Even as her heart spoke the words, a shiver of fear slipped through her. What would God require of her? To face Hugh and Louis? To make atonement for her sin? Part of her wanted to stop this constant running. To stop this incessant fear of being caught.

Lord, I didn't mean to kill Raphael. It was self-defense. God knew her heart. Surely He knew her innocence better than anyone.

Why hadn't He gotten her out of this mess? *Show me how to trust You better, Father. Show me what I'm to do, because I can't see it.*

She sat huddled in the blanket, watching the rain fall in a steady curtain, trying to let her mind go numb. But that lasted only a few minutes until her belly made its own request heard. The sun must be near the noon mark. Time to eat again.

As she unwrapped the food, a sensation in her middle gave her pause. She stilled, focusing on that part of her body. The feeling had been different than the ache of hunger. More like… something moving within her.

She settled a hand on her middle, finally shifting her gaze down to focus on the area as well. "Is that you, little one?" She brought her other hand up to cup her belly too, cradling the child as she would one day. *I hope.*

All this running—this suffering—was for a very good reason. For this life growing inside her. A life she would one day hold, and always cherish. Always protect, no matter what came.

A motion outside the cave, separate from her horse, grabbed her attention. She squinted to see through the downpour. Maybe the flash had only been a trick of the raindrops.

But then, her breath caught in her throat. A man stood beside the rock wall outside the cave. With the rain falling in such a thick curtain over the cave's entrance, he was too blurry to make out more than a dark head and buckskins.

He must have just rounded the far bolder and come upon her horse. He didn't seem to have spotted her yet. Maybe with the rain running in his eyes and the darkness of the cave, he wouldn't see her at all. If she stayed perfectly still, would he pass on?

Of course not. No one would be up here on a leisurely stroll. He must've come looking for her. She reached for the rifle beside her.

But then, the man stepped nearer the cave, and she caught sight of his face.

Jean-Jacques.

A cry slipped out before she could stop herself. She threw the blanket back and scrambled to her feet, barely stooping in time to keep from bumping her head on the low ceiling.

He must have heard her, or seen her move, for he ducked through the cave opening. "Colette?"

As much as she should feign anger and send him away, she couldn't make herself do it. Her exhausted, weary, cold-numbed body longed for his protection. For his arms to come around her, to hold her and warm her and take away the nightmare that had become her life.

He opened his arms, and she stepped into them. No matter that they both had to bend under the low ceiling. No matter that water dripped off of him.

She pressed into his hold, and he held her tight, his strength wrapping around her, warming her. She breathed in the scent of him, the safety she'd always found in his arms. Tears stung her eyes and easily broke through her defenses.

"Shh." He rocked her, then shifted one arm as he eased down to sit on the stone floor. That way neither of them had to duck to keep from bumping against the ceiling.

He pulled her onto his lap and cradled her, wrapping both arms around her. She laid her head on his shoulder, no longer trying to stop the flow of tears. How had she ever thought herself strong enough to leave him behind?

After a few minutes, she managed to quench the flow, then lifted her head, pulling back enough so she could see his face. She swiped the moisture from her face and sniffed, doing her best to restore her voice to something like normal. He would have questions, and she had to decide how to answer them.

The worry in his eyes sent a new dose of strength through her. "I'm sorry." She had to get herself under control. After clearing her throat, she tried again. "How did you find me?"

His brow lowered. "Why did you leave? What happened? Was it those men camped near us?"

The earnest worry in his tone brought a fresh surge of heat to her eyes. He cared too much. How would she ever keep the truth from him? *Should* she tell him everything?

She couldn't.

But even as her mind made that choice, her mouth opened in a flood of truth. "I killed him. I did, and they want me to pay."

The shock on Jean-Jacques's face was everything she'd expected. It would morph to horror as soon as her words registered. Maybe telling him the truth had been best, for now he would leave of his own accord. She braced herself, pulling back as far as his hold would allow.

But the surprise on his features shifted to questions in his eyes. "What do you mean? Killed who? The man who murdered your husband?"

He would make her reveal all in detail. Even as her belly churned, she shook her head. She couldn't quite meet his gaze anymore. "I killed Raphael. My husband."

She should say more. Explain that she hadn't meant to strike him. But knowing Jean-Jacques, he might absolve her of the crime.

And no matter how innocent she might be in his mind, that wouldn't change the fact that Raphael's brothers would demand retribution. Better she make Jean-Jacques think her wicked so he would leave on his own.

"Tell me what happened, Colette. The whole story." His voice had turned soft, almost drowned out by the rain splashing on the rocks outside. But she heard him, every word. And that gentle tone called to her. She made the mistake of glancing at his face, his earnest expression.

The moment his luminous eyes caught hers, she pulled her gaze away, but the damage had been done. The words formed on her lips even though she wasn't sure she wanted them to. "He would drink sometimes. It wasn't always like that, but after his father died.... I had just found out about the baby, and I was afraid." Memory of that fear washed through her, and she pressed her mouth shut against the weight on her chest. She really hadn't meant to strike Raphael, but her emotions had been such a jumble.

"You were afraid of him?" Jean-Jacques's voice, so soft, called to her.

How could she explain the chaos of that night without making Raphael sound like an ogre? She pressed her eyes shut. "He wasn't usually violent. He just...when he started drinking, he became a different person. I never knew how he would be. And when he came at me, all I could think about was the baby, what a blow to my belly might do. I didn't mean to hurt him. I grabbed a metal bar. I only meant to raise it, to defend myself. But when I hit him... When he fell...." She wrapped her arms around herself. He still held her, and though his hand ran up and down in a gentle motion, she couldn't let herself feel his warmth.

She should pull away, put space between them. Jean-Jacques hadn't spoken, so maybe now she would see that horror on his face.

"Who are these men, Colette?" His tone had lost the earnest gentleness of before, though it stayed quiet. She couldn't quite place what emotion resonated there.

She chanced a look at his face. His jaw was set, but not with disdain. He looked...determined?

"Who are they?" He locked his gaze with hers.

Telling him this last detail wouldn't make a difference. "Raphael's brothers. Louis, the younger one, came upon me right after it happened. I was still in shock, and I said more than I meant to. I was trying to explain what happened, but from the moment he saw his brother's dead body, I don't think he heard anything else. I packed a bag the moment he left and sneaked out of the fort that night. I wasn't sure if they'd come looking for me, but when I saw them a week later on the trail behind me, I knew they must have come for revenge.

"I traded for a horse, then met Young Bear's group not long after that. I think God put them in my path to protect me. I thought Hugh and Louis had given up the search. It's been months now. I thought I'd finally found freedom."

His eyes widened when she spoke Young Bear's name, and he straightened. "I forgot about Elk Runs." He released her and even went so far as to lift her off his lap. "I'm sorry, Colette. I forgot about Elk Runs."

Her story must have finally sunk in. Now, he seemed like he couldn't get away from her fast enough.

But then he paused in the middle of standing. He looked at her, locking her gaze with his. "Stay here. I'll be right back. Please don't leave. All right?" Confusion swirled in her mind. He was coming back?

He didn't move, waiting for her answer, so she nodded.

That satisfied him, and he nearly sprinted out into the rain.

CHAPTER 23

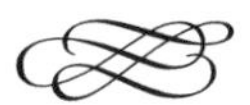

French slipped on a wet spot as he rounded a boulder beside the trail. He grabbed onto a crevice in the stone to keep from slamming his head into the rock. For a long moment he clung there, sucking in a breath to ease the racing in his chest.

He'd better slow down, or he'd not make it back to Colette at all. He'd been so caught up in finding her and hearing her awful story that he'd completely forgotten Elk Runs might be putting his own life in danger, climbing over wet rocks in this downpour, thinking each turn might uncover her.

He eased away from the rock and started forward again, this time a little slower. Would Colette try to sneak away while he was gone? Surely not. She'd confided in him—hopefully everything now. That meant she trusted him, right?

He'd not had time to respond to her story, but he had a host of things to say. If she trusted him enough to tell him everything, didn't that mean she wouldn't try to run again? Had she finally realized they could work through this together? *Lord, help her see. Give me the right words. Give us the right plan. And thank You for leading me to her.*

If they hadn't followed this trail up the mountains, he never would've found Colette. That possibility washed through him with a new dose of awareness. Elk Runs's wisdom may well have been heaven-sent. *Thank You for guiding us.*

The man was waiting for him in the place where they'd separated. He sat on a rock, as though he'd been waiting a while. As French approached, Elk Runs stood.

"I found her. She's in a little cave this way." French motioned back the way he'd come, then spun. Elk Runs followed him back up the stone staircase and around the side of the mountain.

When French rounded the last boulder and saw Colette's horse standing as it had when he left, head down and water running in rivulets from its sides, he eased out a long breath.

But he didn't fully relax until he peered through the rain into the shadows of the cave and saw Colette's form.

She was standing, her head ducked under the low ceiling. She'd not run again.

He ducked under the shelter, and Elk Runs stepped in behind him. French blew out a long breath as he studied Colette.

She eyed them with a hint of wariness, not the same open desperation from before he'd left. *Don't let her close me off again.*

He motioned toward Elk Runs but spoke to Colette. "He had gone the other way around the mountain, looking for you."

She nodded, flicking her gaze between the two of them. "Where are the others?" Definite wariness in her tone. Too much like a cornered rabbit that might bolt any moment.

He motioned toward the stone floor. The cave tilted downward toward the opening, so no rainwater had run inside. "Let's sit so we don't have to duck."

She seemed hesitant, so he made the first move, settling himself on the rock floor. Elk Runs did the same, and finally Colette eased down as well. She sat across from them, and the way she braced her hands behind her to lean back a little showed roundness in her belly, even through her coat. The bump swept warmth through him. The anticipation when he thought of the babe was stronger than he would have ever expected. Even now that he knew more about the child's father.

He lifted his focus up to her face, and the way she eyed him expectantly brought her question to his mind. "The others went upriver to talk with those two strangers." But they weren't strangers to her. "What did you say their names were?"

Her expression didn't soften. "Hugh is the elder. And Louis, the younger. What did they plan to say to them?"

French leaned forward. "We were looking for you. We thought maybe they'd taken you somehow, though I couldn't figure out how they would have stolen you from under our noses."

At that last comment, a hint of embarrassment slipped over her face. She didn't say anything on the subject though. She must have gone to great lengths to sneak away without anyone hearing.

But the embarrassment quickly sharpened into intensity, and she sat straighter. "They asked Hugh and Louis about me? Told them I've been traveling with you?" Alarm stiffened her tone, sending a warning through his chest.

He'd need to tread carefully. "I doubt they would have given your name. They only meant to see what the men were about, to make sure they hadn't kidnapped you."

Elk Runs spoke up for the first time. "I go make sure all is well."

As the man pushed up to his feet, Colette leaned forward like she might also stand. "In the rain?"

The man nodded. "Wet already." Then he cast a gentle look toward Colette. "I make sure all is well." Though almost the same words, this time they seemed to mean so much more. He would make this right for Colette, as best as he and the others could. They may not know who the brothers were to Colette, but Elk Runs must sense her fear.

After studying Elk Runs for a moment, she seemed to relax. "Thank you."

For a heartbeat, a twinge of jealousy pricked French. He wanted to be the one to protect her. But Elk Runs was more capable of descending the mountain in the downpour, and the braves would work together for Colette's good.

That gave French the chance to stay with her and work through the details of her past and what they should do moving forward.

As the Indian slipped out into the rain, French turned his focus back to Colette, leaning in. Now was his chance to say everything on his heart. He could only pray Colette was ready to hear it. *Don't let me mangle this, Lord.*

He met her gaze, letting the truth of his words filter through his tone. "I'm so sorry, Colette. I'm sorry for everything you've been through. I'm sorry I wasn't there when you needed me."

His voice graveled rough with his emotions. "I'm here now, and I'm not letting you go. Not this time. I made you a promise when I was thirteen, and I've never changed my mind. I never will. You're the woman I love more than life itself. I'll take care of you, no matter what we have to do."

A tumult of emotions clouded her eyes, so many he couldn't decipher them all. Concern maybe? Perhaps a tinge of happiness.

But the hesitation marking her expression was impossible to miss. He waited, making himself sit still, though everything in him wanted to take her hand and beg her to say yes.

She had to choose this herself. She had to commit fully, or she might try to run again.

When her lips finally parted to speak, his chest squeezed, cutting off his breath as he waited.

Her lips seemed to tremble before sound finally slipped from them. "Won't your wife mind?"

The words wouldn't penetrate, or at least, his mind couldn't sort them into anything that made sense. *She* would be his wife. Hadn't he said that? He replayed his statements from a moment before.

Realization settled in. He was a blithering idiot. He hadn't asked her the most important question.

He reached out and took her hand in his. She let him, but there was no emotion in her touch. "I didn't say that right, Colette. I'm asking you to marry me. I've always loved you, and I want desperately to be your husband. I want to take care of you and the baby. I will do that, whether or not you say yes. But please, *say yes*."

She wouldn't be able to miss the desperate hope in his voice. Maybe he shouldn't lay himself out so vulnerable, but he'd never been able to hide anything from her. He didn't want to.

Yet she still held a barrier between them. Her eyes still showed hesitation, that shield to protect herself. From what? How did she think he would hurt her?

She didn't make him wait as long this time. Her chin raised a notch, and her eyes positioned that shield more tightly in place. "What about your wife, Jean-Jacques. Where is she?"

Confusion washed through him. "What do you mean? I don't have a wife. I want *you* to be my wife." He'd said it plainly this time hadn't he? How much clearer could he get?

Now all the confusion crowded into her eyes. "Did she pass away?"

Frustration seeped in. "Colette, I'm not married. I never have been. What are you talking about?"

She looked as befuddled as he felt. "Then who's Susanna?"

What did she know of her? Had he spoken any of the women's names to Colette without making it clear who they were? "She's Beaver Tail's wife. One of my friends I was traveling with." He softened his gaze on her. "There's never been anyone for me but you."

Her lips parted, then closed, then parted again. "But…you were. Mama said…"

As she snapped her mouth closed, an awful inkling crept through him. Her mother told her he'd married? Why? Had she meant to separate them completely…forever?

He'd known her parents weren't overly fond of him. They'd offered Christian charity to the poor neighbor boy, but when he and Colette grew closer and closer, they'd seemed uneasy about the bond. He'd wondered if that had played into their sudden desire to move west, though they'd said her father's work was the cause. But this…

He focused on Colette's face, on the myriad of thoughts swirling across her expression. Her features molded into a look of dismay. Then, incredulous, horrified shock. Her perfect lips formed an O. Then his name slipped out in a whisper. "Jean-Jacques."

She'd really thought he deserted her? That he would turn away from his promise—from their love—and wed another?

Then another thought seeped in. Was that why she'd married another?

When he met her gaze again, her eyes confirmed it.

"Oh, Colette." Moisture clogged his throat and stung his eyes. He tugged her hand, and she came to him. He wrapped his arms around her as the tears pressed harder. How much had they lost? How much had she endured? And why? It all seemed so senseless, so unnecessary.

As he clung to her, cradling her close, his tears dampening her hair and hers his shirt, he released the pain of the years he'd spent missing her. Searching for her. Desperate for her.

No matter what, he would never…ever…let them be parted again.

CHAPTER 24

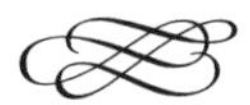

Colette had no tears left to cry. Jean-Jacques had let them fall, soothing away the pain, refilling her heart with the love she never thought she'd feel again. This seemed far too good to be possible. Why had they taken so long to come to this point?

And to think, she'd tried to run away. To leave him far behind. She never would've known the truth.

The truth shall make you free. She nearly laughed at the Scripture that slipped in. Jesus's words, if she remembered correctly, and how true they were. She should have told Jean-Jacques the truth from the beginning. A bit of honesty between them had cleared away all the barriers. If only they could have reached this point long ago. If only they could've avoided all the pain.

Another verse crept in. *But we glory in tribulations also: knowing that tribulation worketh patience; And patience, experience; and experience, hope.*

She leaned back, just enough so she could see his face. This hope was so much better than anything she'd thought possible.

Jean-Jacques caught her expression, and a smile eased the corners of his eyes. "What are you thinking?"

She raised a hand to his cheek, relishing the feel of him, warm and sturdy beneath her fingers. "At first, I was thinking how much pain we could have missed if we'd reached this point sooner. But then God reminded me how much I've grown through the hard times. This moment is so much better for who I've become. Who we both are now."

Some of the smile slipped from his eyes, and sadness tugged the corners. "I wish you hadn't been forced to go through what you did. I wish I could have protected you from it."

She shook her head. "It wasn't always hard. I've grown so much through it. And I wouldn't have…" She broke off the words even as another tiny flutter tickled her insides. She wouldn't trade this little one for anything.

Jean-Jacques's gaze slipped down—and yearning crept into his expression. He didn't say anything though. Was he thinking of the babe's father?

Her mind wandered to Raphael so many times when she thought of the little one. Would the babe have his eyes? That dark hair? She needed to speak of it with Jean-Jacques. They had to be able to communicate these hard things.

She swallowed and forced the words out. "Raphael wasn't always… Things weren't always hard. He was a good man at heart, especially before his father died. Before the drinking. I only wish things hadn't ended the way…"

There was one more thing she had to say, and she sent up a prayer for strength. "That's why I can't stand to be around anyone who's overindulging in strong drink. I can't even stand the smell of the stuff."

His eyes turned sad. "I know what you mean. Those smells always remind me of my father. I've never had a desire to drink." Relief washed through her, and he must have seen it on her face.

He leaned near and pressed a kiss to her brow, so gentle that the touch sent a wave of warmth through her. This man…

Could he really be back in her life forever? How could he still love her so much? *Lord, You are too good to me.*

Jean-Jacques held her for long moments. But too soon, he pulled back, enough for her to see his face. "I think we have some things to decide, but first, I need an answer. Will you marry me?"

Joy sluiced through her, pouring onto her face in a smile. It would be fun to be coy, but the best she could manage was a giggle and, "I suppose so." Happiness pulsed too strongly within her.

"All right then." He pulled her closer, and his glance at her mouth was her only hint before his lips met hers.

Their power washed through her with a surge, and she returned the kiss.

But he stopped far too soon, pulling back with a glint of humor in his eyes that didn't quite match the longing there. "You can expect more of that to come, but we have details to work out first."

A smile tickled her mouth again. She liked this new in-charge Jean-Jacques. She raised her brows as she waited for what he had to say next.

His expression grew serious, and worry formed a line across his brow. "I just need to know one more thing, Colette. Is there anything else you haven't told me? Any other secrets?"

Pain speared her. If she'd only been honest from the beginning. She'd known deep down she could trust him. Why had she been so stubborn? Maybe God sent him specifically to help her out of this debacle with Raphael's brothers.

The truth of that jolted her. It had to be God. How else would Jean-Jacques have come across her in all this vast mountain wilderness? And recognized her for who she was, despite the fact that she had been nearly covered up with men's clothing?

She could see the Lord's hand so clearly now. If only she hadn't fought it before. *I'm sorry, Father.*

Jean-Jacques was still waiting for her answer, and she searched herself for anything she might have forgotten to tell him. Then she shook her head. "No more secrets."

A sigh seemed to escape from him, though she didn't actually hear it. How much had her holding back hurt him? Never again. She deepened her gaze. "I'm sorry. For not letting you in sooner."

His expression turned gentle, though his eyes still held a tinge of sadness. "No secrets for either of us. Not even tiny ones." He lifted her hand to his mouth and pressed a kiss to her fingers.

A thought slipped in, one that had needled her since he'd first showed up in their camp. Maybe this was the time to ask. "Tell me..."

His gaze lifted to hers again, and he held the look as he turned her hand over and pressed another kiss to the flesh of her palm.

The touch sent a skitter through her that made every thought flee her mind. She wouldn't be able to speak coherently with him doing that. But then he pressed her hand to his chest, and she forced herself to focus on his face and recall her question. "Why did you tell the men to call you French? Did you really mean it when you said that's what your friends call you? Why not Jean-Jacques?"

She'd always loved his name, the rolling cadence as it flowed from her tongue. She almost never shortened it, except for very rare occasions when a nickname felt right.

His gaze grew distant, as though he was sinking into a memory. His throat worked in a swallow.

Her chest tightened. She'd not meant to raise painful memories. But she wanted to know this part of him. To understand. To help, if she could.

His gaze moved past her when he finally spoke. "I told you my parents died. My father was drunk that night. It was about six months after you left, and I had sneaked out to our place at the creek. Missing you." He sent her a sad, wistful smile.

Then he looked away again. It seemed to be easier for him to tell if he wasn't looking at her. "I smelled the smoke first, then when I got to the edge of the trees, I saw the flames. It was too late to save them."

Pain built in her chest, rising up in her throat. So many awful things he'd experienced. She'd been blind to many of them, and not there for others.

His throat worked again. "After that, I had no reason to stay, so I went to find you." Again, he sent her a sad smile. "I couldn't find you at Fort York. People said your family hadn't stayed there long, that you'd gone farther west. I searched every fort and settlement I could find. Ended up joining on with a trapper named LeBeau so I could travel with a little more safety and enough food in my belly. Though he was a Frenchman, he had a rough temper. Eventually, I left him to join on with McCann. He found my name too much of a mouthful, so he started calling me French."

Finally, his gaze came back to hers, and his eyes had lost some of their sadness. "Maybe I should have been offended, but the name made me feel more connected to home. For some reason, it reminded me of those days back when we were together. I guess it made me remember who I was. Who I am." He shrugged. "Everyone started calling me that, and I let the name stick. I haven't been called Jean-Jacques for eight or nine years at least. Not until you." His thumb stroked across the back of her hand, sending another shiver through her. His eyes held hers with warmth that soaked all the way through her.

"So what will you go by now?"

He was quiet for a moment, and his thoughts were hard to read. "I think, maybe I'll stay with French...for my friends. And

Jean-Jacques"—he lifted her hand from his chest and pressed another kiss to her fingers—"will be special for you, the one who knows me best."

The love burning within her for this man might overcome her. Emotion rose up with so much power, her chest ached, and her eyes burned.

Jean-Jacques drew her close again, holding her. And in his arms, she finally let herself rest.

~

French would be content to hold Colette like this for the rest of their days. And Lord willing, he would be able to do just that.

As much as he'd wanted this connection, it seemed hard to fathom they'd worked through all they had in these few hours together. She finally trusted him. He could see God's hand now, working together for their good, bringing them back together, then helping him find her twice more. *Thank you, Lord. Even despite my resistance and distrust, You gave me my heart's desire.*

In a way, God had been doing with him as French had longed to do for Colette. No matter how many times he'd pushed God away, kept himself separate, locked his pain inside him, the Lord had been there. Waiting for him to open his heart, waiting for him to finally trust.

A new round of emotion rose up inside. *I'm so sorry, Lord. I'm so sorry.* There weren't words enough to describe the pain in his heart for what he'd caused the Father. What a relief to finally be reconnected with Him. What joy.

As the rain slowed to a trickle, then only steady drops falling at the edge of the cave, Colette's breathing grew even and deep in his arms. He cradled her like that, letting their new reality soak through him fully while she slept.

The sun revealed itself at last, and another quarter hour

passed before Colette stirred in his arms. She straightened and stretched like a little girl. Like the girl he still loved.

When her sleep-hazed eyes finally settled on his face, and her mouth curved in a sweet smile, the joy in his chest nearly burst through him. He brushed her cheek with his fingers. "Sleep well?"

She nodded, then straightened, pulling out of his arms and settling on the stone beside him. Her attention turned to the cave opening and the dazzling sunlight outside. "The rain stopped."

"I've been thinking about what we should do next."

She snapped her attention to him, the smile slipping from her expression. Worry pressed across her brow. "What are you thinking?"

He moved his hand to take hers, weaving their fingers together. "First, what were your plans? Did you have a specific place you were intended to go?"

Her mouth pinched, and that line in her brow deepened. "Only far from here. I was going to start over again, this time with a completely new name."

A shiver slipped through him. He'd come so close to losing her forever. God had been on his side, leading him to her. No matter how much courage it took him to hand over the reins and submit to the Lord's leading, listening to His guidance was the only way this good could have come.

He brushed his thumb across the back of her hand. "I told you about the friends I've been riding with. They're from all over—Adam and Joel traveled here from Spain, Caleb from Missouri. Beaver Tail is part Blackfoot, and his wife Susanna is from Boston. And Elan, Meksem, and Otskai are all Nez Perce. They're expecting me to meet up with them in Otskai's village on the other side of the mountains."

He motioned toward the west. "They would love to take you in—take in both of us. Susanna is expecting a babe also, though

I think she's farther along than you. And Otskai has a little son already. We'll find a quiet place to settle, and Caleb's even an ordained reverend. He can marry us." He studied her face for any sign of hesitation.

The hesitation was there, with indecision clouding her eyes. "Would we be safe? Staying in one place like that? At one point, I'd thought to go back to Young Bear's camp with him and the others. I had hoped to make a home there, that I might be able to hide among them. Become one of them. But that was before Hugh and Louis showed up. I'd hoped they wouldn't come this far, that they might have given up."

She planned to become an Indian? He almost smiled at the thought of her pale hair trying to hide in the midst of a black-haired camp. This woman possessed spunk, and she never ceased to amaze him. "I'm sure Young Bear and his people would welcome you and protect you. However, I don't think there's any place in the world you would be safer than among my friends. We take care of each other, and Beaver Tail and Meksem are both strong warriors. The others are more than capable too."

He tightened his fingers around hers, longing for her to feel that protection. "I think you'll like them." The more he thought about it, the more right this felt. The band of brothers who'd started out two years ago had grown into a family who felt more like kin than any people he'd ever lived among. Having Colette by his side would make the group complete.

At last, she nodded—a tentative bob of her chin. "If you think it's the right choice." The weight of her trust settled over him anew.

He met her gaze with intensity. "I wouldn't take you there if I didn't know in my heart this was best. I feel a peace, God's leading, I think." *Lord, don't let me get this wrong.*

She nodded again. "I think so too."

He closed his eyes with the relief sweeping through him.

Following God's will was hard—finding that right path. He'd have to pay close attention not to go astray.

He squeezed her hand again. "I need to go back to camp and get my things. I'll thank Young Bear and the others, too, and let them know we're off. Anything you want me to pass along? To bring back for you? Your traps, I suppose. I'll bring all the furs Giselle can carry."

Her expression turned anxious as he spoke. "Are you sure you should? What if Hugh and Louis are there waiting for you? What if they follow you back here?"

He'd thought of that, but he would be careful. "I won't let them see me. Young Bear and the others will have taken care of them, I have no doubt. And I won't return here if I think there's even a chance of them following."

Her eyes widened as the anxiety seemed to shift into something else. "You don't think the braves would hurt them, do you? I don't want more bloodshed, not on my account."

She paused, and that line spread across her brow again. "I only want the baby to be safe. If it weren't for him or her, I would go back and settle things with them. Let them do whatever they think will bring justice for their brother's death. I didn't mean to hurt him, and I would tell them that, but it doesn't change the fact that I killed their brother. My husband." Her voice hitched on that last word, and it eased a bit of anger that sluiced through him every time he thought of her in that position, having to defend herself from the man who'd pledged to care for her.

She was so good, this woman he loved. Even with what she'd gone through, she didn't seem to hold bitterness—not toward God or the man who'd put her through so much.

And something in her words pressed him. Revenge came too easily as his first thought. Yet hadn't God said in the Scriptures that vengeance belonged to Him? Those words Jesus spoke to his disciples about forgiving had never felt comfortable, nor did they now. Somehow, Colette seemed to have mastered that virtue fully.

Could he let her face these two men who meant her harm? Did she really want to? Yet she'd been running—maybe this was only passing thought.

He forced himself to pray one of the hardest prayers he could imagine. *What is Your will here, Lord?*

He waited, watching Colette as indecision crossed her face. Her free hand crept to her belly. She'd said she would face the men *if* she didn't have the baby to protect.

Guide us, Lord. Take us on the path You want us to go. He'd just finished telling himself how, even though submitting to God's leading took all his courage, the Lord's plan truly was best. He'd not expected another testing so soon.

Colette's arm crept farther around her belly, as though trying to shield the wee one inside as much as she could. "I have to protect the baby." Her words came almost in a whisper. And she was right. Was this God's leading? He couldn't tell—his spirit didn't seem to be settling in one direction. But maybe Colette felt peace with this choice.

He nodded. "I won't let Hugh or Louis see me, and I won't come back until I'm sure I'm not followed. I need to get my horse, though, and enough supplies to travel across the mountains."

Though reluctance marked her features, Colette gave a slow nod. "Tell our friends thank-you for me."

He gave her hand a squeeze. He would say it from them both. From the bottom of his heart, he was grateful for this group of unlikely protectors God had led her to.

CHAPTER 25

As Colette watched Jean-Jacques go, she could barely sort through the churning of emotions inside her. The joy of a future with him still flowed through every part of her, but watching him go, knowing the danger he was headed toward....

And what of Hugh and Louis? All this time, she'd been intent on running from them. Determined to keep from facing their retribution. But something in Jean-Jacques's words made her picture what Hawk Wing and some of the other more hotheaded braves might do to them—all to ensure her protection.

The image had turned nausea in her belly. That wasn't what she wanted. They couldn't die on her account. They were only avenging their brother. Caring so much about family wasn't wrong, was it?

And Louis was so young. She could still see his face as he stared at Raphael's dead body. Louis had always been kind to her, like a little brother. For that matter, Hugh had been kind as well. Though his manners might be a bit rough, he'd treated her with respect.

Could she really stand by and let them be hurt—or worse—because of her? She had no idea what the braves would do to them. Maybe it depended on how much of a fight the two put up. They'd come this far, so they likely wouldn't turn away easily.

She had to do something. Had to intervene before their blood, too, would be counted toward her.

Lord, I'm so afraid. How will I protect the baby?

She forced herself to stand quietly. She'd run without thinking the night of Raphael's death.

And since then, she hadn't stopped running.

She'd raised her defenses so high, she'd not stopped to listen to the Lord's guiding. She'd not even recognized the gift of Jean-Jacques, whom He'd sent when she needed it most. *Don't let me do that again now. Don't let me run ahead without following Your will.*

She let her eyes drift shut as the sun beamed down on her. Like a kiss of warmth, the rays soaked through her, soothing her raw nerves, easing the tension in every limb. The peace that soaked through her could only come from the Father. *So You would have me go back and face Raphael's brothers?*

The sense of peace—of rightness—deepened.

Will You protect my baby? No audible voice sounded, not even a firm whisper in her spirit. Only that lingering certainty that she had to go back. The Lord wanted her to go back and face Hugh and Louis.

Could she place her child's life in His hands too? Even without having His word that the babe would be safe?

Though the nausea tried to rise again, the sensation didn't hold the same power as before.

At last, she opened her eyes and breathed in a deep, cleansing breath. She would go. And whatever came of it, she would leave in God's hands.

Gathering her things didn't take long. She still needed to dry the wet items in her pack, but that would have to be done later. Would she ever have the chance? She pushed that thought back and took out a bit of smoked meat to eat on the way.

Once everything was packed, she turned her horse and stroked the animal's neck. "If by some miracle we get out of this alive and I get to keep you, girl, you're going to get a name."

The mare bobbed her nose as though agreeing. Although, maybe she was only hungry.

"Let's get down this mountain, then I'll let you graze a minute." But not long, because two men's lives could be in danger.

Leading the mare around the side of the mountain wasn't as challenging in daylight as it had been during the night. But once they maneuvered the stone steps and descended the mountain goat trail down the slope, she began praying in earnest for their safety. *Don't let us tumble down these rocks.*

Not many horses would have ventured, slipping and sliding, down that stone face. Either the mare trusted her far more than she deserved, or the animal sensed that this was the only way off the rocky peak.

They splashed into the water, and her horse stumbled, going down to her knees in the river. She scrambled back up to her feet, though.

They both stood in the flowing water, heaving in deep breaths, thankful to have made it intact.

Now came the hard part.

They had to trudge through the water a little way before the spot where the opposite bank was low enough to climb up to the grass. Colette walked beside the horse through the river instead of riding. The mare had endured enough already without carrying her against the current's flow.

Once they finally reached dry ground, she let the mare graze a couple minutes. Then she gathered her reins and climbed aboard. "You can graze more when we get back to camp."

The horse seemed eager enough to stretch her legs, so Colette pushed her into a lope over the grassy stretch. Soon, though, trees hugged the bank's edge, and they had to rein down to a walk.

Anxiety pulsed through her, knotting her belly with fresh worry. Part of her itched to ride faster, regardless of the terrain. Hugh and Louis might die if she didn't reach them in time.

But the rest of her wanted to spin the horse and run as fast as the mare could travel—away from the two who demanded recourse for their brother's death. She could hide by the river, where Jean-Jacques would come looking for her. When he returned, they could head west.

But she'd run too many times these past months. She wouldn't let fear control her any longer. She had to do this.

She kept her attention focused ahead, searching for signs of Jean-Jacques or anyone else. On horseback, she should reach him long before he arrived back at camp, even though he might be running.

She never saw him, though, and as she reached the first of his snares at the farthest end of their trapping area, a new worry pulsed through her. Had she missed him somehow? Or had something happened to him? Maybe he'd fallen down the rocky slope and been knocked unconscious…or even killed. The water could have carried his body downriver. *Lord, no.*

She had to push these thoughts away. Surely God wouldn't have reunited them at last only to separate them forever. He wasn't so cruel, was He? Maybe Jean-Jacques had run the entire way and was already with the braves. With all the lean muscle he possessed, he could have managed it. If he'd been impressed with the same worry for Hugh and Louis that twisted through her, maybe that urge had driven him.

A cluster of trees stood several strides away from the river, and she pointed her mare toward them. She could hobble the horse behind the grouping and let the mare graze while Colette went ahead on foot. Better to keep herself hidden until she knew what was happening.

The horse crunched hungrily in the thick grass as soon as Colette fastened the hobbles and removed the bridle.

A quick departure shouldn't be necessary. She wouldn't be running anymore.

Would Hugh and Louis let her return with them to the fort and receive a proper trial, or would they kill her then and there? If she did go north with them, would Jean-Jacques follow?

Yes. She had little doubt of it. *Thank You for him again, Lord.*

Leaving everything with the horse except her rifle and shot pouch, Colette crept forward, staying away from the water's edge but moving upriver in the direction of camp. Staying this far back would allow her to see any activity before she was spotted. Hopefully.

There was no sign of anyone. She came all the way abreast of the path from the river to their camp, but no one was working in the scraping place by the river. Had she really expected them to go about their business as usual?

Elk Runs had said he would make sure all was well. Did that mean he would push for bloodshed so Hugh and Louis couldn't come after her? She'd seen Hawk Wing, and sometimes Cross the River, show their tempers. Left Standing had been her champion, translating for her and sometimes letting his façade drop enough to show her the warmth of friendship. Would he be even more loyal than the others—to the point of bloodshed?

She had to learn where they were. Would it be better to check the braves' camp first or follow the river up to where Hugh and Louis had bedded down? If all was peaceful, Young Bear and the others might be working or relaxing around their own campfire. It would be better to look in the clearing beside the cliff first.

Easing away from the trees protecting her, she bent low as she strode to the river. Where was Jean-Jacques? She still hadn't seen any sign of him. Maybe he was also at the camp with the others, packing their things and saying a final farewell.

Of course. That would be why no one worked in the scraping area. They were all gathered to see Jean-Jacques off. If not at camp, maybe the men would be with the horses.

She used the familiar stones to step across the river, probably for one of her final times. She'd used this route more often than she could count over the past weeks. This time in the valley had been a blessing in so many ways—the rest, the chance to reunite with Jean-Jacques.

And now the clarity of purpose for what she must do next.

Her feet traveled the barren path through the woods toward the braves' camp. She strained to hear voices, but no sounds drifted from ahead. The men must be with the horses.

Even as her heart pounded about the other possibility—the very bloody prospect—she refused to let her mind travel there.

As she reached the edge of the trees, she peered into the clearing that housed their camp. All appeared almost as she'd left it in the night, except that men no longer slept on their pallets. Had that really been less than a day ago? That fear-filled flight seemed another lifetime.

She stepped into the clearing and scanned her things. Everything was in its place. Jean-Jacques's belongings seemed untouched as well. Even his bedding still lay out, with the top cover rumbled.

He'd not come to pack up yet.

A new frisson of fear washed through her. Could her wild imaginings be true? *Lord, protect him. Show me what to do to help both Raphael's brothers and Jean-Jacques.*

She wanted desperately—again—to turn and sprint back the way she'd come.

But this time to search out Jean-Jacques's wounded body. She forced herself to stay put. She'd come this far to help Hugh and Louis. She had to fulfill her mission as the Lord had prompted and leave Jean-Jacques in God's hands.

Along with her baby. *God, would You really take everything I love?*

She couldn't let herself dwell on that thought. Trust meant not snatching back the reins every time worry spiked.

She refocused on the packs and supplies in the clearing. Everything seemed to be here, although she didn't see any of the braves' weapons. They must be carrying them all. Her heart thumped harder in her chest and she turned toward the path leading to the horses.

Moving as quickly as she dared, she strained for any motion or sound from ahead that signaled people. When she neared the clearing where the horses grazed, a flash of brown showed through the trees. The figure might be one of the animals, but it *could* be a man wearing leathers.

She eased from one tree to the next, straining to see more each time she darted forward. Those *were* horses. When she'd reached the edge of the clearing, she paused behind a trunk and peered around to count the animals.

Two…four…five. All the horses except her own mount stood there.

No men among them.

She lifted her gaze upward, above the tops of the trees on the other side of the clearing. Jean-Jacques had said he saw the smoke from that direction.

No smoke drifted from that way now. There did seem to be the faintest scent of woodsmoke in the air, though that could have come from their own smoldering campfire behind her.

There was no other place to look. She had to advance forward and find where Hugh and Louis had camped. The braves must be there. The thought clenched the knot in her belly even tighter.

She started across the clearing, gripping her rifle tight and sending up a steady stream of prayers as she walked.

"Colette."

With her thoughts so intense, she nearly missed the whispered call. The moment the sound registered, she spun to find its source.

Behind one of the horses, a man straightened.

"Jean-Jacques?"

He wasn't hurt. Relief soaked through her.

She strode toward him, and he pressed a finger to his lips in silence. Though he came around to the front of the horse, he stayed by the animal, seeming hesitant to leave the cover it provided.

When she reached him, he opened the arm not holding his own gun, and she came into his hug. She soaked in his familiar scent as he held her tight.

His breath ruffled the hair at her ear. "What are you doing here?"

Reality pressed in, and she pulled back to see his face. "I can't let Hugh and Louis be hurt because of me. More bloodshed won't make what I did right. I don't know what Elk Runs and the others intend to do with them, but I have to face this."

She expected shock to cover his expression. Or maybe worry, or anger, or…anything but the grim determination that settled over him. "Are you sure?"

Part of her wanted to be affronted by the fact that he didn't try to stop her. Didn't he care she might be killed, or at the very least, might have to stand trial for her actions? What about the baby? *Lord...* Her spirit strained, the weight of fear pressing so hard. Yet she had to do this.

She nodded. "It's the right thing. I have to trust that God will protect me—us."

Jean-Jacques's eyes drifted shut as a pained expression twisted his face. He didn't make a sound, and finally he opened his eyes to meet her gaze. "I felt God nudging us that direction too, but I couldn't stomach it. I told Him that He'd better take it up with you if that was His leading."

If not for the fear twisting her belly, she might have smiled. The Lord had just confirmed His guidance, and she loved the way Jean-Jacques was open to His voice. *Please don't let me lose him.*

"I think they must be at the camp." He motioned upriver toward where he'd said Hugh and Louis were staying. "I can't find anyone elsewhere."

She inhaled a strengthening breath as she nodded. "I thought the same. You know the best way to approach so we can learn what's happening?"

Jean-Jacques nodded as he stepped forward. "Stay close and walk quietly."

He took her hand and led the way. She savored the feel of his strong, calloused palm. This might be the last time she would ever hold his hand.

CHAPTER 26

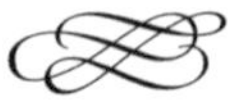

French had never experienced so much pride and fear twisting through his gut at the same time.

He was leading Colette toward an unknown danger. How could he not only allow her to put herself in this position, but lead her willingly toward men who probably sought her life?

He had no idea the character of Raphael's brothers. Were they the kind of men who would hurt a woman? Maybe not. Though the fact that they'd come this far to find her…that didn't bode well.

He and Colette crept along the edge of the woods beside the river. Neither of them spoke, and the grass silenced most of their footsteps. But his heart thundered loudly enough to be heard across the water.

Voices sounded from ahead, the low murmur of deep undertones. Young Bear's speech possessed that rumble, but he couldn't be sure.

Colette's grip tightened in his own, and he gave her an encouraging squeeze. No matter what came, they would face it together. And if the men tried to atone for their brother's life by taking hers, he wouldn't allow it.

She'd not killed the man with malice aforethought. Back in Montréal, the act wouldn't warrant the death penalty. Would these men abide by civilized laws? There weren't any such regulations in the vast territory of Rupert's Land where they'd all lived, nor here in the Idaho Territory. But surely they could be made to see reason.

As they crept closer, another voice distinguished itself. Left Standing, though he was speaking the Blackfoot tongue, and French couldn't hear well enough to interpret.

One silent step at a time, they moved forward. He kept a solid grip on his rifle with one hand and Colette with the other. Maybe he should have the gun raised and aimed, ready to shoot.

But Colette had said no more bloodshed. Was he really ready to place her life completely in the Lord's hands? *God, help me. Help us both.*

Another voice rose now, louder than the others and more passionate. Hawk Wing, for certain. French strained to make out words. Something about an animal, but the man's outrage made the sounds more staccato than usual. Through the trees ahead, he glimpsed motion, but couldn't identify figures.

They had to get closer. Once he could see what was happening, he might understand the conversation better. At least it sounded like no harm had come to Young Bear, Left Standing, and Hawk Wing. He didn't really expect that the two Frenchmen would be able to harm five braves, especially when these Blackfoot had probably had the advantage of surprise. But it was still a relief to know his friends hadn't been harmed.

A few more steps, and he finally reached a place with a view between the trees that showed him the activity in the camp. He jerked to a halt as the scene came clear, and his heart seized.

Two white men were tied to trees and looked so much rougher than they had the evening before.

The younger—Louis?—was positioned nearest him and Colette. A gash marred his temple, with a line of blood dripping down his face. More crimson leaked from a line across the boy's throat. Someone had pressed a knife there, hard enough to draw blood. Thankfully, *not* deep enough to sever an artery.

The other man, Hugh, was tied a few trees away from his brother. The fellow's hair had been mussed so it spiked in several directions, with leaves and grass mixed in. He was already gathering a good-sized black eye but didn't seem to be bleeding anywhere.

French shifted his focus from the captives to the others in the clearing. Hawk Wing, Young Bear, and Left Standing were clustered together, talking. Elk Runs and Cross the River stood a little apart, focused on the white men like guards.

Left Standing murmured something, but the idea didn't seem to please Hawk Wing, for he jerked his head away and spat toward Hugh. He spoke a string of louder impassioned words, and French focused on the sounds to decipher them. Something about a woman.

Colette pressed into his side, and French shifted to allow her a better view. He wrapped his arm around her waist, as though he could hold her in safety that way.

But he couldn't. He had to listen for the Lord's leading in this. Had to be willing to follow that prompting, no matter how awful the direction seemed. *Show us, Father.*

Colette sucked in a breath just loud enough for him to hear, and her body stiffened under his hand.

The captives did look awful, especially at first sight. Louis must have fought a great deal to be so roughed up. But then, if French'd had a brother, he would have given his life to protect him. And would have wanted justice for his death.

In response to Hawk Wing's rant, Young Bear bit out a sharp "no" in their tongue. That, at least, French could decipher.

Hawk Wing's face twisted in a rage fiercer than anything he'd seen from the man. The brave spun with a piercing yell. Raising his knife in the air, he charged Louis.

Another voice bellowed. Hugh writhed against his bonds, twisting. He struck out with both feet.

One caught Hawk Wing's knee, throwing the brave forward so he had to scramble to catch his balance.

With another roar, the Indian spun on Hugh and charged him with the raised knife.

A scream erupted, and Colette jerked from his arm.

Before French could stop her, she charged forward into the clearing. He dove after her.

"Stop!" Her scream pierced the melee.

Hawk Wing spun to face her, every eye turning with him to stare at Colette.

She jerked to a halt in front of the men. "Stop. Don't hurt him."

Hawk Wing slowly lowered his knife and straightened. "They come to hurt you."

French stepped up beside Colette even as she squared her shoulders and raised her chin. "I will speak with them." Determination hardened her voice.

He glanced at the two white men. Louis stared at Colette with eyes wide, as though seeing a vision. Even Hugh looked a bit shocked at her sudden appearance.

Then the older brother's expression turned wary. "You know these men, Colette?"

She nodded, her chin still lifted in a way that made her look just like a French princess. "They are my friends. They've given me shelter and protection since I left Fort Pike." Her gaze turned tender as she scanned the braves around the clearing.

Then she looked back at the two. "I'm so sorry about Raphael. I never meant to hurt him. I was only trying to protect —" She bit off her words.

Did she not want them to know about the baby? Something about that didn't sit right with him. These men deserved to know they would have a niece or nephew.

Just as Raphael should have known he would be a father.

Another layer of pain pressed on French's chest. As much as he wasn't sure how he felt about the man, the fellow should have known his child. What would it be like to raise the baby in his place? Could French be the papa he wanted to be and speak of the child's blood father with respect?

He would have to find a way, but that battle could be waged another time. He forced his focus back to these men.

Hugh sent his younger brother a weighty look. Louis barely spared him a glance before turning earnest eyes on Colette. "We don't blame you, Colette. In fact, I'm sorry we didn't step in sooner. I didn't realize how bad he'd gotten until I came that day. I'm sorry. I should've seen it before."

Colette stood motionless, her eyes rounding as she stared at the man. French knew exactly how she felt. Were these men serious about not blaming her? Then why had they come such a long distance?

She shook her head as though trying to shake away her shock, and her voice trembled when she spoke. "It's not your fault. We are each responsible for our own actions." That was the closest French had heard her come to condemning the man.

But she was right. This half-grown boy wasn't responsible for his elder brother's actions. Neither of his brothers were.

Hugh straightened—as much as he could while still tied to the tree. "When Louis told me what you said…about the…babe." He dipped his head toward Colette's midsection, and his cheeks turned ruddier. It seemed odd to watch this rough frontiersman befuddled by a woman.

French glanced around the group at the braves to see if they'd caught the word and understood. Their stoic faces were impossible to read, so he returned his focus to Hugh as the man spoke again.

His earnest gaze locked on Colette's face. "We didn't mean

for you to leave on your own. We came after you to tell you we want to take care of you and the little one."

His words slammed into French's belly like a punch, knocking him off balance. These two wanted to care for Colette?

The fellow was already speaking again. "When you kept running, we got worried. We figured there might be something else wrong." He sent the group of braves a scowl. "We only meant to help. Didn't expect to be scalped."

French struggled to take in the full import of his words. Like puzzle pieces, they fit in place, yet they changed the entire picture.

A sob slipped from the woman beside him, pulling his focus to her. She pressed a hand to her chest and another over her mouth, probably to hold in more sobs.

French stepped nearer and rested a hand on her back. Seeing her pain brought out every one of his protective instincts.

She glanced his way, and her eyes spoke a tumult of words. What she'd thought would end so badly had turned out to be so good.

He slipped his hand farther around her waist and tugged her to his side. If all these people hadn't been watching, he would have pressed a kiss to her hair. Once again, the Lord had led them to the best outcome possible.

She turned back to the braves. "Please. Let them go free."

Left Standing shifted, drawing her focus to him. "You are sure?" Ever the protective brother.

French had liked him from the first few times they met, and even more so now.

Colette nodded, her chin rising again as determination settled over her features. "I was married to their brother. I killed him by accident and thought they were coming to make me pay for that act. But I had to face what I'd done. I can't run from hard things any longer."

The man nodded, then turned and moved to Louis, using his hunting knife to cut the leather straps binding him to the tree. Hawk Wing did the same with Hugh.

As the brothers stepped away from their trees, Louis shook out his arms and twisted his shoulders. Hugh was much more reserved, standing with his feet spread, glaring around the group. He looked ready to take on any man who came at him.

Colette must have seen it too, for she stepped toward the man, motioning around the group of Indians. "These men have become good friends. They gave me protection and taught me how to trap and provide for myself. Without them I wouldn't be here today."

French sent a glance to Young Bear and almost smiled at the twinkle of pride in his gaze. Maybe for what Colette was saying about his people, or maybe simply because of Colette and the strength she now showed.

Silence settled over them all. No one seemed to know quite what to do next. Hugh still looked ready to take on any of them, maybe all at once. Louis wore a nervous smile. The Indians simply watched, ready for when they might need to step in again.

Maybe this was French's turn. He swept his gaze around to include all. "Anyone hungry? It's been almost a full day since I had a bite, and my belly is complaining."

That eased the tension in the air like a needle bursting an abscess. Colette turned her face up to him with a smile that warmed him all the way through.

CHAPTER 27

Colette sank into the moment as they sat around the campfire, early dusk tinting the light. Jean-Jacques had worked his usual magic to throw together a meal, and the group now gathered around the fire in the camp beside the cliff wall.

The men sat in their usual places, with Jean-Jacques on one side of her and Young Bear on the other. Louis and Hugh sat on Young Bear's right, still looking a bit concerned about the tawny-skinned men surrounding them.

She couldn't blame them. Sitting in a group of Blackfoot braves had to be unnerving, especially since all had left their weapons with their packs around the outer edge of the camp. After all, the braves' initial introduction had been to string these two brothers up to the nearest stout trees.

But Young Bear had made an effort to extend an olive branch to them, asking about the town they haled from and their work there. He also had his pipe nestled beside him. She had a feeling that, after the meal concluded, he would light the tobacco and maybe offer the two a smoke. A true peace offering.

They ate with few words, mostly because all seemed ravenous. She certainly was, even though she'd been nibbling on meat most of the day. The babe seemed desperate for food of late, and perhaps that was why her belly had expanded more each time she looked down.

When the cups of food had been emptied and set aside, Young Bear did light his pipe. As she suspected, he offered it to Hugh and Louis, and eventually they passed the implement around the circle.

Louis turned to her with an earnest expression, more like the younger brother she'd known. "How are you? And…the little one?" His gaze dipped to her belly for a heartbeat before surging back up to meet her eyes.

She smiled and stopped herself just before moving a hand to her belly. Maybe that wouldn't be proper among all these men. "We are well, both of us. I didn't think you'd heard me when I spoke of the baby…that night. I'm sorry I gave you so much worry and brought you so far into the wilderness." She still couldn't fathom that they'd traveled all these weeks just to make sure she was taken care of. These men were so much better than she'd given them credit for.

Hugh leaned forward so he could see her better around those sitting between them. His gaze flicked from her to Jean-Jacques. "I take it you two have known each other a while?"

The smile seeped off her face. She'd wondered, back in the clearing when Jean-Jacques put his arm around her, what Raphael's brothers would think. Now was her chance to make it clear.

She met his gaze. "Jean-Jacques and I grew up together. The last time I'd seen him was when my family moved when I was thirteen. We happened to pass him on the trail a few weeks ago." Hopefully she'd made it clear she'd been faithful to Raphael. Now she needed to be equally clear with this next part. "He's asked me to marry him, and I've agreed."

Though Hugh's gaze flickered wide for a heartbeat, she couldn't read any thoughts beyond surprise on his face or

Louis's. What would they think of her even considering an offer of marriage so soon after Raphael passed? There wasn't anything typical about this situation, and she certainly hadn't been wearing mourning gowns. Mama must be turning over in her grave. But this was the way things were.

Beside her, Jean-Jacques leaned forward, matching Hugh's posture, though not his accusatory tone. "I've been looking for Colette since her family moved eleven years ago. I'd almost given up ever finding her again until we crossed paths a few weeks back."

She held her breath, tensing with every word. Would he speak of his love for her? As much as those words stirred her insides, her deceased husband's elder brother might not appreciate hearing them.

When Jean-Jacques spoke again, his voice deepened. "It will be my honor to care for and provide for Colette and the babe. I'll do my best to be the father the little one needs—and help him appreciate the man who gave life to him."

A burn crept up her throat and stung her eyes. Jean-Jacques couldn't have said it better. Did he really mean those words? She'd seen his earlier battle when she spoke a little about what her life had been like those last months. Had he truly forgiven Raphael?

Jean-Jacques was every bit the man she'd always thought him. So much more. *Lord, you've blessed me abundantly.*

As much as she would love to stay in that place of joy, she glanced at Hugh and Louis to gauge their response to Jean-Jacques's words.

A look passed between the brothers, and she couldn't begin to decipher its meaning.

Then Hugh turned to her. "So you two are planning to marry? Where will you live?" He didn't seem angered, but his questions were...a bit nosy. She didn't mind answering them though.

She glanced at Jean-Jacques to see if he wanted to reply.

He must've taken her look as request to speak for them both. "We're planning west, at least for now. The group I've been traveling with for the past couple years will be summering in a Nez Perce village across the mountains. One of my friends is a reverend who can marry us. We'll stay there, at least until the baby is born, then decide where we'd like to settle."

Colette cast a look around the group at their Blackfoot friends as Jean-Jacques spoke. Would they think she was abandoning them now that she no longer needed their help? Would they be upset about her going to the Nez Perce village? She'd heard the two tribes didn't always get along.

Young Bear met her gaze, and the corners of his mouth curved in the hint of a smile, no doubt meant to set her at ease. She did her best to send him a *thank-you* with her gaze. She would make sure to say those words aloud to all of them before she and Jean-Jacques headed out.

Again, Hugh and Louis looked at each other, a message passing between their gazes. This time the look seemed to be agreement. Hugh turned back to her, clearly the spokesman between them. "We'd like to travel along with you and stay nearby, at least until the baby is born."

He sent a look to Jean-Jacques that might be almost respectful. "Not that we don't appreciate what you intend to do, but we want to help if there's any way we can. And we'd like to meet the baby."

Louis finally spoke up. "This might be the only niece or nephew I ever have." He sent a teasing sideways glance to his brother.

Another round of emotion clogged her throat, but she smiled through the tears stinging her eyes. These two… How far she'd misjudged them.

But before she could speak, Hugh's gaze intensified. "If we'd paid more attention before, we might not be in this situation.

But we'd like to do everything we can to make up for it and to see you well settled." His gaze flicked to Jean-Jacques, then back to her as he gave a final nod.

Jean-Jacques's hand found hers on the ground between them, and he gave her a little squeeze.

The support was what she needed to bolster her emotions. She sent him a grateful glance, checking to make sure his face didn't hold concern. He gave her a nod that bespoke so much trust that she didn't want to look away. He was giving her the freedom to choose whether to accept the offer or not.

Hugh wasn't presenting it as an offer exactly, but she knew beyond a doubt that if she declined, Jean-Jacques would support her decision and send the men packing. As would the braves around them. And she also had a feeling that these two brothers wouldn't force their presence if she asked them to return north. Was that what she wanted?

Would it be wise to let them come with us, Lord? She'd learned her lesson about charging ahead without seeking God's will. The idea of having these two travel along, though it had seemed so foreign at first, now settled like a comfortable blanket. This would be good, this time to get to know her brothers-in-law better.

And though she and Jean-Jacques would certainly wait until marriage vows had been spoken before anything intimate passed between them, having a couple of chaperones along the trail would keep things very proper.

She nearly laughed at the thought. Mama would *not* think traveling with three unmarried men proper, no matter how she presented the plan. But having her deceased husband's brothers along would certainly keep her and Jean-Jacques from crossing any lines they shouldn't.

She met Hugh's gaze, then looked to Louis. "We would be honored to have you come along. Are you sure you can be spared from your work that long?" Hugh had been traveling with a group of trappers for several years now, and Louis worked in the livery back at Fort Pike.

Hugh nodded. "I live off the land. I imagine I can do that as well from a Nimiipuu camp as anywhere." He looked to his brother, and she did also.

Louis shrugged. “I told McMahon I would be gone for a while. As busy as we were, I suspect he's already hired a man or two to replace me. I might start trapping like Hugh does after this."

Though Louis’s boyish tendencies made her smile, she couldn't help the pain that pressed her chest. Hugh had lived a hard life in his line of work. Jean-Jacques probably had too, though he didn't wear the scars of it the way Hugh did. The idea of Louis also taking up that occupation didn't settle well. Maybe she could share her concerns with the lad over the next few months.

"All right then." Jean-Jacques’s voice beside her sent a shiver through her. Just having him near made her love him a little more each day. She could only imagine how she would feel years from now.

She wasn't naïve enough to think life would always be comfortable, that trials wouldn't come to test them. She'd ridden that path before, but she'd learned through every hard time. She would be a better wife to Jean-Jacques than she’d been to Raphael. With God's help, she would be his partner, his helpmate. They would take each challenge as it came —together.

~

Colette swallowed down a lump as she stared at the line of braves before her. How could she express to them what they’d meant these past weeks? God had brought them into her life at one of her most vulnerable times. They'd taken her in—a weak white woman—taught her, fed her, and protected her.

But now the time had come to leave.

She stepped to Young Bear first. Did Indians shake hands? The older man answered the question for her, extending both hands to her. She placed hers in his, and he clasped them in his large calloused palms. She met his gaze but had to blink to clear her vision. "Thank you. For everything. You took me in when I had no one else. I'm so grateful."

He squeezed her hands. "You are strong, my daughter. You will do many great things and raise a strong son."

She raised her brows. "A boy, you think?" She'd taken to calling the babe *he* as well. But she really had no idea.

The older man merely smiled and gave her hands a final squeeze before releasing them.

She moved to Left Standing and took his hands as she had Young Bear's. "Thank you for all your help translating and teaching me your language. And teaching me to set my traps." And so much more, but her voice was threatening to crack.

He seemed to understand, for he released her hands and placed a palm on her shoulder. Just like a brother.

She turned to Cross the River next and clasped his hands as she had the others. "And you taught me how to skin my catch without damaging the hide. I would have made a mess of my pelts if you hadn't stepped in to help me."

His eyes twinkled as his mouth curved. "The cut hide is good only to braid rope. We would have had enough rope to fence these mountains."

She managed a laugh even as she sniffed away emotion. Then she moved to Hawk Wing. "Thank you for teaching me the way of the beaver and how to read their sign. I should have told you before, but a predator was stealing the catch from my traps too. I just couldn't imagine riding another day in the saddle."

A swirl of reactions crossed his face, his emotions flicking from one to the next. Then he gripped her hands tight and raised them, as though in victory. "I am glad you did not tell me. Better I lose half my catch then cause you harm, my sister."

A new rush of emotion surged up to sting her eyes. Finally, she turned to Elk Runs. He took her hands as the others had, and the calming wisdom in his gaze soothed her like she hadn't allowed it to before. "I might still be hiding in that tiny cave on the mountain if it wasn't for you. Thank you for coming after me. For using your great skill to bring back my wayward self." She managed a smile, even through her tears. "I won't run anymore."

He released one of her hands and reached up to cup her cheek, the gesture almost fatherly. "If you ever need us, send word with the raven. We will find you."

These men… God had blessed her abundantly beyond what she deserved. Nodding her thanks, she stepped back.

"Or send word by the hawk." Hawk Wing's voice brought a smile, even as she turned away.

When they'd mounted—all four of them—they turned for a final farewell wave. The braves still stood as they had before, a line of bravery. Of refuge. She'd needed it for a time—needed *them*. But she'd grown so much in her weeks with them.

With God before her, and Jean-Jacques at her side—not to mention Hugh and Louis guarding their flank—she was ready to face a new adventure.

EPILOGUE

Anticipation surged through French as the Nimiipuu village appeared ahead. After three weeks riding through the mountains, he was more than ready to rejoin his friends. They'd been taking it slower than he was accustomed to because of Colette's condition, but she still seemed exhausted each day by an hour or two after noon. She'd insisted they keep riding though. Maybe she wanted to finally reach a place where they could be settled.

They'd stopped at Otskai's village the night before, and he'd been hoping against hope the others would still be there. But according to the chief, they'd all gone on to the northern village a day farther. Even Otskai and her son had accompanied the group.

Now, the lodges of that town stood like welcoming beacons in the late afternoon light. What would the others think of Colette? Maybe he should have told them about her. Their surprise might make her think he'd not missed her enough to speak of her.

In fact, the opposite was true. He'd have to make sure she

understood. He never wanted her to question his love for her. And he'd happily spend the rest of his life showing it.

When they drew about twenty strides from the outer lodges, a small figure toddled from the edge of camp. A boy, but surely not…

Had Otskai's son escaped again? He shot a glance at the river. Thankfully, it flowed on the other side of the town. The lad had a penchant for landing in water, no matter how dangerous.

But a much larger figure strode around the side of the lodge, his long legs covering the same distance as five of the lad's strides. Caleb bent low and swept up the boy, then in the same motion, lifted him high in the air above his head. Giggles filled the air as the boy writhed. Caleb held him up for another moment, then lowered him to perch on his arm.

Then Caleb turned their direction.

A smile hovered on French's lips as he waited for the man to recognize him. The moment awareness settled, Caleb's expression formed a wide grin, and he strode with that same long step toward them.

French slipped off his horse and moved forward on foot, meeting his friend with a firm shake.

"It's about time you showed up." Caleb's deep voice rumbled. "We were about to come looking for you."

French gave the man a backslap, then stepped back, settling into the camaraderie in a way he hadn't in so long. "I thought maybe you'd give up on me. Decide I wasn't coming back."

Caleb met his gaze, his voice turning serious. "We wouldn't give up on you. We're family. If you're up against a battle and need reinforcements, we'll come after you every time. Don't think otherwise."

The words pressed through him, striking a chord of familiarity. Wasn't that exactly how he felt about Colette? Exactly the way God felt toward *him*? God had placed these brothers—this unlikely family—in his life to reinforce his understanding of unconditional love.

French nodded. "Thank you." The words seemed paltry, but he meant them from the core of his being.

Caleb shifted his gaze past French. "Now you can introduce me to your friends."

The grin surged forward again as French turned and motioned to Colette. "Colette, I'm pleased to introduce my good friend, Caleb Jackson."

He turned to Caleb. Maybe he wouldn't say everything during this first introduction, but he could start the story. "Colette and I were childhood playmates."

Caleb nodded, a knowing glint settling in his eyes. "She's the one you've been pining after all this time."

The shock of his words splashed through French, and his first instinct was to deny them. But Caleb seemed so sure of himself, maybe French hadn't been as good at hiding his emotions as he thought. Besides, if he planned to show Colette what she really meant to him, this would be a good start.

He turned back to Colette with a grin and a wink. "She's the one."

A throat cleared behind her, and Hugh rode forward.

French pressed his lips together to hide a smile. Maybe he shouldn't be quite as blatant in front of her brothers-in-law.

French motioned toward both men. "This is Hugh Charpentier and his brother, Louis. They're…family of Colette. I told them there would be plenty of room for all." A glance at Colette showed a softness in her expression. Yes, he needed to do better to honor these men who cared enough about her and their unborn niece or nephew to chase her across the mountain wilderness.

Turning back to Caleb, he raised his brows. "You are all here?"

Caleb turned, and they began the final steps to reach the

village. "We're all here. Otskai and this fellow decided to come along too."

French slid a glance toward him. "So we heard when we stopped at her uncle's village. You're married then?"

A grin stretched Caleb's cheeks, and his ears turned pink. He kept facing forward though. "Just waiting until you get here for that."

A weight pressed in French's chest. Caleb had been waiting for *him*? That possibility had never entered his thoughts. He'd been so wrapped up in his own thoughts and worries.

He dropped his voice. "I'm sorry I made you wait. You're a better brother to me than I am in return."

Caleb sent him a look. "That's not the way it works." He straightened and nodded toward the village. "There's someone else here you know."

French raised his brows at the man. There weren't many they knew who weren't also part of their group.

"Telipe." Something in Caleb's manner, and his weighty tone, pressed like a hand to French's chest. Telipe was Meksem's sister, the one they'd rescued from the Blackfoot war party a few months ago.

He searched Caleb's eyes. "She's here? Her baby must be coming soon. Why did she leave her husband and village so close to her time?"

Sadness entered Caleb's gaze. "Her husband died. Apparently, not long after we left her in the Salish village. She's moved here permanently, living with her brother's family. You're right about the baby. She looks big enough to birth twins."

That hand pressed harder on French's chest, and his gaze shifted back to Colette. Telipe's situation bore an uncanny similarity to Colette's. They were both with child, both the babes' fathers deceased. The difference was, he would be there for Colette in every way possible. She wasn't alone, not like Telipe probably felt.

Colette's gaze glistened, probably comprehending more about the situation than most would after hearing Caleb's brief summary. Her eyes said she would help this Indian woman she didn't even know. That she would be a friend, a sister, as they both navigated the path of new motherhood.

A fresh wave of love for this woman surged through him. The little girl he'd known all those years ago had matured into so much more than he'd imagined. He couldn't wait to see what adventures their life together would hold.

Did you enjoy French and Colette's story? I hope so!
Would you take a quick minute to leave a review where you purchased the book?
It doesn't have to be long. Just a sentence or two telling what you liked about the story!

To receive a free book and get updates when new Misty M. Beller books release, go to https://mistymbeller.com/freebook

And here's a peek at the next book in the series (remember Telipe, Meksem's little sister who the group rescued form the Blackfoot kidnapping party?), Honor in the Mountain Refuge:

Chapter One

SUMMER, 1831
CLEARWATER RIVER VALLEY, FUTURE IDAHO TERRITORY

The fine hairs along Telípe's neck stood on end, and she turned to scan the woods around her—not an easy feat with the babe weighing down her belly.

Was there an animal watching her? Or could there be a person scouting out there, unseen?

She peered through the summer leaves covering the trees, but all appeared still. Maybe the sensation had only come from sweat trickling down her neck.

Turning back to the fruit bushes, she pushed aside the branches and reached for a cluster of chokecherries. At least the trees offered shade and a bit of a breeze, unlike the hot, smoky lodge she'd escaped. With all her family lounging or milling about the place, she could barely breathe, much less think.

Of course, she couldn't breathe well anyway, as the baby filled every empty space inside her. She slipped a hand under her belly to better support the mass at her middle, then reached for another cluster of cherries.

She'd never expected her final days before confinement to look like this. The home she'd thought would be hers to tend for the rest of her life, gone. Just when she'd finally found a measure of fulfillment caring for her new husband, he'd been taken away too.

Now, she'd returned to the lodge of her family. Actually, her eldest brother's home now, for when their parents died, he'd taken over as the principle man of the family. Thankfully, he'd married, bringing his new wife and her grandmother to live with them. Both women were kind and generous. Ámtiz willingly took over care for Telípe and Síkem's two younger brothers, and the young woman's patience with the boys never ended. They'd all taken to calling the older woman simply *the grandmother,* and the entire group had found a comfortable rhythm.

One that Telípe wasn't quite part of. Since she'd returned, she seemed to be more in the way than anything.

She used the back of her wrist to swipe the sweat trickling into her eyes, then waved off a mosquito and reached for another cluster of cherries. After pushing a branch aside, she studied what remained of the fruit. All green. Better to wait for them to ripen.

Turning to slip out of the thick brush, her sleeve caught on a limb. She elbowed the branch aside, then waddled forward, grabbing a tree to help her up the hill.

Every move took more effort with the babe so large in her belly. She couldn't possibly get any bigger in the final few days. There was no room. Once she pulled herself out of the hollow, she paused to catch her breath, leaning against a trunk for support.

Her gaze wandered through the woods around her. In the past, the leafy growth had been a sign of new life. But she couldn't summon the strength to feel hopeful now.

A movement snagged her focus, and she narrowed her attention to that spot. Perhaps only a squirrel, but all kinds of animals roamed these trees. Big predatory creatures.

And predatory men.

The movement stilled, but something didn't appear right among the limbs overhead. Thick leaves covered much of the area, but something showed between the green.

Leather? Was that the brown of buckskins? She gripped a tree as she strained to make out what she was seeing.

Then another movement flashed. A face appeared between leaves. Not a bear or a wildcat. A man.

Her heart thundered in her chest. *Not a man. Not again.*

She turned to flee, though the futility of the act swept through her as she faced thick tree growth that would only slow her down. In her condition, she could barely toddle, much less run. She was more likely to fall down the wooded hill than to outrun an able-bodied man.

But she couldn't let herself be caught again. She may not fare so well this time.

Grabbing her belly to support its weight, she reached for a tree to push off from. Yet she'd barely taken two steps before a voice sounded from behind.

"Tayógosa." Wait.

He'd spoken the word in her tongue. Did that mean he *wasn't* part of another Blackfoot war party come to take captives as slaves for their people? Maybe he was only one of the braves from a neighboring town out hunting.

But she still felt the urge to flee. She paused and made herself turn to face him.

He'd come down from the tree and now stood beside the trunk. Definitely a full-grown man, taller than most with broad shoulders. A flash of memory slipped through her. She knew another brave with wide shoulders like that.

But she didn't allow her mind to form his shape or his handsome features.

Instead, she honed her gaze on this man's face. A jolt coursed through her. *It couldn't be*. Was this a vision? Surely...

He took a step nearer, moving into a patch of sunlight. A gasp slipped out even as her heart raced into her throat.

Hope and panic warred through her, and she stepped back, though her feet were too frozen to the ground to turn and run. Had he returned to recapture her? Maybe he'd realized he shouldn't have been so kind the last time, shouldn't have protected her from the other warriors when his band had kidnapped her before.

Had they sent him on a quest to retake the captive himself in order to keep his place among them?

Fear overtook every other emotion, and she spun away from him. Grasping for first one trunk, then the next, she scrambled through the trees. Down the hill.

"Amkakáiz."

The word he barked only slowed her down a tiny bit. Surely he wasn't saying that he came in peace. Did he even know what that idea meant? His people prided themselves on how many captives they took of her tribe. And how did he know so much of her Nimiipuu tongue? He'd spoken only a couple words the last time she'd seen him.

She kept running, sliding down the slope, nearly seated and gripping the trees to keep from tumbling.

"Telípe!"

Her name on his lips slowed her more than anything else. Something in his tone reminded her of his kindness before.

He'd been so careful with her, especially after he learned of the baby, always making sure she had enough food and furs to keep warm through the snows.

She finally let herself stop, struggling to take in breaths. The need to run away fought against her exhausted limbs. She craned to look back at him, though her bulky body couldn't turn with the awkward position she was in.

Chogan took another step forward, his hand outstretched as though to calm a flighty horse. "Amkakáiz." This time he accompanied the word with the sign for peace. Did he really mean it?

She stared at his face for signs of his true intentions. Though he looked every bit the strong warrior he had before, his eyes held kindness. And also something more, a shadow they hadn't possessed before. Maybe the distance between them caused the expression.

He motioned for her to stand. "I will not hurt you."

She'd trusted him before, but only because she had to. She and the four other captives had been at the mercy of him and his Blackfoot comrades. He'd never showed anything but kindness, though he could have been as cruel as he wanted.

In truth, his companions had goaded and jeered at him for his gentle actions. *Weak*, they'd called him. Though nothing about this man appeared weak. His height, the breadth of his shoulders tapering to a lean waist, all wrapped in sinewy muscles. The buckskin tunic and leggings he wore disguised none of his strength.

No, the man wasn't weak.

But could he be trusted? As before, she was at his mercy now. Though she could try to run, her cumbersome body wouldn't take her far if he really tried to catch her. Better she stand and face him like a woman of strength.

Grasping trunks on both sides of her, she did her best to pull herself up with more grace than she could usually manage these days. The weight of her belly tugged her, and she braced her feet as she turned to face the man.

She was downhill from him now, at least a dozen steps away. With him positioned so much higher than she, he looked as large as a grizzly standing on its back legs, pawing the air.

Maybe he realized the fear his position might plant in her, for he started walking downhill. Not directly to her, but a little sideways. When he reached the same level as her, he came to a stop with about five steps separating them.

She could see his face well now, the earnest expression marking his handsome features. He looked almost…worried.

He motioned toward her belly. "Are you well?" His brows rose in question.

She cradled the swell, her hand finding its usual place to support the babe. Even before, he'd seemed worried about the child inside her, taking extra care with her and stepping in when the others grew rough in their treatment. His gentleness hadn't won him any favors with the other braves, and she'd been so grateful for his kindness. Grateful enough to ensure her sister and the others spared his life when they came to rescue her.

In answer to his questioning gaze, she nodded. "The babe is well. It will be coming soon." Did Chogan understand her? He'd spoken four times now in her language, so maybe he'd learned more than he knew before. His eyes showed understanding.

If so, it was time he answer a question for her. She lifted her chin. "Why have you come?"

His gaze narrowed, not in animosity but as if he were trying to decide something. Maybe deciphering her words in his mind. Just in case, she asked the question again using the common language of signs all the tribes understood.

He still hesitated. Trying to decide what to say? Or attempting to find Nimiipuu words to speak it? Would he tell the truth? Did he have reason to lie? That would depend on his motive.

At last, he leveled his chin, holding her gaze with directness in his own. "My people have sent me away. I've journeyed a full moon through the mountains, asking the great spirit to show me my purpose. I did not realize how far I'd come. But I now see he's led me to you."

She worked to take in his words. Though he stumbled through some of them, he spoke her language. Had he known it all along? Why had he hidden his understanding from her before? Maybe that was how he'd known she was with child, even though she'd taken pains to wear clothing that wouldn't reveal her condition. But perhaps he'd overheard her speaking to the other captives of the babe. She'd assumed it was the one time she'd rested her hand on her belly that gave her away. He'd been watching and had given her a look of full understanding. But maybe he'd known before that.

Forcing her focus back to the present, she studied him as she mulled through his words. "Why did your people send you away?" Surely it didn't have to do with his kindness during their kidnapping.

The sadness that had cloaked his gaze before grew thicker now, confirming her fear. She gripped the tree harder as words tumbled out of her. "Because of me? Us?"

He shook his head once. "I have never agreed with my people's desire for war. That campaign was my last chance to be the man of bloodshed my father would have me be. I will not go against how I feel here." He pressed a fist to his chest. "I do not regret helping you." He lifted his chin. "I know my place is not with people of war. I have been following the great spirit's leading to show me what he would have me do."

A swirl of conflicting emotions tangled in her chest. Chogan was here. What would her family say? Her brothers couldn't even speak the word *Blackfoot* without spitting. Yet he'd been so kind to her in those fearful days of the kidnapping last winter. Now he'd been cast out from his village for his actions.

And he spoke of the great spirit's leading. She'd never questioned the beliefs she'd been taught from her earliest days, but her sister Meksem had been speaking to her of the God Meksem now served. A God stronger than the great spirit. A God who made every person and thing that existed, with all power, far more than the sun or any other being. Yet Meksem said this God cared about every part of her life, wanted good for her, and was guiding her to that good path, even through the hard times.

If the great spirit had led Chogan here, did Meksem's God have any part in it? And why here, to a quiet Nimiipuu village with good cause to hate the Blackfoot?

Chogan wouldn't know of her husband's passing. The last time she'd seen this man, Heinmot had been alive, and she'd not even known how bad his sickness had progressed. A pang pressed her chest.

Should she speak of him? She didn't want this man to think she was asking for help.

She wasn't. In truth, her family had been kind to take her back into their lodge. No matter how much the cluster of bodies and heat and smoke nearly suffocated her.

Chogan must have seen something of her thoughts on her face. He certainly watched her closely enough. "Your brave, he is recovered?"

Had she spoken of Heinmot to this man? They'd communicated mostly through signs before. Chogan must have overheard her speaking with one of the other women who had been taken with her.

She narrowed her gaze at him. "You know our language."

A sheepish grin slipped over his face, and he shrugged. His actions more than confirmed the truth of her words.

Anger slid through her. Why had he lied about his understanding? He'd never actually *said* he didn't speak their language. But his face had never revealed comprehension when they spoke to him in Nimiipuu. That naturally made her assume.

Again, he seemed to read her thoughts, for his brows dipped as his gaze turned earnest. Troubled. "I did not want my brothers to know I could speak your language. I did not want them to make me use that against you. I also knew if they heard me speaking much with you that they couldn't understand, they would become angry and not believe what I told them you said."

She studied him as she took in his reasons. This time, she was careful to let her face show only distrust. At least until she was sure whether she *could* trust him or not. "Why wouldn't they believe you? You were one of them." But not anymore? Could she dare believe what he said now? She might have been more willing before learning that he'd lied about their language.

His hand cut through the air. "They have long been displeased with me. This was my last chance to show myself as bloodthirsty as the rest of them."

Nothing in his face made her think he was lying, but it took more than a few words to prove a man's true character. Still, she would be civil to him as long as he did the same.

She gave him a nod, which wouldn't commit her one way or another—she hoped.

He seemed to accept the response. "Is your brave recovered?"

She'd been distracted before and hadn't answered him. She would speak the truth now. It was what she wanted from him, so she should do the same. "He has been gone these four moons."

Chogan's expression shifted. Softened. His brows drew close again, and his eyes glistened. "I'm sorry."

Was he? About the death of a Salish man, the known enemies of the Blackfoot?

But whether everything he said now was true or not, Chogan had already proved himself different from the others who'd kidnapped her. Why would he feign sadness now if he didn't feel it?

Again, she nodded to acknowledge his words.

His gaze dropped to her belly, then lifted again to her face. "His family has taken you in?"

Maybe that was the way his people handled such matters, but thankfully, she'd been allowed to return to her own family. She shook her head. "I have come back to the village of my people. To the lodge of my brother."

Curiosity flickered in his gaze, but then it slipped away. "Do you need anything? Have your men found enough hunting? I can bring you meat."

Again, a jumble of emotions churned through her. Why would he offer more kindness? Did he truly think the great spirit brought him here to help her? Meat wasn't what she needed. And what she did long for was certainly not something she could seek from him.

Her own life again.

It didn't even have to be the life she'd thought would be hers for the rest of her days—to keep the lodge for Heinmot until he grew old and passed away. By then, their future sons would have grown enough to provide for her. She'd not expected it to all end so soon, before even the first of those children had the chance to see the world.

She pushed those thoughts away lest Chogan decipher them on her face. "We have enough meat. I am well." Hot, weary, and as large as a community lodge, but he could help with none of those.

It was time she end this unusual meeting. Her family would worry if she didn't return soon.

Before turning away, Telípe sought out Chogan's gaze one

last time. "I must go now. You will not stay in this place?" Surely he knew what an uproar would be raised if a Blackfoot warrior was found hiding in the woods outside their village.

Chogan's eyes drilled into hers. "I will not leave yet, not until I know the great spirit's purpose for me."

Another press of fear weighed her chest. "If they find you, they'll not wait to ask your purpose. My people detest the Blackfoot." *Hate* would have been a more accurate word, but she couldn't bring herself to say it. Not about him.

His expression remained calm, though still intense. "I won't be found. And I won't do harm to your people. You may tell them so, if you think it wise."

She shook her head. "They would hunt you down if they knew you were here."

"I won't be found." He repeated the words in a steady tone with a peace that belied the determination in their meaning.

He was such a mystery, this man. Enemy, yet friend. Fierce warrior, yet gentle and kind. Undecided, yet determined.

Well, he would have to make his own choices. If she stayed away much longer, one of the boys would be sent to find her. If the lad spotted Chogan, she'd be putting him at great risk.

"I must go." With a final nod, she turned away.

She'd once thought she'd never see this man again. Yet she'd been granted one more chance. Was this now their final farewell?

And why did the thought make her chest ache?

Get HONOR IN THE MOUNTAIN REFUGE at your Favorite Retailer!

ABOUT THE AUTHOR

Misty M. Beller is a *USA Today* bestselling author of romantic mountain stories, set on the 1800s frontier and woven with the truth of God's love.

She was raised on a farm in South Carolina, so her Southern roots run deep. Growing up, her family was close, and they continue to keep that priority today. Her husband and children now add another dimension to her life, keeping her both grounded and crazy.

God has placed a desire in Misty's heart to combine her love for Christian fiction and the simpler ranch life, writing historical novels that display God's abundant love through the twists and turns in the lives of her characters.

Connect with Misty at www.MistyMBeller.com

ALSO BY MISTY M. BELLER

Call of the Rockies

Freedom in the Mountain Wind

Hope in the Mountain River

Light in the Mountain Sky

Courage in the Mountain Wilderness

Faith in the Mountain Valley

Honor in the Mountain Refuge

Brides of Laurent

A Warrior's Heart

Hearts of Montana

Hope's Highest Mountain

Love's Mountain Quest

Faith's Mountain Home

Texas Rancher Trilogy

The Rancher Takes a Cook

The Ranger Takes a Bride

The Rancher Takes a Cowgirl

Wyoming Mountain Tales

A Pony Express Romance

A Rocky Mountain Romance

A Sweetwater River Romance

A Mountain Christmas Romance

The Mountain Series

The Lady and the Mountain Man

The Lady and the Mountain Doctor

The Lady and the Mountain Fire

The Lady and the Mountain Promise

The Lady and the Mountain Call

This Treacherous Journey

This Wilderness Journey

This Freedom Journey (novella)

This Courageous Journey

This Homeward Journey

This Daring Journey

This Healing Journey

Made in the USA
Columbia, SC
12 June 2021